FIONA GRAPH lives in London. *Things That Bounded* is
her first published novel.

THINGS THAT BOUNDED

Fiona Graph

SilverWood

Published in 2020 by SilverWood Books

SilverWood Books Ltd
14 Small Street, Bristol, BS1 1DE, United Kingdom
www.silverwoodbooks.co.uk

ISBN 978-1-80042-007-6 (paperback)
ISBN 978-1-80042-008-3 (ebook)

British Library Cataloguing in Publication Data
A CIP catalogue record for this book is
available from the British Library

Page design and typesetting by SilverWood Books

Over these things I could not see;
These were the things that bounded me;
And I could touch them with my hand,
Almost, I thought, from where I stand.
And all at once things seemed so small
My breath came short, and scarce at all.

Renascence and Other Poems (1917)
by Edna St Vincent Millay

1

The policeman was chasing her down the street. She was running as fast as she could, twisting and turning, but suddenly she was in a dead end and he was on her, grabbing her roughly by the arm and shouting, 'Now you're for it, you suffragette bitch!' He started blowing his whistle, a long triumphant blast. Ellen jerked awake, her heart thumping, and reached over to turn off the alarm. Of course, it must be Hilda's funeral that had made her dream of those days. She lay still while her breathing calmed, then rolled out of bed and went to run the bath.

She was drying herself when Freddie tapped on the door and stuck his head around. His red hair huddled in dishevelled clumps and dark smudges haunted his eyes. Clearly, another sleepless night. But he greeted her cheerily enough. 'You've still got it, Ellie! That Myra's a lucky woman.' Ellen laughed and threw her sponge at him.

'Cup of tea?' he suggested, and disappeared.

He came into her bedroom with tea and toast as she was buttoning up her skirt and stood appraising her. 'I'm pleased with this design. The silk falls nicely and that shade of green suits you. I'm making up a similar style for Mrs Drummond, although with more panels, her body being considerably larger than yours. Your white blouse goes well with it.'

Ellen said, through a mouthful of toast, 'Hilda left instructions no one should wear black. I know it's sentimental, but I wanted to have the suffragette colours. It feels important for her funeral.'

'White for purity, hmm?' he quizzed, raising an eyebrow at her. 'Well then, you need a touch of purple, my dear. I know just the thing,' and he delved into her wardrobe, coming out with a violet scarf which he tied at her throat. He stood back and cocked his head. 'There, perfect. How are you feeling?'

'Oh, Freddie – it seems so wrong to be going to the funeral of someone who was just fifty, who was so brave and full of life. She was such a lovely woman ... but I can't help feeling relieved her suffering's at an end. Ever since she had the stroke – well, you know the story. Each time I saw her it was more distressing.'

'I know, sweetie. She was very kind to me. I'll never forget that. But I think she was ready to go. I hope she never regretted the way she martyred herself for the cause. She never was the same after all that ghastly force-feeding. Thank God you never put yourself through it.'

'At the time I thought I was a coward, but looking back, I wonder if the results were justified. When I think of the physical damage and suffering ... So we got a bit of sympathy from the public – was it worth it?' Ellen sighed and shrugged her shoulders.

Freddie held out the jacket for her, instinctively smoothing down the fabric on her arms. 'Will all the old suffragette glories be there?'

'I hope you don't include me in that,' Ellen said mock sternly, thinking all this bright chatter was a bit forced. She knew he was miserable. If only he weren't so stubborn – but Freddie's laugh broke into her thoughts.

'Good God, no. But then, you were so young when you got involved. How innocent we all were then …' They were briefly caught up in their memories, then he asked, 'Do you think Kate might turn up? I'd love to see her again.'

Ellen's eyes widened in surprise. 'It never occurred to me. I don't see why she would, after all these years, considering the way she vanished from our lives. I just wish I could know she's all right. Hilda used to get cards on her birthday with a Paris postmark, but there was never an address. Short of wandering the streets of Paris, I don't know what I could do to find her. God, I haven't thought of her in ages. What made you mention her just now?'

'I suppose because the three of you did everything together. Remember the time you broke those shop windows in Regent Street and escaped the police by jumping on a bus?'

Ellen laughed at the memory. 'And Hilda hit a policeman over the head with her umbrella!'

'To think you were just fifteen when you first met Kate and Hilda. And now you're more than twice that age.'

Ellen said lightly, 'Older but wiser,' but Freddie retorted, his tone hard, 'Speak for yourself, Ellie. I'm more of a fool than ever.'

'Oh, Freddie … Why don't you—?'

He cut across her. 'No. Let's not go through that again.' He gave one of his nervous coughs and they looked at each other. In the silence, she could hear banging on the stairs as their weekly charwoman, Gladys, lugged the hoover up from the shop. Freddie forced a smile. 'You'd best go, Ellie. Don't want to be late. And I need to get myself presentable and open the shop.'

'No,' she agreed, looking in the mirror while she applied lipstick and settled her cloche hat over her hair. 'I hope you won't be run off your feet. Do you have many appointments?'

'Just two. The fitting for Mrs Drummond and a new client, plus any walk-ins. I'll be fine, don't you worry. Hester will be around and it's better to keep busy. I hope it all goes well.' He gave her a wan smile and left the room.

Ellen's eyes drifted to her framed photograph of the funeral procession for Emily Wilding Davison. Hilda was holding a banner while Kate stood in the front, dressed in white like the others, her face unusually solemn. Ellen, a few rows back, had been caught by the camera in the act of peeping around at Kate. She had arrived in London weeks earlier and that was the day they had met each other. For one eventful year they had been best friends. And now Hilda was dead and she hadn't seen Kate since 1914. Sudden grief tightened her chest. A sob rose in her throat but she blinked back the tears, chiding herself. Now was not the time to get sentimental. She had a train to catch.

Why did people always walk so slowly? Out on Piccadilly they grouped together like camels ambling along in the desert. Ellen snapped at their heels, impatient, at the first available opportunity overtaking them with long strides. Coming up to Green Park tube, her eyes sought out the tender green of the spring leaves clothing the trees. She heard the song of a blackbird over the traffic and paused to listen, her face lifted in quiet enjoyment. Then she hurried down the steps, calculating the time she had left to catch the Southern Belle at Victoria.

Ellen knew from experience how bumpy the trip to Brighton could be. As the train lurched about, the day trippers in her carriage laughed merrily. The train was surprisingly full, considering it was a Friday, and she guessed some of her fellow travellers had taken an illicit day off work. Who could blame them? After the recent cool weather, it was a lovely May day, more appropriate for a picnic by the seaside than attending the funeral of an old friend.

Her latest library book was open on her lap, but she could not concentrate. As she looked out the window, clouds of steam fitfully obscuring the fields and late-blossoming trees, her thoughts went back to the first time she had met Hilda. Ellen had come down to London from the Norfolk Broads as soon as she left school, freshly apprenticed and determined to do her bit to support the suffragette cause. When she went to hear Mrs Pankhurst talk at a public meeting, an older woman with soft brown hair dressed in the latest style had come up to greet her warmly, asking, 'Is this your first time?' and drawing her into a group. Ellen had quickly lost her shyness and by the end of the evening she had committed herself to future actions. Her fellow suffragettes became a surrogate family, with Hilda and Kate the sisters she'd never had. Freddie's frequent visits to stay with her in her Clerkenwell lodgings completed the circle. As the train pulled into the station, she gathered her things, knowing she would do it again in a heartbeat. She regretted none of it.

It was a short walk through The Lanes to the Quaker hall where Hilda's funeral was taking place. Ellen looked with interest in the shop windows as she passed by. She dawdled in front of a window display of women's hats, making a mental note to tell Freddie about an unusual design. As she turned to go, she caught her reflection in the glass, stylish in Freddie's suit and jaunty scarf, her face a pale oval and her blue eyes looking back seriously.

Her steps lagged when she arrived at the hall in Ship Street, the sea a tantalising glimpse to her right. Walking up the path past fig trees and flower beds, she surveyed the red-brick building. The windows were all at different heights, as if they'd been haphazardly thrown on as an afterthought. So, this was where Hilda had found consolation in the last years of her life. Reluctant to go in, she hovered at the steps leading to the twin arches. Groups of women and a few men were talking quietly by the front door. The usual "old glories", she thought wryly. Older women who appeared conventional at first glance, many clinging to their old-fashioned hair and fusty clothes – but oh! what strength and courage they had, what sacrifices they had made in the cause of women's suffrage. Underestimate them at your peril, she thought fondly as she scanned their familiar faces.

But then Ellen stiffened with shock. At first, she thought she was seeing things, her mind conjuring up an illusion thanks to her conversation with Freddie. But no, standing quietly in a group of chattering women, seemingly back from the dead – it really was Kate.

2

How changed she was! Her thick dark hair was short in an Eton crop and she was dressed in the latest style, with smart trousers and a jacket, but it was not this that made her nearly unrecognisable. Kate looked thin, unwell, with a sallow colour and lines of tension on her face – so unlike the vivid girl Ellen had known. Why, Ellen thought, she looks unhappy.

At that moment Kate looked over and saw her. The spontaneous delight on her face gave a flash of her old friend, and Ellen grinned at her in relief. She came forward to take Ellen in a firm embrace. 'Ellen! I was so hoping I'd find you here. How wonderful to see you!' They hugged each other tightly, then Kate held her at arm's length and scrutinised her from head to toe. 'Let me take a look at you. My God, Ellie, you look – fabulous. So elegant!'

'You mean, so unlike the gawky girl I used to be?' Ellen tried to give a nonchalant laugh but blushed in spite of herself. She was aware of feeling knocked off her usual balance, and surprisingly shy, at this unexpected reappearance of her old friend.

'God, it's been so long. Too long. But I can see time has been good to you. You're positively blooming. Are you well? Are you happy?' Kate's voice was serious, almost insistent.

'Yes, life is good. Oh, Kate, I can't tell you how glad I am to see you. Where have you been? Quite a few of us made enquiries without any luck. It was as if you dropped off the edge of the world. I was worried sick. Why didn't you at least write to let me know you were all right?' Ellen tried to keep her voice steady but some of the remembered pain must have come through, because a shadow crossed Kate's face.

'I'm sorry if you were worried, Ellie. It didn't occur to me people would care.'

Ellen stared at her, at a loss for words. Just then, Hilda's husband came up to say the ceremony was about to start and she realised people were filing into a room off the hallway. As they started to follow the others, Kate grabbed her hand, asking, 'Can you stay to talk afterwards?' and she replied, 'Yes, of course.'

She hadn't expected the service would be so moving, or that she would have her ideas about the Quakers so challenged. She had imagined boringly devout, po-faced people. But the ceremony was simple and honest, with little talk about God. There was no priest giving a sermon and it became apparent they didn't believe in the afterlife. One man read a poem, then people just stood up and talked about Hilda. Her husband and daughter described her warm and loving nature. Women who'd been active with her in the suffragette struggle spoke of her courage and unquenchable commitment. There was little talk of the last years of ill health and suffering – everyone wanted to focus on the happier times.

Ellen found herself on her feet telling stories of the actions they had taken together: smashing windows, putting glue in post boxes. The time Hilda climbed onto a roof and threw slates at policemen. Hilda's kindness towards others, her clear analysis of the injustice they needed to redress. How, even in the darkest times, such as her spells in prison when she was weak from hunger strikes, she would keep up the spirits of her fellow suffragettes.

The room was plain, the windows set up high as if to avoid worldly distractions, although Ellen could still hear the cries of seagulls sounding like lost souls, both mournful and mocking. There was a large photograph of Hilda on a nearby table and she gazed at it sadly. Several times, she found Kate's eyes on her with a quizzical expression.

After the ceremony, they became caught up with old suffragette comrades. The conversation was lively, with fond reminiscing of Hilda and their adventures before the war. During a lull in the chatter, one woman said to Ellen, 'My dear, I hope you don't mind my curiosity, but I've been admiring your beautiful suit and that slit skirt. Where did you buy it?'

Ellen switched automatically into business mode. 'Why, thank you, Anne. It was designed by my brother. We have a women's fashion shop just behind Piccadilly, Fernsby Fashions. He'd be pleased to make this up for you. Would you like a card?' She produced one from her bag and handed it over. 'Would anyone else like our details? We do special rates for suffragettes, you know!'

Kate gave Ellen an amused glance, which also showed some surprise. The women now switched their attention to Kate, expressing pleasure at seeing her and politely hinting in roundabout ways at her absence. But then Millie, who had always been nosy, asked directly, 'Where have you been for so many years, Kathleen Shergold? We all wondered what on earth had happened to you, ever since—'

Kate spoke over her. 'I've been abroad, mostly in Paris.'

'I hope that doesn't mean, my good woman, that you missed your first opportunity to vote in the election last year?' There was a hectoring note in her voice. Kate's eyes suddenly sparked from under her lashes.

'On the contrary, Millie. Do you think, after all we went through to get the vote, I'd turn down the opportunity to exercise my right? I came back specifically to vote and did so with great pride.'

'And are you only back for another visit now?'

Kate tensed but replied pleasantly enough, 'No. I moved back permanently last August.'

Ellen had to look down to disguise the shock on her face. They were joined by Hilda's family and the conversation became more general. She smiled and nodded in the right places but couldn't stop brooding. Kate had been back for nine months and hadn't tried to contact her. Why? As if she had read her mind, Kate touched Ellen's arm and said quietly, 'Would you like to duck out? I know a nice tea room in front of the sea.' Her warm tone didn't show any signs of anger, although there was the same puzzled expression on her face.

Ellen replied soberly, 'Yes, let's go now.'

The streets were crowded with a mixture of Londoners down for the day and workers out for their precious lunch break. As they walked down to the seafront, frequently separated by clumps of people on the narrow lanes, Kate asked about Hilda's last years. She listened in silence to the tale of Hilda's declining health, the move to the seaside in a vain attempt to redress this, and her growing interest in the Quakers. Ellen commented, 'When Hilda first told me about the Quakers, I was astonished. She was always so questioning about things, I'd never imagined she'd get involved in an organised religion. But, I admit, it did appear to bring her a sort of comfort.'

Kate looked over at Ellen. 'How unjust it is to hear her last years were difficult. She was still so young – she should not be dead. But she was never the same after that last bout of force-feeding, was she? Do you remember how awful she looked when she got out? Her skin like yellow paper, her sunken eyes ... and that sickly smell ...' Their eyes met. After negotiating their way around a group of men outside a pub who loudly invited the "young ladies" to join them, Kate continued, 'But as far as religions go, the Quakers seem to be the best of the lot, although I know that's not saying much. I've come across some quite decent ones.'

'Where was this?'

'When I was driving ambulances in France during the war.' Ellen looked at her curiously, but they had arrived at the tea room and the next few minutes involved finding a table and placing their order. The waitress, a red-cheeked woman, was inclined to be chatty. When she finally left the table, Ellen looked over at Kate ready to question her further, but was temporarily silenced by Kate's smiling contemplation of her.

'I can't tell you how good it is to see you again, Ellie. So, what is this about you and your brother having your own business? The last time I saw Freddie he was, what, fourteen? So funny to think of him all grown up.'

Ellen laughed. 'Well, he turns thirty next week! You might remember my mother's a seamstress and we both learnt the trade from her. Freddie worked in a tailor's shop after the war, and when Mr Perkins retired five years ago we decided to jointly take over the business. I trained as a nurse during the war and was still doing that, but I fancied a change. It was hard going at first, but just in the last year or so we've started making a decent return on it. There's a workroom and flat above the shop so it gives us everything we need.' She paused for breath and Kate nodded encouragingly. 'Freddie's really creative – he goes well beyond my limited skills – and he's passionate about design. In fact, he's sent in drawings to the Old Vic for the costumes in a ballet they're putting on next year. I hope he gets the work – he'd love to get more into that sort of thing.' She stopped, aware she'd been rattling away nervously, but Kate's eyes were fixed on her face and she appeared interested.

'Thank God he got through the war unscathed.'

'I was hoping he'd escape it altogether, but he was conscripted in 1917 even though he was still too young. He went through some terrible times, but yes, he survived. What about your brothers?'

Kate's voice was flat. 'Both dead. Harry died first, in the Somme, and Reginald died of his injuries the following year.'

'Oh, Kate. I'm so sorry. All that death and suffering in the war … Such a dreadful time, and all so bloody unnecessary.' Kate stared silently out the window at the sea, sparkling in the sunshine. Ellen added, 'It must have been terrible for your mother. How is she?'

'Dead. They're all gone now. My mother died soon after the war ended, and my father had a heart attack last year.' Kate stated this calmly enough, but Ellen sensed deep emotions. The waitress returned to the table with tea and sandwiches, and a short silence fell while Kate poured the tea. She had beautiful

14

hands. Looking at them, Ellen had a sudden memory of Kate's hand gripping hers and pulling her along as they sprinted from the police after one of their marches on Parliament. Always she had been so bold and brave, so full of life. Smiling at the memory, she lifted her eyes to find Kate observing her with an expression she couldn't quite decipher.

'I was never close to my brothers. They were too like my father, all of them nasty bullies. I used to envy your closeness with Freddie and wished I had a brother like him. Does that sound heartless?' Ellen shook her head. Kate went on, 'If you're living together, then presumably neither of you is married?'

'Married? Good God, no.' Ellen's emphatic reaction was spontaneous. She hesitated, then said, 'Freddie lost someone dear to him in the war, another soldier, and it affected him badly. He has his adventures now, but nothing long-term. Well, when I say nothing – he did get serious about a good man a few months ago and I hoped it would work out, but no.' She met Kate's gaze steadily. 'Yes, he loves men.'

'I always did think he was heading that way.' Kate smiled and continued looking at Ellen. 'What about you?' But Ellen's patience, never her strong point, had worn thin and she could no longer stop herself.

'Kate, it's so wonderful to see you again, and we have a lot of catching up to do. But there's something we need to clear up first. Where have you been all these years? Why didn't you let me know you were alive? The last time I saw you was when you came to visit me in Holloway just before the war. When they released me a week later, you'd disappeared from sight and no one knew where you were. All I could find out was that you and Hilda were involved in an arson attack on a church and it went wrong. Where did you go, for God's sake?'

The smile left Kate's eyes and she stared at Ellen bleakly. 'The facts are easy enough. I went up to Scotland to lie low for a few months until the police operation was shut down. Ironic to think the start of the war helped to divert interest ... then I ended up working in France with the ambulance service organised by Toupie Lowther. Did you hear about that?'

'Of course! I told you I trained as a nurse. I worked in the hospital in Endell Street run by Flora Murray and Louisa Garret Anderson. Do you remember them from the movement? We used to get lots of patients sent over by Toupie's ambulance service. We all thought they were marvellous.'

Kate's face relaxed momentarily. 'Just think, we were both working in services run by women and I helped deliver soldiers to your hospital. That's a nice connection ...'

Ellen waited for her to continue, but Kate seemed to be caught up by some private musings, gazing at her then giving her head a small shake. She asked, 'Did you come back to England after the war?'

'Yes, temporarily, but it was no good. After my mother died, I went back to Paris and made my life there.' She hesitated, as if to say more, but was silent.

'But why did you stay away? Why the silence? Did I do something to offend you?'

Kate impulsively caught her hand and exclaimed, 'Offend me? Impossible. How could that be? I thought about you constantly.' She was silent for a while, crumbling a sandwich between her fingers, then looked up at Ellen with a desolate expression. 'Don't you see, Ellie? Thanks to my stupidity, I could have destroyed everything the suffragettes had worked for. It was sheer luck the war started a few days later and took everyone's attention. Otherwise, the newspapers would never have let it go. Can't you see that's why I didn't contact you? You always had such strong ideals. We'd argued about the use of arson – you said it was too risky. You said it couldn't be justified. And you were right. How could you forgive me, if I can't forgive myself for having murdered someone?'

3

There was a light breeze by the seaside and the clouds were scudding along. Intrepid groups of people had arranged themselves for picnics on the beach among the fishing boats pulled up from the water line. Small children ran squealing in and out of the shallows. A portly day tripper balanced precariously on a donkey being led along the pebbles, apprehension and delight quarrelling on his face. Watching them, Ellen's expression lightened as she recalled her own childhood in Norfolk, where water was never far away. She and Freddie had learned to swim at an early age and spent much of their free time in and around the Broads. The pier was ahead and she could hear screams and laughter coming from the funfair. She and Kate were slowly pacing along, instinctively moving in unison, and she remembered the countless times they had walked like this in the year before the war, arm in arm, discussing suffragette actions or their future hopes and dreams.

She spotted a quiet bench up ahead and turned her head to Kate, who was staring in front of her. 'Let's sit here.' Kate nodded and they settled, looking out at the sea. Ellen said, as if continuing a silent conversation, 'It's ridiculous to talk about murder. It was just a tragic mistake. You have no reason to feel guilty. You had no way of knowing that man was in the church.'

Kate response was swift and irritable. 'Oh, so now you're a bloody legal expert as well? You know better than the police and the courts? Perhaps you should go and teach them criminal law ...'

Ellen just looked at her and Kate turned her head away. After a short silence she turned back. 'Forgive me, Ellen, you didn't deserve that.' She took a cigarette case out from her pocket and offered it to Ellen. 'Do you smoke?' Ellen shook her head. 'No, quite right. Filthy habit, really.' Kate stared with dislike at the cigarette she'd taken out, and put it back into the case. She continued looking down at her hands. Her next words were quiet. 'Do you know what happened?'

'Only from Hilda, after I got out of Holloway and you'd disappeared. She told me the two of you went to burn down a church in Shoreditch. You checked thoroughly to make sure it was empty before you started the fire, but it later turned out the police found a man's body in the ruins.'

Kate gave a deep sigh. 'That's about it. We waited nearby for a few minutes to check that the fire took hold, then we left. I've gone over this a thousand times in my head, and each time I come to the same conclusion. It was my fault, my responsibility. I thought I'd looked everywhere but I forgot to check the vestry. I suppose he was asleep in there. I hope to God he didn't wake up ...'

Ellen stared at her in surprise. 'Are you sure? Hilda told me she searched the vestry and it was empty. She said she could never work out how he got in there.'

'Well, she must be wrong. What does it matter, anyway? A man is dead because of me. He was someone's son. He had a right to life. It's my fault. I killed him.' Kate's voice sounded harsh.

Ellen said slowly, 'Kate, I think it could be important. Hilda was emphatic about this point. Don't you think you should investigate—?' But Kate interrupted.

'Leave it, Ellen. It happened and I have to live with it. No more to be said.'

Ellen realised this was not the time to push the issue. She asked instead, 'Is that the reason why you didn't come back to England?'

Kate gave a short laugh. 'Oh, Ellen, there were lots of reasons. Because of that – because I was mad with grief after my mother died and couldn't bear to be near my father – because I was sick of everything. I wanted to be in a place where no one knew me. I went back over to France the week after my mother's funeral and ended up staying there for nearly ten years. For a long time, it seemed just what I needed. I found a community of like-minded women and I found love of a sort. I thought the world could go hang. And then ... Well, let's just say it went sour. I knew I had to get out to preserve my health. I tried Berlin for a year but it was even worse.' Ellen waited for her to say more, but she scowled out at the horizon with her lips firmly closed.

Dark clouds suddenly blotted out the sun and small waves with white caps appeared on the water. A huge seagull hovered balefully in front of them, a malevolent flying chicken, before wheeling away to intimidate someone else. A breeze ruffled Kate's straight hair, defiantly hatless. Ellen took a surreptitious glance at her watch but Kate must have seen this, because she asked, 'You have to go, don't you?'

'Soon, yes. I have an appointment in town. Kate – we still have so much to talk about. You're not going to vanish again, are you? You must know you've been very much missed.' She was surprised to see tears in Kate's eyes.

'You don't know how good it is to see you, Ellie. You really are a tonic for the soul! No, I promise you I won't disappear again. I'm here to stay, I hope.'

'Are you living in London? We can get the train back together,' Ellen suggested, but Kate shook her head, smiling ruefully. 'I'm afraid I've arranged to stay tonight with a friend in Hastings.'

A tired-looking nanny, walking past with her charge in a pram, stopped and sat at the other end of the bench. The baby instantly started wailing and the nanny gave them an apologetic look, jiggling the pram handle vigorously. They got up from the bench in silent agreement. Ellen took one last look at the sea before they turned to start walking up the hill to the station. Kate asked, 'Do you still like to swim?'

'Oh yes, Freddie and I swim in the Serpentine. Women aren't allowed there, of course, but the other men know me by now and accept me. The police nearly arrested me once, but some of the men distracted them so I could get away. And I sometimes go to the ladies' pond on Hampstead Heath.'

'Do you remember that water carnival we organised at the Serpentine in 1914? The police were so determined to stop us getting in the water. But you swam out to the boats with some other women and waved the suffragette banner.' They both laughed at the memory.

'God, I haven't thought about that in years. The police didn't know what to do with us when we came out. Luckily, there was a crowd watching, or who knows what might have happened. What adventures we had!'

She put her arm in Kate's who pressed it close to her, saying only, 'Ellie!'

As they came closer to the station, Ellen broke the silence to ask, 'Are you free tomorrow evening? Could you come to supper with Freddie and me?'

'Thank you, I'd love that. You must give me one of those impressive business cards.'

Ellen smiled and did so, explaining, 'You'll see a dark blue door with a bell just to the right of the shop. If you need to telephone, give me time to run down the stairs to our workshop where the phone is. Come any time after seven thirty.'

Kate was staring at the card oddly. 'Good God, Ellie, you live in Jermyn Street. We're just a few blocks apart. I can't believe it! To think we've spent the last months so close – perhaps we passed each other on the street without knowing ...' In response to Ellen's questioning look, she explained, 'I have a flat on Curzon Street.'

Ellen had so many questions but asked only, 'Are you working? What do you do with your days?'

'I do a few hours each week teaching French and German in girls' schools. I've got some private pupils as well. And I've become interested in photography. I love to walk around London, watching people and taking pictures, observing the different communities in their villages. You can walk two streets in London and find a whole new world. Or I'll take a bus to the end of its route and sit on the top deck watching everything. I can easily pass a whole day just doing that.'

Ellen felt such sadness she could not speak. What had happened to the feisty, vibrant Kate who grabbed at life and laughed at danger? Who was never alone, always in the centre of a group? Who lightly wore a fine arrogance matched with great personal charm and warmth? But they had arrived at the station and she saw from the board her train was leaving in a few minutes. Kate pulled her in for a hug and said in her ear, 'Till tomorrow,' then walked briskly away.

Myra was chatting animatedly as they emerged from the Garrick with the theatre crowd. 'Isn't that Tallulah Bankhead absolutely divine, darling? She was the best thing about the play, rather dreary otherwise if you ask me. But one could just gaze at her all day long. I hear she may be leaving us soon for Hollywood …'

Ellen tried to appear interested, but her attention was elsewhere. She'd sat unseeing through the play as she had on the train journey back from Brighton, her mind turned inwards. It occurred to her now that Kate had invaded her subconscious in ways she hadn't realised. For many months after the beginning of the war she had missed and worried about Kate grievously. Over the years, her concern had retreated to a private part of her mind, but it had never completely gone away. And now she was back, Ellen realised just how important it was for her to have Kate in her life again.

They had been unlikely friends on the surface: Kate, not quite a year older but far more sophisticated, having grown up in Bloomsbury with an easy assumption of access to privilege and education, her father a well-to-do banker; Ellen, from a quiet rural background, accustomed to helping out in the family grocery shop and her mother's dressmaking business, needing to leave school at fifteen and go out to work. And yet, something between them clicked from their first meeting. Over time, their similarities had become clear: both strong, curious characters, impatient, fearless and with a certain indifference to society's opinion. Hilda had dubbed them "the inseparables". Now, their friendship stood in front of them, seemingly strong and untarnished by the sixteen years of separation.

Just then, she thought she glimpsed Kate on the other side of Charing Cross Road, and her heart quickened. But even as she opened her mouth to call out, she realised it was someone quite different, with a rounder face and curled hair; just a superficial similarity, after all. She laughed to herself at her mistake and wondered about the friend Kate was seeing in Hastings.

'Ellen, my dear, wherever are you tonight? Who was that woman you were staring at? Did you hear a word I've said?'

She came out of her thoughts to see Myra observing her in amused exasperation. 'Sorry, I was miles away. What did you say?'

Myra gave an exaggerated sigh and smiled at her brightly. 'I said, where shall we go for a drink? A group of people are going round to the Savoy. It should be fun.'

'I think I'll just go home. I don't really feel up to socialising.'

'Oh, Ellen, don't be such a sad sack! You were the one who suggested we have this evening out, rather than always staying in. It's far too early to call it a night,' Myra protested with a small pout of her scarlet lips.

'I'm sorry, Myra, I'm just not in the mood. Please, go on without me.'

'If you insist, but I think you're being a great bore. You haven't forgotten our date next Wednesday, have you? Frank's going to be away. He says it's for some dull work thing, but I know he's having it off with his new secretary. You can stay all night – it will be such a luxury!' But even as Myra spoke, she sneaked a look at her society friends who were starting to move off.

Ellen looked at her without speaking and then smiled. 'Go and enjoy yourself with your friends. I'll see you Wednesday.' She kissed Myra on the cheek and got a whiff of her expensive perfume, bringing back memories of a different sort.

The night was mild. She crossed the street and walked into Leicester Square, relishing the chance to pursue her thoughts uninterrupted. Yet she found herself distracted as she walked through the streets, full of people emerging from cinemas and theatres, going to eat or drink. A waiter leaning against the wall next to an Italian restaurant, smoking on his break, gave her a weary nod. It was nearly ten. Women in turbans and bright scarves tottered past a man in threadbare clothes, begging in the Square. This was becoming a familiar sight since the stock market crash and Ellen felt a flicker of dread, knowing things were likely to get much worse.

In Piccadilly Circus, the usual flower sellers had gone but a lone shoeshine boy waited forlornly for a customer. It was as busy as rush hour and she was amused to see a horse-drawn cart waiting, alongside smart automobiles and cyclists, for the policeman to operate the lights. Neon signs proclaimed, "Guinness is good for you", and the virtues of Gordon's gin. When she'd first arrived in London from the country, she had found it overwhelming; now, she couldn't imagine living anywhere else. She crossed over to the island and stopped by the statue of Eros to observe the lights and constant movement. There was a skinny fair-haired boy, no older than sixteen, sitting on the steps nearby. Poor kid, he's on the rent, she thought and reached for her purse to give him money for a hostel. But when she looked up again, he had gone. She turned down Piccadilly and into the lane by the church in a chastened mood.

As usual, she paused outside their shop with the words *Fernsby Fashions* proudly written in gold at the top. Freddie had made some changes to the window display and she stood admiring it. Looking up at their flat, she half expected to see it in darkness, but a light in the sitting room was shining out through the half-closed curtains. As she came into the flat, there was Freddie smiling at her and turning off the wireless. Thank God! Always, they could talk to each other about everything.

'You've had a long day, Ellie. Did you go straight to the theatre? Would you like a drink?'

'Yes, yes and yes. Oh Freddie, I've got so much to tell you. Kate is back!'

An hour later, Ellen was curled up on the sofa in her pyjamas with her second gin fizz, having related all the details of the day. Freddie was regarding her with raised eyebrows. 'What are you thinking, Ellie? I can see you're plotting something.'

'I just feel there's something not right in all this. Obviously, I wasn't there when it happened, but Hilda and I discussed it several times afterwards when we were so worried about Kate. Hilda was positive she checked the vestry before they set the fire, and said no one could have come into the church without them knowing. She just couldn't understand how someone could have been there.'

'Perhaps he was hiding in a cupboard? Or under a table?' Freddie suggested.

'Why would he be hiding?'

'Mm … lots of reasons. He thought it was robbers? Or he had no right to be there himself, and he thought it was the vicar coming back.'

'Possibly … But Hilda said she checked everywhere. She'd had experience at that sort of thing – she'd helped to burn down the tea pavilion in Kew Gardens the year before, you may remember. She knew what she was doing. Anyway, I wouldn't expect there are many places an adult man could hide in a vestry.'

'Well, sadly Hilda's not around to ask and it sounds like Kate doesn't want to discuss it, so I don't know what more you can do. Anyway, isn't it up to Kate if she wants to revisit all this? From what you say, she feels bad enough about the whole thing.'

'But that's just the point,' Ellen said, leaning forward with a frown. 'It's upsetting to see her so changed. She looks unhappy, Freddie. She's full of remorse and it seems to be ruining her life. I hate to see her like this – so … so diminished, somehow. I want to help her.'

'Yes, well, the things that control us …' Freddie's voice was suddenly flat. They were wordlessly entangled in their memories until he stirred and asked, 'So, what do you want to do about it?'

Ellen took the plunge. 'I'd like to ask Alec if he could help us to investigate it.'

At the mention of his name, Freddie gave a start and flushed deeply. She'd half expected him to be angry or to instantly reject the idea, but to her relief he merely sighed and said, 'Why him?'

'He's a solicitor, and he knows all about the suffragettes. I thought he could find a way to, I don't know, get the inquest or police report, find more details about the death. It's crazy that Kate knows so little about what happened.'

'But you can't do all this without Kate knowing. You know we've talked about this before, Ellie. You do have the tendency to take charge of things, with the best will in the world of course,' he said, giving her a smile, 'but sometimes you forget to check if it's what the other person wants.'

'I know I can be bossy. I know I can overdo the big sister thing. But I did listen to you when you said I shouldn't contact Alec about you, and I'm not suggesting it now for that reason. Do you believe me?'

His blue eyes looked at her searchingly and her heart contracted. How handsome and dear he was. He deserved so much to be loved for himself. If only he hadn't pushed Alec away … He answered, his voice rather hoarse, 'Yes, I believe you, Ellie. But I, I think it's unlikely he'll agree to help, considering he's so angry with me. He pr-probably wants nothing to do with either of us.'

'I can only try. I was thinking,' she hesitated, nervous about his reaction, 'I could go to see him first thing in the morning. If he agrees to help, I thought – well, he could come to supper tomorrow night along with Kate and we could discuss it then?'

'To-tomorrow?' Freddie's stutter was mostly under control now, the only sign an occasional pause in his speech, but it sometimes recurred when he was nervous or upset. Ellen noticed a glint of hope cross his face. He got up jerkily and stared out the window to the street, coughing. She waited for his answer. 'Let me think about it for a while.'

'Of course, sweetie. Well, I think I'll take myself off to bed. Are you going out?' He was dressed in his street clothes.

Before Alec, this was often the time he would head out for one of his pickups, either to the nearby Turkish baths or one of the discreet queer bars in the West End.

He said absently, 'What? Oh – no. I think I'll turn in too.' She was heading for the stairs when he turned and said, 'Ellie, have you considered your plan might end badly? You say Kate's troubled by remorse now – once she knows more details about the man who died, she may feel even worse. You could be stirring up a hornet's nest, you know.'

She nodded gravely. 'I know, Freddie. I've thought about this. Of course, Kate must have the final decision. But I believe it's a risk worth taking. She already knows her actions resulted in a man dying, so if that's confirmed, nothing changes. But there's also the chance something could come out to help free her from this – this thing that seems to have her tied up in knots.'

4

The following morning, Ellen was up early. When she came downstairs to the kitchen she was surprised to see Freddie there, ready for work and frowning over a list.

'Good morning!' he greeted her. 'Did you sleep well?' There was colour in his cheeks and a brightness in his eyes, which had been missing for many weeks. 'I've decided it's a good idea to invite Alec. Perhaps we can become amateur sleuths, like those Agatha Christie novels you bring home. Or like that aristocratic git with the eyeglass.'

Ellen laughed, surprised and pleased. 'What have you got there?'

'I'm working on the menu for tonight. I'm going to prepare corn soup, then poached salmon in a horseradish sauce. For dessert we can have something simple like strawberries with cream, that's if I can find any. Could you pop to the fishmonger this afternoon to get four good pieces of salmon?'

'Of course, my dear. Does this mean you're cooking?'

'Well, we don't really want to poison our guests, do we, so I think it's best if you stick to arranging the drinks.' Ellen made a face at him, pretending to be cross, but secretly delighted to see his sense of humour coming back. Impulsively she gave him a hug, saying, 'Thank you, Freddie. I think I'll go to see him now, before he gets busy with his clients.'

As she turned to leave the kitchen, he added, 'By the way, I forgot to ask you last night. Did you have a nice time with Myra?'

She admitted, 'To be honest, the play was pretty boring and I wasn't in the mood for socialising. She went off with some of her friends to have cocktails at the Savoy.'

Freddie gave her a wicked grin. 'Your outing was supposed to be the chance to discover if you had anything in common with Myra other than bed, wasn't it?'

'You don't have to put it quite so …' She paused, looking abashed.

'Let's face it, I think she's history now, don't you?'

Ellen had no answer to that.

The bus journey was quick. It was eight thirty when Ellen alighted in Marylebone High Street. She hadn't been to Alec's office before, but knew it was just around the corner from his small flat in Moxon Street. It was easy enough to find, located above a bookshop with a brass plaque, *Gastrell & Medley, Solicitors*. Climbing the steep stairs to the second floor, she was relieved to see no one there, apart from a young woman setting up the reception who greeted her pleasantly. Ellen asked, 'Is Mr Medley available for a few minutes? My name's Ellen Fernsby. I don't have an appointment.' The receptionist disappeared into the office next door.

Before she could sit down, Alec was in front of her, looking alarmed. 'Is it Freddie? Is he – did something happen?'

Ellen said quickly, 'No, no, everything's fine. I wanted to speak to you about another matter.' It hadn't occurred to her he might respond to her appearance in that way, and she cursed herself for her thoughtlessness. Yet again, she was rushing into things without considering the impact on others. When would she learn? She smiled at him reassuringly and added, 'I was hoping you might have a couple of minutes free now. Or I could make an appointment …'

Alec had regained his poise. 'Of course I have time for you. Please, come into my office.' As she walked to his room she heard him ask the receptionist to hold all calls. Then he shut the door and gave her a kiss on the cheek. 'It's lovely to see you, Ellen. You look very well.'

He was subdued, but had recovered from his shock and the colour was back in his face. It was a nice face, with hazel eyes and a sensitive mouth, but she noticed he was thinner than the last time she had seen him. He sat down next to her. 'Now, how can I help you?'

Ellen explained the situation while Alec listened silently. He nodded as she came to a halt. 'Yes, I remember the church arson and the reports of a dead man. It was just before the war started, wasn't it? I was fifteen at the time and it went over my head a bit, but I remember my mother was worried it would put public opinion against the cause. But once the war started, I didn't see anything further in the papers about it – or maybe I just didn't notice. God knows, there was a lot going on at that time.'

'Well, I'm not sure either. I was in Holloway myself, so I only know what I heard from others afterwards.'

'Oh yes, I forgot about that. Were you in prison for long?'

'I was lucky, I suppose. I was out in three months, thanks to the war.' For a moment, the memories washed over her. She'd left prison to find she'd lost her job and her lodgings, suffragette actions had been suspended, the country was at war and Kate had disappeared. For many months she had felt lost, utterly bereft. She dragged her thoughts back to the present. 'What I wanted to ask, was if you could help us find out more about what happened?'

Alec spoke slowly, thinking it through aloud. 'Yes, I'd be glad to help. I'll need the details of the man who died and the police investigation. I've got contacts in the police. They should be able to help with that. I could ask for the autopsy report and the inquest findings, because there must have been one. But I can't do it off my own bat. I need to be acting for someone who has a right to know. That would probably mean one of the family. I couldn't do it on behalf of Kate. What does she think? How would she like to go about this?'

Ellen had the grace to blush. 'Well, the thing is, I haven't yet suggested this to Kate …' Her voice trailed away.

'Oh!' Alec looked at her, puzzled. 'Well, it's pretty essential she agrees to all this. Is she a close friend, or …?' He seemed to be hinting tactfully and Ellen remembered how she had always found him sensitive with others.

'We were best friends at the time, but she left London after the fire and we lost touch. She only came back to England recently. I'm just concerned about her and want to get to the bottom of this, that's all,' she stated firmly. 'I was wondering if you'd like to come to supper tonight to meet Kate, and we could talk it through then?'

Alec looked pleased. 'Well, I – well, yes, that would be

lovely.' He hesitated, then asked in a casual tone, 'Will Freddie be there?'

'Yes, he's cooking the meal.' The surprise was clear on his face and Ellen couldn't stop herself from adding, 'He thought you might not want to come, though. He thought you might be too angry with him.'

'Angry? No. Not any more.' He appeared caught up in his thoughts, sadness etched on his face. Ellen made herself stay silent. She could hear the receptionist outside talking to someone, and guessed he had a client waiting, but he didn't seem in any hurry. After a minute or so, he asked quietly, 'How is he?'

Ellen chose her words carefully. Freddie had made her promise not to interfere, but, surely, replying to a direct question was different. 'He's unhappy. He has a lot of regrets.' Alec gazed out of the window but said nothing. Ellen waited, then asked, 'Shall we see you tonight?' and he looked blank for a second before smiling. 'Yes, of course.'

When they stood up, he said, 'Ellen, I won't take any payment for this. I want to make it clear now.' She opened her mouth but he stated, 'No arguments. I'm doing this as a friend, and because Kate was a suffragette. That's my condition if you want my help.'

Ellen looked at him gratefully. 'Thank you, Alec. You're very kind.'

They walked out to the reception, now occupied by an elderly, red-faced gentleman. Alec said to him, 'I'm sorry to keep you, Sir John. It was good of you to wait. Please go in and I'll join you right away.' He had a kind, courteous manner but Ellen suspected he could put it to good use when necessary. The man gave a harrumph but looked mollified and marched straight-backed into the office. Turning to Alec, she saw him give her a quick wink, but all he said was, 'I don't know if you've met my sister, Rose? Ellen is a good friend,' he explained to the receptionist, and she realised now the family resemblance.

'Pleased to meet you. Let me guess, are you the one studying medicine?'

'That's right. I'm in my final year,' Rose replied. 'My sister Alice is still at school. Alec lets me work a few hours here to earn some money, and I do my best not to mess up his appointments.'

Alec said, 'I'd better go in before my client blows a gasket. What time shall I come tonight?'

'Oh, seven thirty, thereabouts,' Ellen replied, noticing Rose look at him, surprised. Perhaps he had another appointment. But Alec seemed almost light-hearted. 'I'll see you then,' he said with a squeeze of her hand before returning to his office.

Ellen said to Rose, 'Will you please give my best regards to your mother? I know her from the suffragette days. Is she well?'

Rose laughed. 'She's extremely well and full of talk about standing for Parliament in the next election. I'm not sure if they're ready for her! I'll pass on your regards.' Ellen smiled and clattered down the stairs, thinking it had gone about as well as she'd hoped. When she came out onto the street, she found a bus pulling up at the stop and ran to catch it.

5

When Ellen got back to the shop, Hester was dealing with a customer and Freddie was nowhere to be seen. Going over to tidy up material left on the bench top, Ellen noticed a boy of about twelve, with pale blonde hair and a dreamy look, delicately fingering the blue silk and humming to himself. He looked up at her with wide green eyes, startled out of his private world, and smiled, revealing dimples. Something about him reminded her strongly of Freddie at the same age. His mother called out, 'Come along Theo, we need to go,' and Hester came bustling over, full of self-congratulation, when the customers left.

'We've been ever so busy, almost run off our feet! That lady has put in an order for a dress and Freddie's doing a fitting with a new client. He's so good with the customers, but then of course he's a very talented man,' she said, a slight blush colouring her round, earnest face. They had taken Hester on as an assistant a few months back and it was working out well. She was an excellent seamstress, efficient, hard-working and determinedly bright and talkative. Her peroxided hair was cut in the latest bob and she always wore bright red lipstick. She beamed at Ellen now with her gap-toothed grin.

Ellen said, 'You're an angel, covering for me in the shop. I hope it hasn't put you too behind on the orders.'

'Oh, not at all! I stayed a bit late yesterday to finish the suit for Mrs Drummond and Freddie helped out, so kind, as always. Let me help you put these away.' Her comments provided the background noise as they tidied the bright swathes of materials.

'How is your mother? Has she recovered from her bilious attack?' Hester was in her late thirties and lived in a small flat in Camden with her mother, a meek, faded woman who doted on her only child. Ellen listened with half an ear to her long explanation, interrupted only when a woman entered the shop. After that, a stream of customers kept them all busy until one o'clock.

'Gosh!' Hester exclaimed as they put the "Closed" sign on the door. 'Thank heavens for early closing on Saturdays! And what a successful morning we've had!'

Freddie confirmed, with a satisfied look, 'Three new orders, although I had to persuade one customer to accept my style of hat. I think she'll be pleased with the result.' Ever since he'd read about the cruelty involved in killing birds, he had refused to use birds' feathers in his designs. 'And one woman's put in an order for a day suit as well as an evening dress. She's a bit of a society hostess so hopefully, if she likes the result, we'll get more customers through word of mouth.'

'I can stay back to help you start with the designs,' Hester suggested, looking at him brightly, but Freddie blinked and said, 'Good heavens, no, Hester – this is your time off. Go and enjoy it! We'll see you on Monday morning.

Have a lovely weekend.' After taking a few minutes to chatter and collect her bag and coat, she departed and Freddie locked the shop door. He turned to Ellen, remarking, 'Bloody hell! It's good to see she likes her work, but I'm sure she has better things to do.'

Ellen said, 'Indeed,' thinking, he has no idea.

'Right, I'm off to the Serpentine and then I'll do some shopping for the meal. Are you coming for a swim?' Freddie had already demanded every last detail of her meeting with Alec and subsequently displayed a nervy energy interspersed with brilliant good humour.

Ellen was tempted to make a sly comment, but managed to stop herself. 'No, not today. I want to go to the library.' Freddie bounded up the stairs to grab his swimming things and left soon after with a reminder about the fishmonger.

It was just a few minutes' walk around the corner to the London Library. Ellen had enjoyed school and particularly excelled in writing and reading. She'd always known further education was not a possibility, so her annual membership of the Library, her only extravagance, had been a source of entertainment and instruction. Over the years she had read her way through a range of novels and literature. Books had often been a solace. But not today.

When she came into the entrance she asked the librarian, 'I need to see the *Evening News* for July and August 1914. What floor is it on?'

The librarian, a smartly dressed woman in her fifties, replied, 'It's quiet today. I'll bring the copies to you in the reading room.'

Ellen thanked her and headed up the stairs to a desk with a view over St James's Square. The walls around her were filled with bookshelves up to the ceiling, and she amused herself watching a man teetering on a ladder as he stretched for books on the top shelf, an ungainly gecko in a suit. The librarian eventually arrived with a pile of newspapers, on her way out picking up books from the floor with a tut. Ellen started working her way through the papers, beginning towards the end of July. She spotted the first mention of the fire in the 31 July edition, beneath advertisements for "Copies of Paris Model Blouses" and henna paste vegetable hair colouring:

CHURCH BURNED DOWN IN SHOREDITCH
SUSPECT WORK OF FRENZIED SUFFRAGETTES

A serious outbreak of fire was discovered yesterday evening in All Hallows-in-the-East church in Shoreditch. The fire brigade was promptly summoned but the flames quickly took hold and the roof collapsed, resulting in the church being completely gutted. Suffragette literature was found near the church and the matter has been passed to the Metropolitan Police Force based in Bow. Police sergeant Percival Blunt has told this newspaper "no stone will be left unturned" in the search to find the "wicked perpetrators" of this heinous deed. Their enquiries are continuing.

A fuller account was given the next day:

THE LAST STRAW:
MILITANT SUFFRAGETTES NOW COMMITTING MURDER
POLICE EXPECT ARRESTS VERY SOON

The Metropolitan Police have now confirmed the shocking news that the body of a man was discovered in the charred ruins of All Hallows-in-the-East church in Shoreditch. The church was burned to the ground last Thursday evening and the police have been carefully sifting through the remains of the conflagration. The body has been identified by his grieving family as that of Cecil Fawdon, 54, a local husband and father.

Sergeant Percival Blunt of Bow Road Police Station has stated there is "no doubt" that fanatical suffragettes are responsible. Their militant literature was found scattered near the church and two viragos were spotted by a member of the public running away shortly before the flames were spotted.

"This has now become a murder investigation following the discovery of this poor man's body in the vestry," he told our reporter. "These crazy shrews have no limits to the depths they will sink to in pursuit of their depraved attempts to obtain the vote. They have shown by their deeds they are no more than common criminals. We are determined to make sure the full weight of the law is brought to bear on the culprits."

Ellen copied these two accounts word for word into her notebook, and continued searching. There were articles the following two days repeating much the same information, and a thundering editorial proclaiming: *All sane English men and women will rise up with one voice in outrage at this latest example of the infamy of these militant suffragettes.* But after that, nothing. She went carefully through all the newspapers for the remainder of August, now taken up with war news, and could find no further item about the police investigation. That seemed strange. She tapped her pen against her teeth and stared absent-mindedly at the people in the square below.

After wandering around the central garden to think this through, and getting sidetracked by memories, she came out of the gates and started to cross the street, just in time to see a Rolls-Royce sweep by. Nancy Astor could be glimpsed in the back, presumably on her way to an evening function. Ellen smiled to herself at the happy juxtaposition of seeing the first woman MP to sit in Parliament, so soon after reading hostile newspaper coverage of the suffragettes. It was now accepted that women could vote and stand for Parliament, yet not so many years before they had been ridiculed, arrested and brutalised for demanding that right. Thank God, things had changed.

Suddenly, she stopped in the middle of the road, her hand flying to her head. Damn! She'd forgotten to buy the salmon. The fishmonger would be closing any minute.

The shop was still open and two women were being served as she came in, breathing rapidly after her quick march. The fishmonger nodded at her and turned his attention back to his customer, a woman in an ugly brown coat, who was being particular about the fish she required. His assistant, a dark-haired young man, was filleting a mackerel for the other customer. There were exactly four pieces of salmon left. Don't buy the salmon, she pleaded silently, tapping her foot impatiently while the woman pondered, then rejected, first trout and then plaice. But luckily, the other customer was leaving and the assistant turned to her with a friendly look. 'What can I get for you today, Miss Fernsby?'

'I'll have those pieces of salmon, Joe,' she said quickly.

When he handed over her change along with the fish neatly wrapped up, he said, 'Do give my regards to your brother,' with a meaningful look. One of Freddie's past adventures?

She smiled at him and said, 'I will. Have a good evening, Joe.' The woman in the brown coat was still deliberating over her order as Ellen walked triumphantly out into the crowds on the street with the salmon, her mind fixed on the evening to come.

6

'Put it down here,' Freddie instructed as they moved the table from its usual corner location to the middle of the sitting room. He pulled out the flap to lengthen it and put the tablecloth on the top. 'There, not bad,' he said, eyeing the room critically. 'Can you do the plates and things?' The doorbell rang and they both jumped. 'I'll get it,' Ellen said. Her stomach was fluttering.

But, in fact, when she opened the street door it was Alec. He gave a tentative smile and asked, 'Am I too early?' When they came into the sitting room, Freddie was standing at the door to the kitchen.

'Freddie. It's good to see you,' Alec said.

Freddie responded, 'Same here, Alec.' They both looked serious, almost shocked.

Ellen asked, suppressing a nervous giggle, 'Is that a bottle of wine in your hand?' then Freddie cleared his throat and said, 'I see my sister has involved you in her latest hare-brained scheme.' Alec laughed and the tension eased. Ellen got Alec to help with laying the table and Freddie opened the wine.

When the bell rang for a second time, it was Freddie who ran down the stairs, returning a minute later with Kate, elegant in tailored trousers and a dark red blouse. She presented a bunch of roses to Ellen who buried her nose in them, with a recurrence of that odd shyness, while Freddie unearthed a vase. She wondered at her memory of Kate from the previous day – she looked years younger than the version Ellen had taken away and worried over. The sallow colour and tension had gone; she was just like the attractive, vital Kate of old. At first, Ellen was conscious of how she must regard their home. Was she noticing the shabbiness in the unmatched sofa and chair, the threadbare carpet and general simplicity; or would she see the artistic touches, the gay tablecloth and curtains Freddie had used to brighten it up? But Kate looked around her and said, with apparent sincerity, 'I love what you've done with this room.' Alec was introduced, there was some chit-chat and then they were sitting down to the table.

After pronouncing the soup delicious, Kate commented, 'I can't get over the change in you since I last saw you, Freddie. And I hear you're a fashion designer! How did you get into that?'

'Well, up until five years ago I was doing men's tailoring, that was my training. When my old boss retired, I decided to take over his shop and make a change by designing women's clothes. It gives me a lot more opportunities to be creative in terms of colours and use of fabric. Ellie coming in with me made it possible – she's got the business brains, plus she acts as a good advertisement for my designs when she goes out.'

Kate smiled. 'Yes, I've seen her in action. Very effective.'

Freddie was always articulate and confident when he spoke about his work. 'And I think it's important, too. People laugh at me when I say this, but I believe women get a raw deal with their clothing. I mean, just look at what you were forced to wear until recently – those ghastly corsets, those long skirts that prevented you from moving freely …'

'Don't I know it! It made it hard when we were being chased by the police,' Kate said with a reminiscent glance at Ellen. 'I used to scandalise my family because I refused to wear corsets. I said they were instruments of torture.'

'Can you believe some people actually thought women were born with weak spines and they'd just slump to the floor without corsets? Isn't that crazy? So much of women's fashion is plain wrong. I mean, just think about pockets as an example.' Freddie was warming to his theme.

'Pockets?' Alec asked, but Kate knew instantly what he meant.

'Absolutely! Our dresses would have no pockets at all, or these teeny slits to hold a hanky, so we had to take bags with us everywhere. We need just as many pockets as men. That's what I love about these trousers, apart from the fact they're so comfortable,' and she stood up from the table to demonstrate the deep pockets.

Freddie asked, 'Are they French?' and when she nodded, said, 'I thought so. They have a definite style. I've done similar trousers for Ellie. Are yours Chanel?'

Kate laughed. 'Well, a copy. I can't quite afford the real thing.'

'It was Ellie who first made me aware of all this. She always refused to buy clothes that weren't practical or which stopped her moving easily. You used to say it was a way to keep women powerless, didn't you?' Ellen nodded. She was enjoying watching the others and the way the conversation was developing. Kate looked happy and relaxed.

Freddie continued, 'So I started thinking, why don't I design clothes for women which are beautiful, but also give them freedom and practicality? What I'm saying isn't new. It's been around for ages. The Rational Dress people were talking about this long before we were born. We can't walk around naked in public, so what we wear is important. Our clothes are a symbol of who we are, or perhaps who we'd like to be, and what we do.'

Alec had been following the conversation with keen interest. 'This all makes a lot of sense. I agree, it's certainly easier for men, but we're limited as well. I hate having to wear boring suits all the time. Our clothes are always so formal and heavy! And we're not supposed to wear anything colourful – it's seen as effeminate. It's terribly restricting. I can't wait to get out of my work clothes at the end of the day.'

Freddie nodded. 'I know what you mean. Perhaps we should both join the Men's Dress Reform Party! Most of their ideas are crackpot, but they make some good points about men's clothing.'

'Well, you've got a nice colour on now, Alec,' Kate remarked. 'That shirt's a lovely shade of green.'

'Yes, it suits you,' Freddie said.

Ellen decided it was time to join the conversation. 'It's not just clothes that have improved for women. All that hair we used to have! Do you remember the elaborate styles – and those ridiculous hats? When I see pictures of those days I want to cringe. Thank God we can have our hair short now. It gives me a real sense of freedom.'

Kate said, 'I agree – but when you let your hair down, Ellie, God, what a sight. Flaming red locks … It was magnificent.'

'And it made it easy for the police to identify me,' Ellen pointed out.

But Kate continued watching her. 'And now your hair is darker, but still so striking, like burnished copper.' Freddie glanced at Ellen with a raised eyebrow. She looked down, momentarily disconcerted.

They got into a lively discussion on the restrictions and importance of clothes. Freddie eventually got up to collect the soup plates. Ellen asked, 'Can I help?' but he shook his head and disappeared into the kitchen.

Now is the time to say something, Ellen thought, realising she felt anxious about Kate's reaction. She decided to introduce the subject in a roundabout way. 'Kate, you might know Alec's mother from the suffragette days. Do you remember Flora Medley?'

Kate looked closely at Alec with a delighted smile. 'I say, how wonderful. Of course I remember Flora. She was very prominent in the movement. So, you're her son? How is she?'

'Very well, still active and involved in women's rights. She's an amazing woman. She used to drag me along to all the suffragette rallies and actions. When I was a small boy, I found it pretty tedious sitting through the speeches, but later on I started enjoying it. My mother always got me to help carry the banners. I'd walk along, singing the anthems, shouting, "Votes for Women!" and handing out leaflets. I used to get all types of comments from men in the crowd.'

'What sort of comments?' Ellen asked.

'Oh, unnatural, a traitor to my sex, that sort of thing. One man loudly called me a "pansy enslaved by harridans". I just laughed at him.'

'Perhaps we were at some of the same rallies,' Kate suggested.

'I'd imagine so. I certainly remember seeing Ellen and Freddie. It was unusual to see another boy around my age, and of course, with their red hair they were quite memorable. In fact—' But Alec stopped suddenly then changed the subject, asking Kate, 'Were you in the bodyguard protecting Mrs Pankhurst, the same as Ellen?'

'For sure,' Kate replied with relish. 'We learned jujitsu and we used it on a few occasions. In fact, it came in handy last year, when I was attacked on the street in Berlin.' She smiled at Ellen. 'Do you remember the battle of Glasgow? What a brawl that was!'

Ellen nodded. 'I had bruises for weeks after.' Alec looked at them enquiringly, so Ellen told him about their attempts to stop the police arresting Mrs Pankhurst. She continued, 'As for the songs, I can still remember every word, although the one by Ethel Smyth was tricky to sing. There was one note I could never get.'

Kate's face was vivid with memories. 'My favourite was the one sung to *Men of Harlech*. How did it go?' She paused, trying to recall the words, but Alec started singing quietly:

From the daughters of the nation,
Bursts a cry of indignation,
Breathes a sigh of consecration,
In a sacred cause.

'Oh yes! We used to sing that while we were marching along. God, we did walk bloody miles,' Kate laughed.

'I always used to sing "daughters and sons of the nation" for the first line, only I had to gabble the words to fit them in,' Alec remembered with a grin.

Ellen said, 'I liked the ending best.' She started singing and Alec joined her in harmony:

Let no ancient custom bind you
Let one bond of suffering bind you
Leave unrighteous laws behind you,
Soon you shall be free!

Freddie emerged with two plates and Ellen hastily got up to bring in the other plates. 'Are you having a sing-song?' Freddie asked tartly, and they all laughed. 'Help yourself to potatoes.' They were quiet for a while, savouring Freddie's salmon.

Alec said, 'God, Freddie, this tastes fabulous! What's the sauce?' Freddie explained how he had made it and Ellen watched them chatting, with a bubble of happiness inside her. Alec told Freddie about a good fish restaurant he'd discovered and she topped up their glasses. She rarely drank wine, and it made her feel sophisticated with a slight sense of floating.

After a while, Kate said, almost as if speaking to herself, 'I do miss the suffragette days.'

'What? All those cumbersome clothes and being beaten up by the police?' Freddie teased.

'Oh, it certainly wasn't easy. A lot of women suffered terribly. But – I just feel our lives had such meaning then. We were united. We had a sisterhood. We were committed to something that was so important. The suffragette movement was like a blast of fresh air into our stifled lives, don't you think, Ellie? For the first time we felt we were part of life – we weren't just bystanders, passively watching life go by. We had a purpose. We were making things happen.'

Ellen said, 'Yes. It gave us such a feeling of freedom and power.'

'I was part of something bigger than myself. And I miss that ...' Kate looked around at the others.

Ellen saw a wistfulness on her face, which made her feel sad. Even so, her dogged insistence on the truth made her say, 'Perhaps we have rose-tinted glasses about those days, Kate. I was shocked at the way most suffragettes blindly supported the war. How could they be so clear about the injustice we suffered, but think that it was right to send men off to die for no reason? How is that a patriotic duty? I got into so many arguments. I lost quite a few friendships over that.'

Freddie's voice was quiet. 'I was given a white feather in the street by a woman I recognised from suffragette rallies. She called me a coward for not enlisting. I'd just turned sixteen. As if I should go off whistling into hell.'

Kate responded, 'You're right. I was disillusioned by the way most suffragettes acted so unthinkingly. I never did understand why we went to war. Does anyone? Who in their right mind could think war is anything other than hideous? The things I saw in France ...' Ellen could see unhappy memories on all their faces. God knows, Freddie and Alec had suffered the most, but she still had nightmares about some of her nursing experiences. She didn't weep easily, but during the war she'd sometimes cried herself to sleep after a day of being cheerful for men who were maimed and in desperate pain.

Alec broke the silence. 'But I know what you mean, Kate, about being part of a cause. I think we all need something that gives us meaning. That's why people have religion. Or football.'

'Or they support war, or political movements,' Freddie added.

Kate looked pensive. 'I spent a year in Berlin before I came back to London. These Nazis are getting a lot of support and it seems to make people ... less human, more animal. Groups of men would sometimes go around attacking anyone who didn't fit in with their ideals of German purity. I had to leave in the end, I found it so disturbing.'

'Did you say something about being attacked yourself?' Ellen asked.

'Yes. I was on the street one day when a couple of thugs were smashing up a shop, I suppose because the poor owners were Jews. They saw my camera and turned on me, calling me a "Jewish bitch" and worse. I managed to get away. But what shocked me was the way people stood there and watched. No one tried to help me.' Kate had inherited her Irish mother's dark complexion; she used to joke she must be descended from a shipwrecked Armada sailor.

'Thank God you were all right,' Ellen breathed. 'I didn't realise it was so bad there.'

'I've been reading about this, and I fear it's going to get worse. These are nasty times,' Alec commented.

Kate went on, 'So, the important thing is to be sure you're supporting a cause that's for the greater good. Something that makes people better, not worse.'

Freddie suggested, 'There are lots of causes to get involved in. Ellie and I teach dressmaking skills every Tuesday night to women in Toynbee Hall. If they have a trade, it'll be easier for them to find work and be independent, and not have to stay with some bastard who's beating them up.'

Ellen added, 'It's part of the work Sylvia Pankhurst was doing for years in the East End, although she's not involved now. These women can lead desperately hard lives. I feel it's the least we can do. We employ a few on a casual basis when our orders pile up. They get work experience and money, but we get something out of it too. Of course, most of the women we teach are in love with Freddie.'

Kate laughed. 'I'm not surprised! You're a lovely man, Freddie.'

Alec seemed to be thinking out loud. 'Yes, he is.' Freddie was thoroughly red and embarrassed by now. Kate observed them both with interest. Alec said swiftly to her, 'My mother's thrown herself into getting more birth control clinics set up. She'd love your help, I'm sure.'

'And what about you?' Kate asked.

'Oh – I provide my services in a free clinic in the East End, and I do a fair bit of *pro bono* work.' On seeing Kate's puzzled look, he said, 'Didn't Ellen tell you I'm a solicitor?'

This is the moment, Ellen thought, and opened her mouth to say, 'Actually—'

But Kate was already saying to Alec, 'That's interesting! I'm on the lookout for a solicitor I can trust. I've been using my father's firm and I hate them. Which is ironic, considering they have complete power over the money that's left. Because I'm a single woman, I'm not allowed to have a bank account, so they act as my male guardian. I have to go to them, cap in hand, if I need money. The whole thing is humiliating. It makes me so angry.'

Ellen forgot what she was going to say, and asked instead, 'Did your father leave the estate to you?'

Kate gave a cynical laugh. 'Yes. Hilarious, isn't it? We hated each other and I had nothing to do with him once my mother died. For years there was no contact. Then I got a letter last summer from his solicitors, saying he'd died and left everything to me. Thank God they changed the law a few years ago so I could at least inherit the property! I can only think he decided the black sheep of the family was better than no family at all. He would never have left his money to charity.'

'Is that why you came back to England?'

'Yes – and no. It came at just the right time, because I wanted to come home anyway. I missed England, London.' She hesitated and Ellen silently urged her to continue. 'At first, I was going to refuse the money, but then I thought no, in a way it's a sort of natural justice. He treated my mother and me so badly, why shouldn't I get something from him in the end? It meant I had enough to buy a flat outright with a little left over for a rainy day. My father's firm was telling me I should have used the money to invest. I had to really argue with them to use the money the way I wanted.'

Alec observed, 'You made the right decision, Kate. When did you buy the flat?'

'September, last year.'

'Good timing, because the markets crashed just weeks later. Far better to have your money in real estate than in worthless shares. You have much more security this way.'

'It was pure luck, that's all. I understand nothing about investments,' Kate said, but she looked pleased.

Freddie had quietly collected their empty plates and stopped to say, 'Now it's stocks and shares, for heaven's sake!

I think I preferred the communal singing. Ellie, come and help me with the dessert.' But when she went into the kitchen she saw he had the strawberries and cream ready in four bowls. He murmured to her, 'Are you going to say something this evening? It's going so well … Perhaps leave it for another day?'

She shook her head. 'I told Alec to come tonight so we could discuss it. I'll mention it now.' Freddie looked at her with a slight frown, but said nothing. They walked back into the sitting room with the bowls.

7

Kate broke off her conversation with Alec to smile at them both. 'This is such a special meal.' Turning back to him, she asked, 'And did you always plan to be a solicitor?'

Alec laughed. 'God, no. I used to have dreams of being a professional musician. I studied the piano all through school and planned to do a music degree. And then …' He shrugged and held up his right hand, so Kate could see the angry scars and missing middle finger.

'The war?' she asked.

'Yes. A grenade went off near me. I had to give up that idea and get a job to support my family. My father died at the end of the war and I have two younger sisters. But I still love music. I sing in a choir and go to a lot of concerts.'

'Presumably you got compensation of a sort?' Kate asked, but Alec shook his head.

'Of course not. They gave a miniscule amount if you lost two or more fingers – mine wasn't considered serious enough. But I don't complain. I wouldn't have taken the money anyway.

I was lucky. Any pension should be going to the poor sods who suffered awful injuries.' He looked over at Freddie. 'These strawberries are really tasty.'

There was a comfortable silence as they ate the fruit. This was it. Ellen took a deep breath. 'Kate.'

Kate looked over at her, smiling. 'Yes, my dear?'

'I thought Alec could help us look into the circumstances of that man's death in the church fire. We discussed it this morning, and he's agreed to help. That's if you want to go ahead ...' She faltered when she saw Kate staring at her, pale and serious.

'Who have you been talking to about this? Are you telling the whole world?' Her voice was quiet but there was a steeliness Ellen hadn't heard before.

'Of course not, Kate! I've only spoken to Freddie and Alec, and you can trust them completely. Don't you see? There's something not right about this death. I read the newspaper accounts this afternoon and it doesn't add up. They don't say the body's there until two days later, and then it's not mentioned again once the war started. Nothing about the police investigation, not another word. Don't you think—?' But Kate cut across her.

'No, Ellen. I can't believe you thought this would be all right with me. We've only just met up again – and you're already trying to manage my life! What gives you the right to meddle? I won't take this. No. I don't agree.' She put her bowl down on the table and stood up. Her voice was still quiet, but she was clearly angry. 'Freddie, thank you for an excellent meal. Alec, very nice to meet you.' She started walking out of the room.

'Kate, please don't go!' Ellen stood up as well, looking after her with distress. 'I'm sorry ...' But Kate had already left.

They heard the front door close a minute later. 'Oh, Christ!' she uttered in despair. 'What have I done?'

Alec said gently, 'If she doesn't agree, I can't take this any further. I'm sorry, Ellen.'

'Best to give her some time to think it over and cool down,' Freddie suggested.

Ellen stared at him miserably, shook her head and made for the stairs.

It was still quite early and the Saturday night crowds were just getting started. Ellen could hear the traffic on Piccadilly and the sounds of people laughing and talking. Someone was playing a jazz tune on a trumpet. But in Jermyn Street it was dark and still, apart from one man crossing over from the church. The moon briefly came out from behind some clouds.

She'd run out without grabbing a coat, and the night air was cool. Shivering in her thin silk blouse, she looked around. She spotted Kate further along, walking rapidly towards St James's Street, and hurried after her. Kate must have heard her footsteps but didn't turn around. Ellen had to run up alongside and grab her arm before she halted.

'Kate – stop. Please talk to me. I'm sorry I made you angry. It was never my intention. I just wanted—'

Kate stared furiously at her. 'Wanted what? To make me feel worse? How could you be so, so—'

'Be so stupid? Is that what you were going to say? I know I haven't had the same education as you. I come from a simple family and I daresay I do appear very stupid to you. But—'

'Oh, for God's sake, don't make this into a class issue, Ellen. And don't play the little victim either. It doesn't suit you. You know bloody well you're an intelligent woman. We've never felt anything other than equals in this and all other respects, so don't start playing that game. It insults both of us.' She paused, visibly trying to gain control of her emotions. 'No, I was going to say: how could you be so thoughtless?'

Two men came out of the restaurant near the corner and looked at them with interest. They remained silent while the men walked past. Ellen heard one of the men laugh at a comment the other made.

Looking after them, she sighed. 'Look, I know I rush into things. I know I have a tendency to interfere. Freddie's always telling me that. But I just … I have this gut feeling about the fire. I can see you have such remorse over it, and it breaks my heart to see you like this. I just thought, if we look into it, what could we lose? If it turns out the man did die in the fire, perhaps knowing more about it will help you feel less controlled by the guilt.'

Kate narrowed her eyes. 'Why is this any of your business?'

'Because I care about you, Kate. Because you're my friend.' Ellen tried to keep her voice steady.

Kate gave a short laugh. 'You haven't seen me for sixteen years! Do you really think you still know me? I've changed. I'm no longer that girl. There's a lot you don't know. I don't think you'd like me if you knew some things about me.'

'You're wrong,' Ellen said stubbornly. 'People don't change in the fundamentals. We've both had experiences that changed us, of course, how could that not be? But you're still essentially the same Kate I loved in 1914. Although … perhaps, yes, you have changed in one way. The Kate I knew always stood up to things, always faced things head on. She would never have been such a coward, running away from the truth, being so passive.' The minute the words were said she could have cut out her tongue, but it was too late.

'Coward? Me?' Kate's eyes glittered from a face as pale as parched grass. She stared at Ellen, opened her mouth and shut it, then turned and walked away. This time, Ellen let her go.

She wandered around the back streets away from Piccadilly, not wanting to be among the lights or crowds, not wanting to go home and admit her failure to the others. Her mind was in turmoil, occupied with staccato bursts of recrimination and regret. If only she could go back in time to Friday and change everything! Eventually, chilly and defeated, she turned for home.

Alec and Freddie were sitting talking on the sofa when she came in. She looked around drearily and saw the table had been put back in the corner and the remnants of the meal cleared away. Freddie asked, 'Did you speak to her?'

Ellen nodded. She wanted to howl or, preferably, kick something. 'Yes. We had a horrible argument. She probably never wants to see me again. I've created a ghastly mess and it's all my fault.'

He got up and gave her a consoling hug. 'It'll come right, Ellie. Don't blame yourself. There are strawberries left over – do you want some?' She shook her head miserably but couldn't help noticing how calm Alec and Freddie seemed. At least something tonight wasn't a complete disaster.

Alec was looking at her. 'I said I wouldn't go ahead if Kate didn't agree. But I'd like to see the newspaper accounts you mentioned. Do you have them here?'

'Yes, I went all through all the *Evening News* and wrote down everything I could find. Hold on …' She ran up to her bedroom to get her notebook, gazing sadly at the 1913 photograph of her and Kate. On her return she saw the two men standing close together and halted, fearing she may have interrupted them. But Alec turned to her with a smile.

'Thank you. I'll give this back to you in a few days. And, obviously, let me know if Kate changes her mind.' He paused, looking at Freddie, then said, 'Well, I'd better be going. I'm sorry it didn't turn out the way you hoped, Ellen, but I've had a lovely evening, and the best meal ever.'

Freddie said, 'I'll see you out,' and they went down the stairs. When he came back a few minutes later, she was staring unseeingly out the window. He came and put his hand on her shoulder.

'Oh, Freddie, she hates me now. I've lost my friend. When will I ever learn?'

He was strangely untroubled. 'Don't worry, Ellie. She'll be back. This isn't the last of it.'

8

Sunday was usually Ellen's favourite day of the week. She would spend it out of doors as much as possible, walking or swimming, or having a picnic if the weather permitted. Sometimes she would go with Freddie or a friend on a train trip out of London to explore the countryside. If the weather proved inclement, she would visit galleries and exhibitions, or curl up contentedly on the sofa with a book. But nothing seemed to be right today. The hours stretched before her uninvitingly. She had gone with Freddie for an early morning swim in the Serpentine, returning with their favourite pastries and the newspapers. They always bought a broadsheet and a tabloid so they could compare stories and laugh about the differences. The papers, full of Amy Johnson's arrival in Australia the day before, were spread out over the floor and her pastry was beside her, half-eaten. Looking down, she could see the broadsheet headline: "Amy Johnson lands in Australia. First successful solo flight by woman pilot", while the tabloid screamed: "Blonde Aviatrix does it!"

'Why is the colour of her hair so important?' she grumbled.

Freddie glanced up at her with a smile. He'd been infuriatingly good-tempered all morning. Just then, she heard a ring. 'Is that the phone?' she asked hopefully, jumping off the sofa, but Freddie said, 'No, Ellie, it was a bicycle in the street.'

'Oh.'

Since she was on her feet, she wandered over to the window and frowned out at the sky. There were rows of little fluffy clouds spread out in a line, almost as if they had been carefully painted onto the blue background. She supposed she could go for a walk. Turning around, her eyes fell on the roses, their deep red reminding her of the colour of Kate's blouse. She averted her eyes with a scowl from the image, and considered instead the top of Freddie's head, bent over his section of the paper. She longed to know what was happening between him and Alec, but had sternly told herself not to ask. Her days of interfering were over.

Freddie must have felt her gaze, because he looked up and laughed. 'Ask the question. I can see you're dying to know.'

'Not at all,' she replied stiffly. 'It's none of my business.'

'It is, really. God knows how many hours I spent crying on your shoulder about him. You were always so kind, so patient. You never once told me to shut up.'

'Why would I do that, silly? It's much better to talk. All right, I admit it. I'd love to know if you managed to sort things out.'

Freddie started coughing and she sat next to him on the sofa, waiting for him to catch his breath. His lungs were mostly healed from the gas, but the wheezing fits had returned two months ago, around the same time he and Alec had parted.

'Well ...' He sighed and then went on, his voice ragged, 'I was so sure he must hate me – he could never forgive me. Thank God I was wrong! I was able to tell him everything I'd wanted to say before – how deeply I regretted my behaviour, how I realised afterwards I'd pushed him away because I was scared ... scared of getting hurt again, scared I was betraying Sam. I'd never properly talked to him about Sam. He listened – he said he understood. We've agreed to be friends.'

'Just friends?' Ellen asked, trying for a neutral tone.

Freddie gave a rueful shrug. 'He told me he's become involved with someone, so I think that particular ship has sailed. I only have myself to blame. But, oh, Ellie ... he's very special. I do care about him so much. If this is the way I can have him in my life again, then I accept it. Perhaps it'll be better in the long run. God knows, I'm a disaster at relationships. Friendships last longer. I only know I can't lose contact with Alec again.'

Ellen squeezed his hand. They were both silent with their own thoughts for a while, then Freddie got up with a yawn, stretching out his arms. 'Up you get, Miss Grumpy. Come out with me. There's an exhibition of Regency clothes at the V&A I want to see. I'll buy you lunch.'

They'd found a bakery open in Exhibition Road; when they walked back from Green Park tube around six, she was carrying a still-warm baguette they could have for supper along with the leftover soup. Freddie was telling her about an idea he had for a design, so it was only when they were at the back of Fortnum and Mason that she looked up and noticed someone waiting outside their door. Her heart leapt, but she had to look again to assure herself it wasn't a trick of her eyesight. Freddie said, 'I told you she'd come back.'

As they came up to her, Kate was pale and grave, her eyes on Ellen. Her tone was abrupt. 'Can we talk?'

'Always.' Ellen's voice was even but her stomach was churning.

Freddie put his key in the door. 'Come on, let's go upstairs.' Once in the flat, he said, 'I'll put the kettle on,' and tactfully removed himself to the kitchen.

Kate walked over to the window, with her back to Ellen. 'I haven't stopped thinking about it, Ellen. I barely slept. I couldn't settle to anything today.'

'Kate, I'm sorry—'

'Will you stop apologising all the bloody time?' She flashed Ellen a quick smile which took the sting out of the words. 'No, I realised you're quite right. I have let this damned thing control me. And, yes, I am being a coward. When you said that to me last night … I was so shocked and angry, I couldn't speak. But when I calmed down, I saw a lot of things about myself I didn't want to accept before.'

She sighed and stopped. Ellen waited. The quiet in the flat was pierced by the whistle of the kettle. Kate went on, 'I've always had this belief that I faced up to things. No doubt that's my arrogance. But instead, I've spent sixteen years running away from something I did. And it's time to stop running.' She turned around and looked levelly at Ellen. 'I'd like to take up Alec's offer and find out more about what happened. Maybe I can make a financial reparation to the man's family. Will you help me?'

'With all my heart,' Ellen replied, and then they were smiling at each other with relief.

Freddie came in with the tea tray, took a swift look at their faces, and said merrily, 'Now, my darlings, it's time for tea. I found some scrumptious biscuits in the cupboard. Come and get cosy on the sofa.' They sat down obediently and he poured the tea. 'Milk?' Kate nodded. 'Sugar?' Kate shook her head. 'No, I suppose you're sweet enough already,' and they all started laughing rather hysterically. How much Ellen loved her brother. She knew he was trying to break the tension in the room with his camp routine.

It must have worked, because Kate took a sip of tea and ate a biscuit. She suddenly grinned. 'I didn't realise, I'm bloody starving.'

'Shall I get supper?' Freddie suggested, but she shook her head and took another biscuit. 'No, thank you Freddie. You can't keep on feeding me! I've got someone coming for a French lesson soon, so I can't stay long. I just had to come here and see you both. I was sitting on your step for quite a while, beginning to think you'd never come back. Either that, or you were here and not answering the bell to me.'

'Why on earth would we do that?' Ellen protested, while Freddie explained about the exhibition they'd been to. Kate listened, wrapping her hands around the teacup, the colour returning to her face. They drank their tea and she said, 'I don't know if you heard, Freddie, but I've decided I want to go ahead with this investigation, or whatever we call it.'

'Why don't I ring Alec to tell him?' Freddie suggested instantly, his eyes brightening. He jumped up and disappeared off down to the workroom.

Kate looked at Ellen. 'I don't know where this will lead. Perhaps I'm mad. I may end up getting myself arrested. But doing nothing is no longer an option. You showed me that.'

'We can stop any time you want. The whole point of this is for you to feel in control. You just say the word if it starts to feel wrong. The last thing I want is to hurt you, Kate, or put you in a worse situation.'

Just as Kate was responding, Freddie called her name from below. They went down to the workroom where he was talking quietly on the telephone. Kate stopped to look around with interest at the sewing machines, bolts of material and half-cut dresses on the workbenches and Freddie's designs pinned up on the walls. The evening sun was slanting through the large windows at the front. But Freddie was saying, 'Here she is,' and handing the receiver to Kate.

Ellen wandered over to the window to stand in the shaft of sunlight, a curious stillness in her mind. Freddie leaned next to her with a look of contentment. After a while, Kate said, 'Hold on, I'll ask,' and turned to them. 'Alec's suggesting he can come over here tomorrow after work so we can talk it through. Is that convenient, or …?'

They both nodded. Kate continued looking at them. 'You look like two red-haired angels standing in that light,' she said unexpectedly, then went back to her conversation with Alec. After further discussion she laid the earpiece on the desk and stood up, saying to Freddie, 'He wants to speak to you again.' Freddie went forward quickly to the telephone and Kate came over to Ellen. 'I'm afraid I need to go.'

'Shall I walk with you part of the way?' Ellen didn't feel quite ready to stop their conversation.

'Yes, I'd like that.' Kate blew Freddie a kiss and they went down the stairs.

Out on the street, they walked along silently for a while. Think of something to say, Ellen urged herself. She was never good at small talk. But then, it had never been necessary before with Kate. 'Isn't it a pain needing to work on a Sunday evening? I love having my Sundays free.'

Kate shrugged. 'I suppose it is. It didn't feel important before. It's not as if my Sundays have been anything special. Dorothy said this was the best evening for her. I suspect she won't last many more lessons, though. I think I'm working her too hard. She's complaining about having to conjugate verbs.'

'Is she nice?' Ellen asked with an absurd stab of insecurity.

'Not my type at all. Very flighty and shallow, a typical flapper. Wants to improve her French before her summer holidays, presumably to help her chances of finding a French husband.' They both laughed and Ellen started to feel more relaxed.

'It must be so useful speaking other languages. I wish I could. Did you ever make it to university in the end? I know that was your ambition.'

'What with having to get away after the fire, and then the war, it wasn't really an option. I did start at Cambridge in 1918. I'd come back from France a few weeks before and managed to wangle a place in Girton College after I was offered a bursary. But my mother got sick not long after I started and I had to go home to nurse her, so that was that. Well, too late now.'

'It must have been the terrible influenza that went around. Endell Street Hospital was packed. It was awful. They were dropping like flies, even healthy young people. It seemed so cruel – men who'd survived the carnage in the war were dying within days.' They waited to cross St James's Street. Ellen looked, embarrassed, at the corner where they'd had the argument the previous evening.

Kate didn't seem to notice. She nodded, her face bleak. 'I'm pretty sure my mother picked it up on Armistice Day. She went out into the crowds to celebrate the end of the war, and the next day she was in bed. I used to think, why didn't my father catch the flu instead of her? It was so quick, she was dead within a week. Believe it or not, after the way he treated her, my father cried like a baby.' Ellen lifted her hand to Kate's shoulder in unspoken commiseration. Kate thanked her silently with her eyes.

They turned into Piccadilly, guarded by its imposing buildings. As they walked under the arch next to the Ritz, Ellen looked through the windows at people having high tea in the restaurant, recalling the different clientele she and Freddie sometimes met in the downstairs bar. Her casual glance came to a halt when she realised Myra was at a table with a group of people. She stopped to look. That must be her husband — she recognised him from the studio portrait in Myra's bedroom, although he looked plumper and more self-satisfied in the flesh. She studied Myra, talking vivaciously with one of the other men, and realised she felt nothing, a blankness of emotion. It was as if she were someone Ellen had known a long time ago, before her life changed completely.

'Do you know her?'

She realised Kate was watching her and shrugged. 'Yes.'

Kate looked as if she would like to question her further, but something about Ellen's face must have stopped her. They continued walking and she noticed how they automatically paced at the same speed. Kate was never one of these people who dawdle along. As they came alongside Green Park she said, 'Kate. Whatever happens now, we go through it together.'

Kate stopped and took her hand. 'Yes.' She was about to say more but noticed her watch. 'Bloody hell, is that the time? I need to run. I'll see you tomorrow,' and she gave Ellen a kiss on the cheek, their eyes meeting for a second. Then she dashed over Piccadilly during a break in the traffic, turning on the north side to wave at Ellen with a smile before striding off.

Ellen lingered at the entrance of Green Park, watching people in their deckchairs enjoying the sunny evening. May was such a beautiful month, leaping and budding, full of promise. She found herself whistling under her breath as she walked home.

9

Mondays were always quiet in the shop. The beginning of the week was probably too busy a time for working women and housewives to think about clothes. Most of the shop's profits came from society women, an irony which did not escape Ellen. She might harbour a secret contempt for what she saw as their pampered, empty lives; she might resent their often patronising attitude towards her; but their money kept the shop going. And, after all, that was how she had met Myra.

It was nearly lunchtime, when business would hopefully pick up. Freddie sat at the counter examining designs in *Vogue*, while she tidied materials and thought desultorily about the administration waiting for her upstairs. She was usually organised and efficient in dealing with bills and orders, but, somehow, she felt unable to settle today. When the bell on the shop door tinkled, they looked up to see Mr Cohen, the next-door tailor, entering. 'Ah, so you're quiet too,' he noted. 'I sometimes think we should close on Monday mornings, they're such a waste of time.' He started telling Freddie about the new clothes press he had acquired. They were on good terms with the neighbouring men's tailors. After an initial bemusement, when Freddie had turned Mr Perkins' business into the only women's clothes shop in Jermyn Street, they'd continued friendly and supportive, possibly relieved to have one less competitor. All talk at the moment was how the economic slump might affect business – the topic came up whenever tailors met. Freddie went off to look at the new press and Ellen sat in his place. Kate's re-emergence in her life had sparked off blazing, insistent memories of the time they'd met, a time when the suffragette cause had been everything for them. Staring in front of her, she became lost in those days.

April, 1913: Ellen had arrived in London a few months after her fifteenth birthday. She'd lined up an apprenticeship with a dressmaker in Bond Street and had argued with her parents for weeks about her decision to come to London. Her father had finally acceded to her wishes, telling her, 'I know how stubborn you can be when you get an idea into your head, Ellie. But you're a sensible girl. You can look after yourself, and you're not the sort to go running after boys. We trust you.' All the same, he had insisted on coming with her to London, a long day's travel involving train and buses, and inspected her lodgings and new employer with careful concern. Grudgingly satisfied, he departed the following day, but hugged her very tight before getting on the train.

Left alone, Ellen revelled in her new-found independence, spending every available moment discovering London, a box full of surprises and treasures after her small village. She occasionally joined the other apprentices for trips to tea rooms, but their giggling conversations about boys soon proved wearisome. Always content with her own company, she joined a lending library and wrote long letters to her parents and Freddie. His replies, full of news, drawings and curiosity about her life, were always welcome, and they planned the expeditions they would take when he came to stay with her.

It was on one of her walks around London that she found a message chalked on the pavement giving notice of a talk by Mrs Pankhurst. She had long supported the suffragette struggle – the previous year, she'd stood up in front of her school to give a talk on the subject. After attending the meeting and meeting Hilda, she was quickly drawn into the movement. She had already known instinctively her status and treatment, as a female, was wrong. Now, she came to understand how the denial of suffrage was part of a wider injustice. For more than a year, the Women's Social and Political Union became her whole life. She marched, leafletted, spoke, fought and was imprisoned for women's right to have a vote. The cause gave her life a meaning, deep friendships and a number of new skills: jujitsu, running a newspaper, keeping accounts and organising large events. But she hadn't anticipated how the suffragettes would help her discover her own strength and courage.

From the start, she'd been impressed by their meticulous organisation. Marches, rallies, fund-raising and the weekly newspaper were all planned and executed with ruthless efficiency. Ellen was initially recruited for the packing and despatching of *Votes for Women* from the Charing Cross Road office, but after a few months she moved on to writing articles and helping with the accounts. These skills proved invaluable when she later came to start the business with Freddie. Sometimes, Ellen felt she had learned everything worth knowing through the suffragettes.

She remembered so clearly the day she met Kate. As usual, the WSPU had organised the funeral procession for Emily Wilding Davison down to the smallest detail: the wreath-covered vehicles, the banners, the outfits. She'd sat up half the night before, sewing the white dress she needed to wear, and was waiting in the Kingsway headquarters when she noticed a dark-haired girl around her own age smiling at her. 'You look tired,' she'd said in a friendly, direct way. 'I bet you were up most of the night sewing the blasted dress, weren't you?' Ellen agreed that was the case, then asked if she had known Emily. The girl shrugged and replied, 'Only vaguely. She was in prison a lot, but I heard her talk a few times. She was absolutely dedicated to the cause.'

Ellen said, 'Yes, but did she have to die for the cause? Isn't it better to stay alive and keep fighting? As much as I want the right to vote, I'm certainly not going to die for it. I don't want to be a martyr. Life is too good.'

The other girl had laughed and looked at her more closely, interest showing on her expressive face. 'I'm certainly with you on that! I'm Kate, by the way,' she added.

They shook hands. She found herself looking into intelligent and humorous eyes. 'I'm Ellen. Pleased to meet you.'

They managed to stay in close proximity during the service and slow procession to King's Cross. Afterwards, they talked non-stop into the evening as they helped tidy up the banners and detritus left in Lincoln's Inn House. Kate grabbed some flowers left in the hallway before walking with her to her bus stop. She pushed them into Ellen's arms as the bus arrived, saying, 'You deserve these.'

After that, they always looked out for each other and arranged to be put onto the same duties. Everything was more interesting, more enjoyable, with Kate. They went out together every Thursday evening to sell *Votes for Women* to the public. She had previously found newspaper selling a tedious task, made worse by regular abuse from men in the street; but now, it became fun. They would stand on the road to avoid being arrested, dodging the traffic, entertaining themselves with jokes and sharp observations about the passing people. Sometimes they were laughing so much, or were so wrapped up in their conversation, they would forget the reason they were there. Ellen was elated to find someone who instinctively understood the way she thought. They started telling each other about their lives and their families. Within a few months, they were rarely apart. And, all the time, Ellen's confidence and self-belief steadily grew.

This was a period of turmoil and disagreement for the WSPU. Their slogan, "Deeds not Words", had become more literal following the move to direct action after Black Friday in 1910. Ellen and Kate heard about the brutal beatings and sexual assaults handed out that day by the police, and male bystanders, when suffragettes tried to march on Parliament. That was the time, Hilda told them, they realised that all the marching, lobbying and public speaking in the world would not bring them justice. Always, after Black Friday, women prepared themselves for routine physical violence from the police. They learned how to defend themselves and put cotton or cardboard over their ribs for protection. Many argued they should meet violence with violence. The issue was dividing the movement.

At first, the plan was to create public disorder. Small groups of women would take bags of stones or hammers to smash windows or street lamps, before making a quick getaway.

Thousands of windows were broken in the West End. Ellen sometimes now found herself walking past a shop window in Piccadilly or Bond Street she had once attacked with a hammer. Women would put lighted rags into post boxes, or throw objects at politicians' cars. Telephone wires were cut, fuse boxes destroyed.

Ellen and Kate became proficient at breaking windows and painting "Votes for Women" on every available wall or building. They learned jujitsu and ways to trick the police so that suffragettes, released from prison under the Cat and Mouse Act to recover from hunger strike, could address the public. They would get the police chasing after a decoy while the real mouse slipped out the back way. Once the police realised and tried to arrest the speaker, they would form a protective cordon around her and fight back. The newspapers called the militants "Sylvia's army" or "female hooligans" – the women were proud to label themselves this way.

But some suffragettes believed this still did not go far enough, and started a campaign of arson attacks. Empty buildings were targeted: politicians' houses, churches or places of historical interest. Paintings in art galleries were hacked with knives. Occasionally, women planted bombs. Hilda and Kate became involved while Ellen held back, unable exactly to explain her reasons, but feeling this had crossed a line. They would debate this issue endlessly, agreeing to disagree, always open and fair in their arguments. By now, they had a deep bond and trusted each other implicitly.

Ellen recalled raging angrily one evening to Hilda and Kate about the arguments used by those opposing their cause. 'They insult and attack us in every possible way! They treat us like children, as if we're mentally deficient, or worse. Even the Prime Minister said we're a "distinct and inferior species" to men. He compared us to rabbits – it's outrageous! How can they justify these comments?'

Hilda's kind smile was absent. Just out of prison and recovering from her latest hunger strike, she looked ill and drawn. 'Unfortunately, my dear, many men hate and fear women, and will do anything to keep us subjugated. They lost the right to own slaves eighty years ago, so they're determined we won't escape our enslavement. The chains may feel like velvet, but they're still chains.' She gave a short laugh when she saw their faces. 'I know what you're thinking. How can I be married and say this? I can, because I know our enemy intimately.'

Ellen protested, 'But my father's not like that. He's always treated me and my mother with respect. And my brother could never treat a woman badly. He's the kindest, gentlest person you could meet.' Kate nodded in agreement. She'd met Freddie several times when he came to stay with Ellen in his school holidays. He would enthusiastically design banners and help out with suffragette work.

Hilda went on, 'Don't get me wrong. Of course, there are good men – like my husband, or your father and brother. They work alongside us for women's suffrage, and thank God for them! But too many women are sentimental about men. They give up everything for them and get so little back. They always forgive their actions, even when they cost women dearly. They become trapped in marriages where they have no rights, and look to their children for compensation. Things will only change when we force them to change.' Kate followed the conversation closely but remained silent, and talk soon turned to their next planned action. The following evening, they replaced all the flags on a golf course with ones in the suffragette colours, and laughed all the way home.

By this time, Ellen knew all about the mental and physical abuse Kate's father inflicted on his wife and daughter. Kate's mother felt unable to leave, having no money or relatives, but she secretly supported her daughter's suffragette activity and covered for her absences. Kate sometimes spoke of getting a job so she could escape her father, but said her mother had begged her, with tears spilling from her eyes, to stay at school and get an education so she could be financially independent.

Kate had also told Ellen she'd realised she was attracted to her own sex. They had an instinctive understanding, absorbed as if by osmosis, that they could not talk about this more widely, not even to Hilda. There were a few passionate relationships between suffragettes, but these were mostly conducted in secret. In public, the case for women's suffrage was argued on the basis they were good wives and mothers. The movement could not be sullied by accusations of unnatural behaviour, or rejection of man's dominion. But Kate and Ellen knew they could tell each other everything. They could at least speak openly of their lack of interest in husbands or babies. Hilda would shake her head whenever this came up, smiling sadly at them. 'One day you'll feel differently, my dear girls.' But, as much as they respected Hilda and her greater wisdom, they privately agreed: they knew their minds. This would not change.

The trip to town, at the end of a working day in May, had started like all the others. They talked sparingly on the bus journey, small hammers hidden in their sleeves, an undercurrent of tension concealed beneath their quiet exteriors. As the bus arrived at Oxford Circus, Kate had turned to Ellen and asked,

'Would you like to come home with me for supper? You could stay the night. My father won't be around.' Ellen had agreed, pleasure briefly damping down her nerves.

Oxford Street was clogged with buses, automobiles and horse-drawn wagons. They walked along to a large department store, checking carefully for police. Hilda indicated with a nod of her head the side streets they could run down afterwards. They knew, from previous window-breaking expeditions, that they needed to act swiftly before dispersing. It had just stopped raining and the wet pavements were thronged with last-minute shoppers. As usual, before an action, Ellen's heart thudded in her chest and her senses appeared to be heightened. The people around them were going about their normal lives, minds on their supper or making that essential purchase. She caught snatches of conversation and wished she could lose herself in the crowd; be someone just like them. One woman asked her friend, 'What story did he give this time?' A harried-looking mother told her children, 'Just this last shop, then we'll go home.' A woman with daringly short hair paused and stared at Ellen with a peculiar intensity before walking on. Ellen looked after her, oddly unsettled. But there was no time to think – they were at the point of no return.

Arriving in front of the store, they paused for one final check, then produced their hammers and started smashing a row of windows. 'Votes for Women!' they shouted, throwing their leaflets. The crack of the glass, shattering into large shards, seemed to split the air. For a few valuable seconds, people stopped and gawped, slow to react. They seized this chance to make their escape, scattering in different directions. Ellen dashed over the road between two trolleybuses and down a narrow street, earning a shouted rebuke from one of the drivers. After a minute she slowed to a fast walk, planning to lose herself in the crowds on Regent Street.

But then, with a sudden, shocking thump, she was sent sprawling. She looked up to see a man in a bowler hat standing over her. He held her down with several other men, shouting out he'd identified her by her red hair. A hostile crowd gathered. Men took the opportunity to punch and slap her before the police arrived, while a few women tried to stop them.

Ellen had dreaded prison. Hilda would speak of the torture of forced feeding and she'd seen the impact of imprisonment on other women. She'd narrowly avoided arrest several times before. Finally, her luck had run out.

After some hours at the police station being shoved and insulted, she was thrown into a tiny compartment in the Black Maria and taken to Holloway women's prison on remand. On arrival, the doctor seemed to take pleasure in humiliating her, making her bend over naked in front of the guards, roughly grabbing at her genitals and asking if she was a virgin. She stared rigidly ahead, hot waves of shame and anger washing over her body, forcing herself not to react. After a compulsory bath, the head warder handed her the heavy dark-green serge uniform marked with arrows and she was locked into her cell for a long, lonely night.

When she saw Kate and Hilda in court the next day, she waved with a brave smile. The usual penalty for a first offence was fourteen days, so there were audible gasps in the courtroom when the magistrate sentenced her to six months with hard labour. Kate stood up, shouting angrily, 'She only broke a few windows!' Ellen had time only for one last glance at Kate's dismayed face before she was taken down.

That second night in her cell was her lowest point: knowing she would lose her job and her home, fearing her parents' shame and disapproval, missing Kate, missing Freddie. She made a vow to herself that night. She would not let it break her. She would survive this.

Prison life taught Ellen many lessons. She learned that small acts of defiance helped her to retain her spirit. She learned how simple things could sustain her: a ray of sunlight coming through the bars, a friendly smile or snatched conversations with the other women. And she learned that she was strong, stronger than she'd ever realised.

She coped with the physical privations: the wooden plank for her bed, the slop pail and meagre food, the constant mice and filth, the enforced silence. Thank God it was early summer – at least she didn't have to contend with the cold. Each day followed the same procedure. After dressing, cleaning her cell and emptying her bucket, she would have thin gruel and a piece of bread for breakfast before spending the day sewing garments. She was forced to attend daily chapel, but at least this got her out of her cell and offered a chance to be with the other women. For lunch she had porridge, followed by more gruel for supper and a long night locked in. She had decided, early on, she could not face a hunger strike. After hearing the screams of women being force-fed, and seeing the obvious physical damage they suffered, she never came to regret that decision.

There were meagre compensations among the hardship and Ellen tried to focus on these. She was allowed books from the prison library, although little time to read them before the lights were switched off. Twice a week she could exercise in the courtyard and used this time to walk around vigorously.

Despite the enforced silence, she managed to chat with other suffragettes, speaking out of the sides of their mouths to avoid attention.

And the monthly visits gave her great comfort. Kate always came, usually with Hilda. On the last visit, in July, she turned up with Freddie, down in the school holidays, an unanticipated pleasure. Ellen hugged them both close to her, ignoring the warder's shouted admonitions, and drank in their every look and word. Kate updated her on their friends and talk of war, while Freddie gave her reassuring news of her parents and home. She had seen his look of distress, quickly hidden, when he arrived, and made a point of being cheerful.

The hardest thing to bear was her feeling of panic at being confined in such a small space. The cell was roughly six feet wide and nine feet long with a stone floor and one barred window, high in the wall, which let in a modicum of light. She was allowed just one hour a day out of the cell. Sometimes, when she was locked in afterwards, Ellen thought she might scream. It wasn't the solitude she minded. Hysteria would claw at her throat, knowing she was trapped in this miniscule room with no possibility of getting out. She would force herself to breathe calmly and spent a lot of time pacing up and down. Three steps across, then turn, five strides down, turn again. She could hear mice scuttling in the dark and sang to herself while walking and turning, walking and turning. When she got out, she promised herself, she would never again take for granted the right to be free, in the open air.

Her early release was a surprise gift. A week after Kate's visit with Freddie, another suffragette muttered as they walked around the courtyard, 'War's been declared. We'll be released any day now.' The hope was almost unbearable. When Ellen heard nothing further, she crashed into a despair as deep as the first days. But it was true. A few days later, a guard opened her cell door shortly before lights out and took her to the governor's office, where the other suffragettes were gathered. The governor announced they would be released the following day.

How soft her clothes felt after the rough prison fabric! When Ellen stepped out of the main gate, her eyes blinking in the early morning sunlight, there was a welcome party waiting for them. Her first thought, on seeing Hilda, was that she looked anxious, unwell. But then Freddie was giving her a tight embrace and Hilda was wreathed in smiles.

Ellen had been involved in several receptions for released prisoners and knew the drill. They all piled into waiting cars and drove to a room the WSPU had booked in a smart West End restaurant. The women in her car talked non-stop about the war and the suspension of suffragette action. Hilda was also quietly speaking to her, confirming Ellen had lost her job and her lodgings, saying she and Freddie could stay with her until she got back on her feet. Ellen nodded and smiled, but found it hard to take in the conversation, the noise and movement, the glare of the light – so overwhelming after the last quiet, dark months. She gripped Freddie's hand and stared out the window. When they arrived and she could talk to Kate, it would all start to make sense.

The dining room was dressed in flowers and there was more food on the table than Ellen had seen in the last three months. Coffee, pastries, fruit … the colours and smells seemed to jump out at her, a feast for her senses. Women came up to hug her and congratulate her on her freedom. She had looked around the room, increasingly puzzled, before turning to Hilda. 'But – where's Kate?'

*

'Hello, Ellie, where are you? You're in a world of your own. What are you thinking about?' Ellen realised Freddie had been speaking to her for a while. She had been caught up in her memories, unaware of her surroundings. He stood in front of her now, with an enquiring expression. She got off the stool and stretched, smiling at him vaguely.

'I know, you were thinking about the old glory days, weren't you?' Freddie continued with a grin. 'You and Kate must have so much catching up to do. Isn't it wonderful she's back?'

Before she could reply, two women entered the shop, and work claimed her. But for the rest of the day, the words sounded in her mind like a chime: Kate is back, Kate is back.

10

'I've already made some progress.' They were in the sitting room after work, serious and concentrated. Alec had centre stage. Arriving in his hated work clothes, he had thrown off his suit jacket, and loosened his collar stud and tie, with a sigh of relief. His smart braces were defiantly striped blue and green. He turned to Kate. 'Before I go on, how much do you already know about Fawdon or his family?'

Kate made a sudden, sharp movement, and bit her lip. 'Nothing, absolutely nothing.'

'You never tried to find out anything?' he persisted, but his face was kind.

'No, and I've asked myself why many times. Do you think I don't feel utter shame over my actions, and the way I ran away from it all afterwards? I had the opportunity to find out more when it was apparent the police were no longer investigating ... I can't explain, or justify, why I never did. But now I want to face up to it and put it right.'

Ellen spoke up. 'Hilda never wanted to discuss it either,

when I questioned her. I think with the war starting so soon afterwards, and all the upheaval in our lives …' Her voice trailed off, then she added, 'And I never looked into it.'

'I suppose you just wanted to put it behind you, after all you'd been through,' Alec said. 'Well, there's a son, William, who's still living in the family home. It was quite easy to trace him. The name Fawdon isn't that common. I had a long conversation with him on the phone this afternoon. He's agreed I can go ahead and get the inquest report.'

Dark clouds were massing outside. Freddie got up to switch on the lamp, asking, 'How did you manage to persuade the son?'

Alec shrugged modestly. 'It was mostly luck and timing. He said that, for many years, he couldn't care less about what had happened. From all accounts, Fawdon was a violent drunkard who'd left the family destitute when William was a child. It sounds like he was living on the streets, or in and out of hostels. William said he'd just thought, "good riddance". But his mother died a few months ago and he started wondering about it. He realised he knew nothing other than what the police had told him. He doesn't remember there being an inquest, but that's got to be wrong.'

Ellen asked, 'How did you explain your interest?'

'Surprisingly, that was the easiest part. I decided to start by saying I was asked to look into the fire by an "interested party", and had a story prepared for when he asked questions. Something vague about the parish, or the council, depending on what he said. But he didn't seem curious about that – all he wanted to know was, would he have to pay for anything? We've agreed I'll go to see him once I have the report. I've already applied to the coroner's office for it.'

Kate was closely following the conversation, pale and tense. 'How was he with you? What do you know about the family?'

'It sounds like William's mother had to work all hours to keep the family home after Fawdon walked out. He's the only child. By the time his father died, William was working, so things were easier for him and his mother. He seems to be doing quite well for himself from what he said. He's married with children. He was perfectly friendly with me, but he made it clear he's not really too bothered. As long as he doesn't have to do anything himself, he doesn't mind my going ahead.'

Kate said, 'I want to come with you when you go to see him.'

'I want to come too,' Ellen added firmly.

Alec thought for a long moment, his face pensive in the glow from the lamp, then nodded. 'All right, but we'll need to make up a story. I can say you're a trainee solicitor, and Ellen, you could be my assistant. And you'll have to let me do the talking. Kate – you mustn't come clean about your involvement, or show you know too much. Do you agree?'

'But of course. You're the man, you must do all the talking,' Freddie said mock-seriously, then gave Alec a cheeky look. They all laughed. Even Kate had a slight smile.

She started to say, 'I can never begin to thank you enough—' but Alec shook his head. 'You don't need to, Kate. I want to do this. We're all in this together,' he said, looking around at them.

'What happens next?' Ellen asked.

'As soon as I get the inquest report and arrange a time to see the son, I'll let you know. It should be quite soon, perhaps by Wednesday. And I've spoken to a contact in the Met Police who owes me a favour. He's going to get the police report for me. Kate, here's my card. I've put my home telephone number on the back. Ring me any time you have any questions – or just want to talk,' he added with a warm smile. 'What's the best way to get hold of you?'

'I'll give you my home number,' Kate said, scribbling it down on a piece of paper.

'Well, it sounds like we have a plan,' Alec said.

'Right, my dears, Alec and I are off to try this new restaurant he found,' Freddie announced.

Ellen thought that would explain his quiet radiance. 'Enjoy yourselves. Kate and I are going for a walk.'

Out in the street, they looked at each other uncertainly. They didn't have an umbrella and the ominous clouds were leering down at them thuggishly. Ellen decided to focus on the practical aspect and asked, 'What would you like to do?'

'I feel like being in an open space,' Kate replied. 'Somewhere green and peaceful. One of the parks? But it looks as if a storm is coming …'

'I know a garden square just two minutes around the corner. It's one of my favourite places in London, a real hidden gem. Let's go there.' But as they turned right past the corner tailor shop with its painted tiles, an inviting glimpse of green at the end of the street, there was a threatening rumble. Fat raindrops started to fall. 'Come on!' Ellen grabbed Kate's hand and they ran the few yards to a pub, arriving just as the clouds opened. They fell inside, laughing.

'Under the circumstances, I think we should have a drink,' Ellen suggested. 'Look, here's a seat by the window. What would you like?'

Kate was staring at her with a frown. 'Ellie, they'll never serve you.'

But she was airy. 'Oh, don't worry. Freddie and I have been coming here for years.'

And, sure enough, when she went to the bar, the landlord greeted her. 'Hope you didn't get too wet, Miss Fernsby. It looks like we're in for a good soaking. What can I get you?' She returned to the table with two gin and tonics.

Kate was impressed. 'I've had several pubs turn me away! It makes my blood boil the way they can refuse to take my money.'

As if to prove her point, a morose, red-faced man nursing a pint at the bar remarked loudly, 'Women in trousers buying their own drinks in the pub. What next, a donkey for Prime Minister?' The landlord ignored him.

Ellen shrugged. 'Just another injustice we need to address.'

They clinked glasses and Kate looked around the pub. The front bar was small and the back room was equally compressed, although mirrors added an illusion of greater space. The elaborate frosted-glass etchings on the windows, and the dark ceiling, gave the pub a cosy, mysterious atmosphere, augmented by the loud claps of thunder and lightning bursts outside. Most of the clientele were in the back room and they had their particular corner to themselves.

'My mother would say it's raining cats and dogs,' Ellen remarked, looking out the window. 'It's not quite the open space you wanted, I'm afraid.'

'No, I love it here. It's charming, a real old gin palace! It should have gas lights,' Kate replied, smiling. 'Ellie, what's the story with Freddie and Alec? I can't work out if they're lovers, or ...'

'Hmm, it's complicated. They met when Alec and his mother came into our shop last November. Flora wanted a dress, but it was obvious Alec wanted the dressmaker. He and Freddie could hardly take their eyes off each other. He came back the next day and suggested going for a drink. That was it, really. It was like a match made in heaven. They were so in love, so good for each other. Freddie was the happiest I'd seen him in far too many years.'

'You told me when we first met up – God, that's just last Friday – he was serious about someone but it didn't work out. Was it Alec?'

'Yes, fancy remembering that. Well, Freddie deliberately ruined it. He picked up a man for sex and managed to make sure Alec found them together. Alec walked out and refused to take his calls. That was two months ago, and they didn't speak to each other again until the meal on Saturday.'

Kate gave a surprised whistle. 'But I don't understand. It's clear they're crazy about each other. Why would Freddie do that?'

A bright flash of lightning spotlighted the pub for a heartbeat. 'I think I mentioned Freddie lost someone in the war.' Kate nodded, watching her intently. 'They met soon after he was conscripted. Sam was several years older, a farmer from Yorkshire. I met him once, when they were both home on furlough. A decent man, obviously mad for Freddie. They were planning a life together after the war. But he died, just a week before the war ended. They were leading a charge across a bridge and Sam was shot in the head, killed instantly. Freddie was right next to him. He told me, a long time later, he'd been covered with Sam's blood and brains ...' Her exhaled breath was close to a sob. 'Oh, Kate. It nearly destroyed Freddie. I brought him to my home and looked after him. For months afterwards, he could barely function. It didn't help that he'd been gassed and his lungs were in a terrible state. He used to stammer as a child, and it came back badly then. He'd wake screaming from these terrible nightmares … Sam was his first love and, for a long time, he didn't want to go on.' She looked out the window, her expression dark with remembered pain.

Kate's tone was soft. 'Poor Freddie. Thank God he had you to look after him.'

Ellen didn't seem to hear, her face shadowed, her thoughts turned inward. She sighed and continued. 'When he recovered, he kept everyone at arm's length, apart from me, but of course I'm only his sister. He told me he couldn't suffer like that again. He'd pick up men, have short affairs, move on. He adopted this cynical, world-weary attitude, which didn't suit him – he was always such a sweet, loyal boy. I think, when he met Alec, his feelings scared him and he just panicked. He regretted it immediately, but Alec refused to talk to him.'

'Perhaps Freddie felt guilty because he survived and Sam died. He may have felt he had no right to be happy with someone else.'

'I never thought of it like that, but – yes, it makes a lot of sense.'

Kate gave a tight smile. 'Yes, well I know enough about guilt myself. And your first love can sometimes have a hold on you. Because Sam was dead, Freddie could idealise him.'

'You're quite right. I liked Sam, but Alec's a much better match for him. They were so good together, Kate. And I missed him myself, as a friend, when they broke up. I'm just making myself stay out of it now and not meddle.' She glanced at Kate self-consciously as she said this. 'At least they're talking and Freddie has explained his behaviour. They've decided they're going to be friends.'

Kate laughed. 'Not a chance, the way they looked at each other! I do hope it works out for them. Drink up and I'll get a refill.' When she sat down again with the drinks, Ellen was still gazing out the window at the rain, conscious of a jangling anticipation.

'Ellen.'

'Mm?'

'What about you? Don't tell me a beautiful woman like you has been sitting at home like a vestal virgin.' Ellen couldn't help a small snort of nervous laughter. 'Come on, tell me. Who have you loved? Who has loved you?'

She turned to face Kate, whose eyes were fixed on her. Strange, she'd never noticed before their unusual colour. She'd just thought of them as brown, but she realised now they were like deep amber, with darker flecks and a violet ring around the outside. How striking they were. Ellen suddenly remembered a tiger's eye gemstone she'd seen in a jewellery shop. Kate's eyes were just like that. But she was waiting for an answer.

'I trained as a nurse when the war started, and met another nurse then. We were together for ten years.'

Kate quietly let out her breath, never taking her eyes off Ellen. 'So, you were with a woman?'

'Yes. I'm queer, the same as Freddie. The queer Fernsby siblings. Our parents must have some very special genes,' she added with a wry smile.

'Ellie – did you know this, when we were friends before the war?' There was an urgency in Kate's voice. 'I used to wonder sometimes – I remember you saying you couldn't see yourself getting married, and you never did seem interested in men ...'

She shook her head. 'Not really. No. Which must sound strange when you were so open about yourself. I think I must be a late developer. That year before the war was so momentous for me. Leaving home and coming to London on my own, starting work, becoming involved with the suffragettes, going to prison – there was so much change, so much going on in my head. And – well, I was still only fifteen, sixteen. You must remember what an innocent I was! It was only when Freddie and I had a talk the following year that it became clear. He told me he'd realised he loved his own sex and I instantly knew, so clearly: but that's me, too. That's what I am. I'd met Beth by then and had these feelings ... finally, everything made sense to me.'

'How did you feel about that, when you realised?'

'Well, obviously I knew it's considered wrong in society. I understood my life would not be easy. But I was used to going against society anyway, with the suffragettes, and being able to talk to Freddie, to support each other, made all the difference. I decided quite soon that I wouldn't change myself for anything. This is right for me. You said much the same to me, all those years ago.'

'Mm ... so, you fell in love with Beth.'

'Yes.' She returned Kate's scrutiny with a lift of her chin. 'We moved in together. When the hospital in Endell Street closed after the war, we both went to work at Guy's. I thought we'd be together forever.'

'What happened?'

Ellen stared back out the window. The rain was starting to thin. 'Beth couldn't accept it, and it got harder as the years went by. She didn't want to be a lesbian. She wanted to have what she called a "normal" life. She was older than me and her family kept on at her about getting married and having children. You know, a woman's destiny, our only function in life', with a sarcastic twist of the lips. 'We started arguing all the time. When Freddie suggested we open the shop, I moved in there so Beth could decide what she wanted. She found a man within weeks.' Ellen smiled mirthlessly. 'Didn't waste time, did she?'

'Do you still see her?'

Ellen shook her head. 'She moved up to Manchester. Her husband works there. I'm still friendly with a couple of nurses from Guy's who keep in touch with her. They tell me she's got two children. So, she has what she wanted.'

'Do you miss her?'

'No.' Ellen's response was decisive. 'We wanted different things. Looking back, I can see there were too many differences, quite apart from that.'

'She's mad to walk away from you,' Kate stated. 'And this was, what, five years ago? You would have been twenty-seven then?' Ellen observed her curiously. Kate's lips were compressed and she looked almost angry, although her voice remained composed.

'That's right. Look, I think the rain is stopping.'

Kate gave a brief, uninterested glance out the window, asking, 'And since then?'

Ellen shrugged. 'I've had affairs. You'd be surprised – or maybe you wouldn't – how many respectable wives secretly sleep with other women. They lead separate lives from their husbands. Happy marriages, eh? Perhaps Beth's doing that as well.'

'Are you seeing someone now?' Kate was watching her closely and she nodded. 'Was it the woman you saw in the Ritz yesterday?'

Ellen looked at her, surprised. 'You don't miss much, do you?' She blushed slightly. 'Yes. Her name's Myra. Another married woman. It has no future, of course, but that suits me just fine.'

Kate tapped her fingers on the table, an enigmatic expression on her face.

'What?' Ellen asked with a nervous laugh, wondering if she'd said something to upset her. Kate opened her mouth, shut it, then seemed to make up her mind.

'Don't you see, Ellie? You're just the same as Freddie. Terrified of getting hurt again, so you keep everyone at a distance. Putting on a cynical act, having affairs you know will go nowhere. And you're such a warm, loving woman. What a waste. You deserve so much better.'

The words were unsparing, but Kate's voice had kindness in it. Ellen looked down, unable to think of a reply. The message had struck home. She finished her drink.

Kate broke the silence. 'It's stopped raining. Where is that garden you were going to show me?'

11

When Ellen unlocked the gate to the garden, they could see they were the only people there. The storm must have driven everyone away. But now, even though the clouds were dark to the south, there were patches of blue sky above and the sun even peeked out for a minute. The air smelt fresh and brand new. Raindrops were still sporadically falling from the stately spreading trees, their leaves emerald-bright in the fugitive sunlight. Kate stood and gazed. 'I didn't even know this place existed,' she commented in a hushed voice.

They started to walk along the right-hand path, which meandered around the trees and shrubbery, heavy with spring flowers. In the centre William III sat stonily on his horse, his right hand outstretched. They spoke quietly, almost whispering, as if not wanting to disturb the stillness of the place. Around them, the grand houses of St James's Square loitered with haughty indifference. Ellen pointed out landmarks: Nancy Astor's house, the building where Chopin had lived, the London Library. 'You're right, it's a little jewel,'

Kate said, smiling at Ellen. 'How did you manage to get a key?'

'Oh,' Ellen laughed a little. 'We've had it for a few years, thanks to one of Freddie's past conquests.'

They wandered along to the end of the garden where there was a small pavilion with a bench. Just then, a squirrel jumped along a branch in the tree above and a cascade of drops fell onto them. 'Let's stop here for a while,' Kate suggested.

They sat down beneath a bronze plaque, looking around them in companionable silence. There had always been an unquestioned level of trust and acceptance in their friendship, although Ellen was aware now of an added edge that was unlikely to go away. She removed her hat and brushed off the raindrops, turning to look at Kate, whose eyes appeared tawny in the shade of the pavilion. 'You know what I'm going to say, don't you?'

Kate nodded, her eyes crinkling as she grinned. 'Yes. You're going to say: I told you my story, now it's your turn. Am I right?'

Ellen laughed. 'You've always known me so well.'

Kate shook her head slightly. 'Mm, I can see there are some new sides to you to explore. But yes, you have told me your story. There are still lots of details I want to know, but they can come out with time. And we have a lot of that in front of us, Ellie,' placing her hand on Ellen's for a second. 'All right. My turn. Do you mind if I smoke?'

Ellen said, surprised, 'Of course not.' Kate's lighter was silver and looked expensive. She was silent for a few seconds, collecting her thoughts, absently stroking her thumb on the fine grooves in the lighter.

'You already know I went back to France after my mother died. I met wonderful women in the ambulance service, quite a few of them like us.' She gave Ellen a warm smile before staring abstractedly in front of her. 'We had a real camaraderie. God knows, you needed that to cope with the horrors we saw … I was devastated when my mother died and all I could think was to get back to them, be somewhere without any memories. So, I moved to Paris. I don't know if you've heard about the salons run by Natalie Barney in Rue Jacob?' Ellen nodded silently, not wishing to disturb Kate's train of thought. 'I met fascinating women, and men too. Writers, artists, people in the theatre. I made good friendships, had affairs. Unlike here, it's not illegal for men so you don't have to hide so much. I had a little flat in Montparnasse and scraped a living by working in a bookshop. I did miss England, and I thought about you a lot, but I more or less decided this was my life now, and I'd left everything behind me. Then things changed – ironically, around 1925, the same time you were going through your own changes.'

Ellen waited, but Kate was silent, seemingly lost in her thoughts. 'What happened?' she prompted. Kate turned to look at her before bending her head to gaze with apparent interest at her cigarette. A few people were returning to the square now the rain had stopped. Two children ran whooping past them, chasing a ball.

'I fell in love with someone. Simone was fascinating, unlike anyone I'd ever met. It quickly became … very intense. She'd have these extreme moods. She'd be ecstatically happy and then in the depths of despair. Artist's temperament, I thought. When I look back now, I can see there were signs early on that it wasn't good for me. But in the beginning, it was all sunshine …'

Kate was talking quietly; Ellen had to bend her head to catch her words. 'She moved in a different set and we spent most of our time in bars and nightclubs. There were lots of drugs floating around. At first, it was just another way to have fun. Slip a hash pellet into your gin fizz and dance the night away. But Simone started using cocaine heavily, and I got caught up in it too. I suppose I was trying to keep pace with her.' She quickly glanced at Ellen and away again. 'It went from being a thing she did occasionally, to something she couldn't do without. Then she started on heroin … It was no longer fun. Simone wasn't working and needed money for the drugs. She didn't have any happy times then, she was permanently in a black hole. I couldn't do anything to help and I felt overwhelmed with guilt – about the man I killed – because I wanted to get away from her. I became sickened by everything and had some sort of a breakdown. I don't know what else you'd call it. I couldn't really function.'

'Oh, Kate, I wish I'd known. I wish I could have been there to help you.' Ellen tried to hide her shock. Kate nodded her head briefly, looking as if she would say something, but thinking better of it. After a while she stubbed out her cigarette and continued.

'I was lucky. A friend came to look me up and basically rescued me. I spent a few months in a sanatorium, and afterwards I went to Berlin. That didn't work out either, but by then I was feeling better, much stronger in myself. I realised I was homesick and wanted to come home. As it happened, when I went back to Paris to pack up, I found the letter from my father's solicitors. Good timing.' She smiled faintly at Ellen.

'And Simone?'

'Didn't I say? She died last year. Her heart was weak, I suppose from the drugs, and it just gave out one day.' Kate's voice sounded casual. She could have been discussing a distant acquaintance.

'Oh!' Ellen didn't know what to say.

'I heard this from someone. I wasn't in touch with her then. A shocking waste. She was a talented painter – she could have achieved so much. Well, that's it, Ellie. Not a very edifying tale, I'm afraid.' Ellen knew there was a lot more to the story, a lot of pain, grief and regret, but Kate would need to talk about it in her own time.

'And … are you seeing anyone now?'

'No. No married women, nothing like that. I'm free and available,' Kate replied, looking directly at Ellen.

There was a breathless pause, which Ellen broke by asking, 'But – your friend in Hastings?'

Kate gave a shout of laughter. 'That's Albert! He's a Quaker, one of the ambulance drivers I met during the war. Just the thought … Oh, no, it wouldn't do at all,' and she laughed some more. 'He's married with children and a dear man, a bit of a saint in his way. You must meet him soon. He's become like family for me. You'll like each other. In fact, now I think about it, you're quite similar.'

Ellen grinned. She realised her assumption had been ridiculous. It was quite funny, really. 'What, are you saying I'm like a Quaker?'

'Oh, not for that, although he wears his religion lightly, at least in front of me. He knows I'm not interested. No, I mean you're like him in your character. You care deeply, and you're a seeker after truth.' Ellen looked down, absurdly touched by her comment. A robin was hopping around on the ground close to her feet, inspecting the wet grass. It pulled up a worm and stopped to watch her with a round, bright eye, the worm wriggling in its beak. 'Look at this bold rascal,' she said fondly.

But Kate was frowning at the slanting rays of the sun and checked her watch. 'Ellie, do you realise it's nearly nine and we haven't eaten anything? Did you have supper?'

Now Ellen thought of it, she realised she was hungry. 'I know a good chippie just off Piccadilly Circus – what do you think?'

'That sounds like a great idea.'

They crossed the grass to the gate. Suddenly, Kate put her hand up to Ellen's hair. 'You had a leaf,' she said, showing it to Ellen. For a moment they stood close, smiling at each other.

12

Twenty minutes later they were sitting on the steps under Eros, sharing a portion of chips wrapped in newspaper. 'I always think food tastes best when you're hungry,' Kate said with a contented sigh. 'Although you couldn't do much better than Freddie's banquet the other night. Does he always cook?'

'We usually share it. I had to learn from a young age, of course, being the girl. By the time I was eleven I could do a whole roast dinner by myself. Freddie learned in the war, funnily enough. He says he finds it relaxing.'

'I'm sorry I didn't get to finish the strawberries. Oh, don't look at me in such a guilty way, Ellie! You were right. I'm very glad I've decided to go through with this.' She seemed light-hearted. The sky was crimson to their right and the street lights were starting to come on. A bus trundled by. 'You must come to my place for supper,' Kate suggested, and Ellen nodded, pleased. 'Not tomorrow night. You're teaching your East End women, aren't you? What about Wednesday? Or are you busy with friends?'

'I'd love to, but Alec said that might be when we go to see the Fawdon son,' Ellen replied, noticing she didn't mention Myra's name.

'I don't expect it to happen so soon. It could take him weeks to get the report. Here, I've written down my address and phone number. Let's say Wednesday and we can change it if we need to. That is, if you can be flexible?'

'I don't really have much of a social life,' Ellen admitted awkwardly. 'I'm not very good at making friends. I'm a bit of a disaster that way.'

Kate looked at her, her eyebrows raised. 'You never struck me as being shy or unconfident. No, you have the last chip.'

'You were always more popular than me. I knew several girls who had crushes on you. Didn't you realise I tended to hang back on social occasions?'

'I certainly noticed you were quieter than when you were with me or Hilda. What I remember is how you were so articulate and clear in your thinking. I always looked to you as my moral compass. Did you know that?'

Ellen blinked, not knowing quite how to respond. 'Freddie says I can appear standoffish. I don't mean to be. I'm just not comfortable in large groups of people. Maybe it's from growing up in a village – I don't know. I have a small number of friends and it seems to do well enough.'

'And you have Freddie. You two are very close, aren't you?'

'Yes, we always have been. I think, to be honest, our parents didn't quite know where we sprang from. Red-haired, bookish, queer. A bit of a deviation from a long line of shopkeepers and fishermen. Sometimes I'd see them looking at us, slightly puzzled – but always loving.' Ellen smiled at her memories.

'And you don't need to worry about not having a million friends, believe me. I've found from experience, people with lots of friends often turn out to be needy and ill at ease with themselves. Far better to have one or two genuine friends. Anyone would be very proud and happy to have you as a friend.'

'Thank you,' Ellen said quietly. She often had to censor herself with others, knowing her propensity to be too direct, but always she could say anything to Kate. Although there was something she needed to consider privately first.

Two drunk men chose that moment to sit down next to them and issue beery invitations to have fun. They got up and left, entering Jermyn Street where it was quieter and darker. Ellen glanced to her left as they passed a small lane. What was that white movement? She paused, peering in the dark and then gasped, grabbing Kate's arm. 'Kate, look. I think it's a swan.' She started walking rapidly down the lane. As she came closer, she could see a swan on the pavement, beating its right wing and banging its head, blood running from the left wing, which was bent at an unnatural angle.

Kate came up behind her. 'Its wing is broken. Oh, you poor darling,' she said to the swan. They realised now there was a pool of blood on the ground.

'It must have crashed into the building. It was probably flying back to St James's Park for the night. What can we do? I can't bear to see it in such agony.' Ellen looked at Kate, distressed.

'We could try the RSPCA, although I don't know if they'd answer the phone at this time. Are you all right to stay here? I'll see if I can find a phone. I'll be back as soon as I can,' and Kate gripped her shoulder briefly before running back to Jermyn Street.

Ellen stared sadly at the bird. Her nurse's training told her it could not be saved – the best thing was to put it out of its misery. How heartbreaking to see such a magnificent animal in this state. She slowly edged closer. The swan now lay exhausted, its long neck and head on the ground. Carefully, she sat down on a step next to the bird. It hissed fitfully when she put her hand out. Close up, she could hear it panting and see the wild beating of its heart. 'You beautiful thing. I'm so sorry you've come to this end. I hope you've had a good life,' she said softly.

The swan raised its head once more in mute supplication and this time did not resist when Ellen gently placed it in her lap. She started to hum a tune, noticing the heartbeats were slowing down. No one else was around. She and the swan were alone in the dim light, surrounded by the quiet gloom. She realised after a while the swan's heart was no longer beating, but continued to sit there, stroking its neck. Its lifeless eye was still open, black and impenetrable. As children, she and Freddie had spent hours roaming the countryside with their father's ancient binoculars. Once, a pair of swans had flown directly over them, so close that one wing tip touched Freddie's hair. They had stood still, mesmerised with delight, feeling the power of the beating wings, hearing the whoosh of the air passing through the feathers, for a few precious seconds getting an exhilarating glimpse into the swans' world.

Kate ran up a few minutes later with a policeman following her. 'It's the best I could do, I'm afraid,' she said with a grimace. Then she saw Ellen's face and looked down at the swan. 'Oh, it died. I'm sorry, Ellie. It's probably for the best.'

'No, I'm glad it died quickly. I couldn't bear to think of it suffering for hours.' The policeman arrived, puffing. She said to him, 'Thank you for coming to help, constable, but it's dead.'

He breathed heavily through his mouth as he peered down at the bird. 'I'm sure it's very good of you to help the poor creature. This'll be one of the swans from the park. It's a cob, the female's probably on the nest. Well, they won't hatch now. What a shame. They mate for life.' Kate stared at him with an angry expression, but Ellen realised he was sad in his way and just expressing it clumsily. 'You little ladies had best get along to your husbands. I'll arrange for it to be taken away.'

They walked on, not speaking, and stopped outside Ellen's place. Their carefree mood had evaporated. 'You've got blood on your trousers,' Kate remarked.

Ellen glanced down without much interest. 'It should wash out.' They looked at each other.

'See you Wednesday,' Kate said. She put her hand up to Ellen's cheek, then walked off.

The flat was empty. Ellen folded her trousers for the laundry, tidied up the sitting room and made a cup of tea, drinking it staring out the window. Her thoughts crawled sluggishly through a sticky miasma of dread. Why had she decided to act like God and start an investigation that might end in disaster?

She couldn't stop thinking about Kate. Her tender compassion, over the death and unhappiness Kate had known, clashed oddly with apprehension over how dull she must appear to Kate. How could she compete with Parisian artists and intellectuals, people who partied all night? She felt naive, boring.

As she wandered restlessly around the flat, the swan's dark eyes prompted a memory from the war. A young soldier had been brought into the hospital with his arm hopelessly mangled. The arm was amputated, but he'd lost a lot of blood and his body went into shock. Ellen had sat with him for hours, giving him water and painkillers and useless words of comfort. He sweated and grunted with the pain, staring at her with terror in his eyes. After he died, his mother's guttural screams had echoed around the corridors. Remembering this, she felt weighed down by a formless anguish. The misery and melancholy of the world seemed to have gripped her by the throat.

Ellen was in bed, attempting to concentrate on her book, when Freddie came back close to midnight. After a few minutes, there was a discreet scratching on her door and she called, 'Come in,' welcoming the distraction.

He poked his head cautiously around the door. 'Were you sleeping?' She shook her head and he perched on the side of her bed. He brought the cool night air of the street in with him, along with a diamond brilliance which seemed almost to light him up from inside. The change in him since Friday was startling. But his first words were for her. 'Did you have a nice evening with Kate?'

'Yes. We did a lot of talking, catching up on our lives.'

'You look sad, Ellie. Is everything all right? Did you have an argument, or …?' She shook her head and told him about the swan. His brows contracted in sympathy. 'The poor thing. I'm glad you could be with it at the end. But don't take it as an omen, sweetie. You don't need to be worried or sad. Kate's back in your life and everything will work out, you'll see.'

She made herself smile. 'How about you and Alec? Was the restaurant nice?'

'I had trout stuffed with almonds and herbs, very tasty. We planned to go to a jazz bar in Soho afterwards, but we talked so long there was no point. They threw us out of the restaurant in the end. There was just so much to say.'

'Anything in particular?' Ellie was careful with her words, remembering her vow not to interfere.

'Anything and everything. We talked more about what happened between us, but mostly we spoke about the war. I told him everything about Sam. You know it's always been hard for me to do that – but it was so easy with Alec. I feel I can say anything to him and he understands. He doesn't judge me. Really, I'm so stupid. I don't know why I didn't tell him about Sam before, when ...' He hesitated, his face contemplative, but his next words surprised her. 'Ellie – do you think Sam and I would have stayed together, if he'd lived?'

She replied carefully, 'Oh, Freddie. That's the impossible question, isn't it? He was your first love. But ... I'm not sure I could see you going up to Yorkshire and being a farmer, or if he would have been happy living here in London.'

'Mm.' Freddie fiddled with her bookmark, staring in front of him. His face was serious, but the unhappiness he'd always shown when talking about Sam was absent. He'd never spoken like this before and Ellen knew a significant line had been crossed. 'I think – well, I accept he's gone and life must go on.'

Ellen patted his hand. 'He would have wanted you to be happy and to live your life fully. You know that, don't you? He'll always be in your heart.'

'I've decided I want to visit his grave in Malton. I feel ready to do that now. Alec said he could borrow his mother's car and drive me up there. Maybe in a few weeks, once this investigation is finished.' He gave her a radiant smile. 'Alec is so kind – he's an exceptional person.'

'Yes, he is,' she agreed, happiness flooding her heart to see him like this.

'Sleep tight, Ellie,' and he was gone. At least something good has come out of my meddling, she thought. But a spiteful voice inside her head whispered: at what cost to Kate?

13

It was a clear night. The first stars were out as Ellen and Freddie walked home from the bus stop. In between each streetlight there was a small dark space where she could look up and see them steadily growing brighter as the last of the blue gave way to black. Ellen loved to gaze up at the night sky in the hope of seeing a falling star, but this evening her thoughts were on more practical issues.

'What do you think, Freddie, if we start giving regular work to a couple of the women? We're getting enough commissions now to make it worthwhile, and it helps them to know they have steady money coming in.' They were both lugging bags full of material and drooped with weariness.

Freddie blew his hair out of his eyes. 'Phew, I'll be glad to get home! How about if we start them on two days a week and see how it goes?'

'Sounds good. I'm thinking of Annie. She's come on really well and she needs the money since her husband walked out. If she can't find someone to mind her baby, I thought she could bring it along too. We could set up a sort of crib in the back of the workroom. I'm sure Hester would love to have more people to fuss over.'

'Other than me, do you mean?' he said, giving a rueful look. Oh, so he'd noticed after all. 'Margaret should be the other one. She's showing real talent. If I'm lucky enough to get the commission from the Old Vic, we can increase their hours.'

'You've not heard anything?'

'No, but I don't expect to yet. I only sent in my designs a week ago.' He noticed her look of confusion. 'I know, it seems longer, doesn't it? So much has happened these last few days, it's been quite revolutionary.' He grinned at her cheerfully.

As they opened their front door, they could hear the telephone ringing. Freddie dropped his bag and raced up the stairs two at a time, leaving Ellen to manoeuvre herself in the door and get up to the workroom with the bags. When she arrived, Freddie was talking animatedly into the mouthpiece, gripping the candlestick neck, his face lit up. But as she dumped the bags and turned to leave, he said, 'Ellie, don't go. Alec wants to speak to you,' holding out the receiver.

She sat down at the desk and exchanged greetings with Alec, conscious of an anxious foreboding about what he might say. She'd slept badly the night before, waking with a start from nightmares where Kate was being dragged off to prison, and had spent the day castigating herself for setting off the investigation. Perhaps Alec sensed her nervousness, because he immediately got down to business.

'Well, you said you had a feeling there was something strange about this business, and I think you were right. It appears there was no inquest, which is extremely odd. An inquest is always held if there's a sudden or unexplained death, or of course if foul play is suspected. They've searched their records at the coroner's office and can't find anything about it.'

Ellen asked, 'Could the inquest have been held somewhere else? Or perhaps they just lost the papers?'

'It should have been held in the district where the death took place, but just to be sure, I tried all the other coroners in East London as well as the City. An inquest usually takes place within a few months of the death, but I checked right up to the end of the war. Even if they'd lost the actual papers, or they were passed to the police for the investigation, they would at least have the inquest listed. The coroner's as puzzled as I am. He wasn't around then. He started about twelve years ago.'

'So … where do we go from here?'

'I'm seeing the coroner tomorrow afternoon to get a copy of the autopsy report. They found that, at least. I've spoken to Kate, and she wants to go ahead with a visit to the son tomorrow on that basis. Hopefully, he can fill in some of the gaps. I've arranged for us to be at his place at seven. Can you make it?'

'Yes, of course. What do you think this means?'

'To be honest, Ellen, I don't know. I checked the archives for all the other newspapers and, just like for the *Evening News*, once the war started there's no mention again of the death or the police investigation. Things weren't so chaotic with the war to explain why the story just disappeared from public view – especially as the newspapers took any opportunity to attack the suffragettes. It's too soon to jump to conclusions, but it's definitely strange. I've got my contact trying to get the details of the police investigation for me, hopefully that'll clear it up. Right, do you have a pen to write down the address?'

'Hold on,' and she opened up the work diary to write down the details. Freddie glanced over. He was putting the materials away in the workroom, his attention obviously on the conversation.

'I'll need to go straight from the coroner's office,' Alec continued. 'Kate's teaching in a school somewhere in the City and said she'll make her own way. I suggested to her we all meet up in front of Shoreditch Town Hall about a quarter to seven and go from there. How does that sound?'

'Fine. I'm familiar with the area.' She hesitated. 'Alec – I've been worrying about whether I've started something that could end in the police re-opening the case, or even arresting Kate. Maybe we could make things worse.'

He replied immediately, 'You don't need to worry, Ellen. I won't let anything happen to Kate. If it looks like it's stirring up things and could end badly, we'll just back away. After sixteen years and no evidence, I don't see how the police could possibly do anything now. Let's just take it one step at a time. We can decide what to do after we talk to the son. What do you think?'

'Yes, all right,' Ellen agreed, feeling a sudden lessening of tension. 'I can only thank you again, Alec. You're doing so much for us. I don't want to impose on your kindness.'

Alec laughed. 'Quite the opposite, my dear. I'm enjoying it! And I love to feel I'm helping you and Kate. I'd far rather use my training to do something like this, rather than wills or conveyancing. If anything—' His voice wavered for a second, before he continued. 'Well, you've done me a favour. Believe me.'

As she was about to ring off, he quickly asked, 'Is Freddie still there? May I have a word with him?' Ellen handed the receiver to Freddie, who was hovering by her elbow. She was aware of a relaxation in her mind, as if a string, which had been drawn to breaking point, had just been loosened.

When Freddie appeared in the sitting room some time later, he subsided with a thankful exhalation onto the sofa. 'So, you're all going off to see this Shoreditch chappie tomorrow evening,' he commented, before adding, 'Weren't you meant to be seeing Myra then?'

Ellen looked at him blankly, then her hand flew to her mouth. 'Oh, my God! I completely forgot.'

Back in the workroom, she reluctantly dialled Myra's number. Conscious of relief when the maid told her Mrs Weston was not at home, she left a message to cancel their arrangement for the following evening. But she knew this was only a postponement of the inevitable. After several discarded attempts, she was satisfied enough with her letter, which she hoped contained the right amount of honesty and sensitivity. She at least owed Myra that.

Her thoughts inevitably led her to Kate and she again picked up the receiver. When she answered, Ellen's mouth somehow felt dry, but she soon got over that, and Kate's calm determination over the following day's meeting provided further balm. They chatted for several minutes about their day, inconsequential matters, and agreed she would go to Kate's place for supper on Thursday instead. When she went back upstairs, Kate's voice wishing her a good night's sleep still in her ears, her steps were lighter.

Freddie was sitting in the same position on the sofa. As usual, over these past days, he looked happy, but with an added layer of thoughtfulness. He silently watched as she got out her address book and sat at the table to write Myra's address on the envelope, adding a stamp.

'I'm going to head out for a walk. Shall I post this for you?' he offered. He obviously guessed what the letter contained, but did not make the expected droll comment. She gave him the letter along with an enquiring look. He sighed and said, 'I love him, Ellie. I just love him.'

'I know, Freddie.' She gave him a consoling smile. He hesitated, as if to say something more, then went out the door. She wondered if he might revert to his old ways and seek comfort in another way, but heard him coming back upstairs minutes later as she was getting into bed.

14

They were kept busy on Wednesday with a regular trickle of walk-in customers. At least it stopped Ellen from anxious brooding. Towards the end of the afternoon, their new client arrived. Mrs Granville, who'd come to them on a personal recommendation, wanted an evening gown for her summer parties. She often featured in the society pages, so her patronage was good business. They ushered her into their dressing area at the back of the shop and Ellen wrote down the measurements that Freddie called out. He then sat down to ask about Mrs Granville's requirements. He used this talk with new clients to get a feel for their personality, which, as much as their physical attributes, guided his designs. Mrs Granville was a tall, imposing woman whose primary interests appeared to be the success of her social life and her husband's status in the City.

Freddie started sketching, making encouraging noises, while she talked. Within a few minutes, he had the design ready. The gown would be cut on the bias with an indented waistline, in midnight-blue crepe with sequins. Mrs Granville was enchanted, but there was a polite stand-off over the extent of the sequins. Freddie's design had these confined to the bodice, while Mrs Granville wanted the entire dress to be thus spangled. Ellen listened admiringly as Freddie used clever diplomacy to persuade the customer to go with his design. That was a skill she needed to learn – she knew she could be too direct.

'Phew!' he remarked to Ellen after they'd seen Mrs Granville out, smiling and satisfied. 'She wants the gown ready next week. Sewing sequins all over the dress would have been a nightmare. And can you imagine every time she sat down or got the dress caught on a chair? As it is, it'll be a push to get it finished in time.'

'Well, we would just have charged her more, but I certainly agree with you. And don't forget Annie and Margaret should be with us next week. We can put them straight onto hand-sewing the sequins once the dress is cut,' she reminded him.

Soon after, Ellen was going over orders with Hester when Freddie came up to the workroom. 'Why don't you head off now, Ellie? We'll be closing soon anyway.'

Hester turned to him with a wide smile. 'Ellen and I have arranged for these new girls to start next week. It might get a bit noisy if we have a baby here as well! But they're both smart girls. I think they'll do well.'

Freddie said, 'Oh, that's good,' but his attention seemed to be elsewhere. He followed Ellen up to the sitting room, where she picked up her bag and jacket. 'Good luck. I hope it goes well,' he said with a hug. She realised he was nervous under his apparently casual demeanour. As she walked briskly up to Oxford Street, she was uncomfortably aware she had dragged three people into this business.

The bus was one of the older models with an open top. Ellen usually loved to sit and watch the world go by, but today the journey passed in a blur. By the time they arrived at Old Street, the bus was packed with people on their way home from work. 'Town Hall!' the conductor called out, and she sidled past a tired-looking woman with a large bag of shopping. As the bus drew away, she stood observing the building, a confused patchwork with random additions of different architectural styles including Doric columns, halls and towers. It squatted on the street like a monstrous grey toad. Up at the top she could just make out the legend, *More Light, More Power*, and hoped it was a good omen. She heard her name being called and turned to see Kate coming up behind her.

'Well met,' Kate said smiling, slipping her arm through Ellen's as they crossed the road. She looked smart in a deep-gold dress with a narrow belt, and a dash of lipstick. Ellen must have shown her surprise because Kate laughed, saying, 'The headmistress looked horrified when I turned up to teach French in trousers, so I thought I'd better conform to more acceptable female dress on school days.' Ellen automatically assessed the cut and style, but couldn't help noticing how well the colour suited Kate. Her eyes glowed golden-brown in the sunlight.

As they came to the steps, they could see Alec waiting. It's not too late to stop this, Ellen thought. But as they came up to him, she realised his usual warm smile was missing. Before she could open her mouth, he said, 'We need to talk first. There's something very strange going on here.'

Ellen gave a convulsive swallow of sick dread, but he noticed the dismay on her face and took her hand. 'Don't worry, Ellen, it's not bad news. In fact ... look, let's sit down here so I can explain.' They sat on the steps, their eyes on Alec.

'I've just come from seeing the coroner and he talked me through the autopsy report. I have it here. It seems to be unmistakeable – Fawdon didn't die in the fire.'

They both stared at him, open-mouthed. Ellen recovered first. 'What do you mean?'

'The report states he died of a heart attack. It mentions cirrhosis of the liver, damaged arteries and so on, but it was his heart that seized up. The coroner says he could have dropped dead at any moment. There's no mention of burning or smoke inhalation, nothing about a fire. It was a completely natural death.' They looked at each other, lost for words.

Kate cleared her throat and asked shakily, 'Does this mean I didn't kill anyone? No one died in the fire after all?'

'At this stage, all we can say is that Cecil Fawdon did not die in the fire,' Alec replied carefully. 'What we don't know is whether they got his identity mixed up with someone else, or what the hell is going on.'

'Well then, do we need to see the son at all?' Ellen suggested. 'He doesn't seem to know anything about his father's death and he didn't appear too bothered.' Her thoughts were gyrating crazily. She couldn't make any sense of it. She'd had a strong sense something was not right about the fire, but this was not what she'd expected.

'I think he has a right to know how his father died. And I'm hoping he might tell us something which could help clear this up.'

Alec's voice was mild and Ellen blushed at her thoughtlessness, saying, 'Of course.' Her concern had all been for Kate; she'd forgotten others also had an interest in this. Just then they heard a clock striking the hour.

'Before we go, I just want to check with you. Shall I give false names for you, or …?' They both replied, 'No,' at the same time.

'Good. Let's go then.'

It was a few minutes around the corner to the small house nestled in a row of terraces. The front door, which opened directly onto the street, was freshly painted. It was answered after a few minutes by a stocky man in shirtsleeves, wiping his mouth. He looked to be around forty with a square, pleasant face, brown hair starting to thin on the top and a sparse moustache.

Alec held out his hand. 'William Fawdon? I'm Alexander Medley, the solicitor. I hope this time is convenient.'

William shook his hand but looked Ellen and Kate up and down with a mildly truculent expression. 'What's all this lot then? I didn't expect the bleedin' cavalry!'

'This is Miss Shergold, a trainee solicitor, and Miss Fernsby, my assistant. If you object to them being present I'll ask them to leave, but it would be useful to have them here.'

He stared at them for a few seconds, then shrugged his shoulders. 'Blooming 'eck, lady solicitors now, is it? No, that's all right. In for a penny, in for a pound. Well, I s'pose you'd better come in. I've just finished my supper.'

He turned and led the way to the front room. Ellen was last into the cramped corridor. As she shut the front door, she spotted a young girl watching with inquisitive eyes from a doorway at the back of the house. She smiled at her and was rewarded with a shy grin before a woman's voice called out, 'What are you doing, Lizzie? Come here at once!' The girl disappeared and Ellen walked into the parlour, which was obviously used for formal occasions.

Busy wallpaper with pink, yellow and white flowers competed for her attention with stiff green brocade curtains. Alec and Kate were settling themselves on a dark red sofa facing the window, next to the fireplace, and William was in the armchair with his legs stretched out in front of him, lighting a cigarette. She sat on a chair in the corner, out of the way. Alec took the report out of his briefcase and she brought a notepad and pen out of her bag to confirm her identity as an assistant. A large carriage clock encased in brown oak ticked loudly on the mantelpiece.

15

'My missus says I'm daft as a brush to be doing this. The old man's been dead a long time. What difference does it make now? But you said I don't have to pay. That's right, innit?' His manner was gruff but not unfriendly. Ellen guessed he was probably as nervous as they were.

Alec nodded in confirmation. 'That's correct, Mr Fawdon. This will cost you nothing and it can take as short a time as you like. When you've had enough, just tell us to leave. But I hope we can have at least a few minutes of your time.' William gave a grunt of assent. 'Could I start by asking you to tell me again what you know about your father's death?'

'Like I said, Mr Medley, he'd left my mum a long time before. I was just a nipper. He stayed in the area and we'd see him around, down the boozer or on the streets. A rozzer turned up one day—' He noticed Alec's puzzled face and explained, 'That's a copper, you see – and said he'd been found in the church what was burned down.' He glanced at Kate. Ellen was forgotten in the corner, which suited her fine.

'Do you remember exactly when they came to tell you this?'

William rubbed his nose as he thought about this. 'I'm pretty sure it was the Saturday before the war started. I'd just started seeing Bessie, who's my missus now, and I remember being fed up 'cos we was planning to go to a show up the West End.'

'Who went to identify your father?'

He appeared surprised by the question. 'No one. They said we didn't have to, on account of he was all burned up. They knew my old man anyway. He was in the nick regular for being drunk. Cat got her tongue?' he suddenly asked, jerking his head at Kate.

Alec smiled. 'She might have some questions in a while. You told me already you're not aware of an inquest having taken place – is that right?'

He nodded slowly, a mixture of suspicion and perplexity on his face. 'Why all these questions? What put you onto this in the first place? Was it the church?'

'Yes, I was asked to look into it,' Alec said vaguely. 'The reason I'm asking, Mr Fawdon, is because I have your father's autopsy report here and it states he died a natural death.'

William stared at him. 'Are you taking the mickey? Give us a butcher's,' he said, holding out his hand for the report. Alec got up from the sofa and gave it to him. William frowned at the paper, reading it slowly with his lips moving. 'A lot of bloody words here. Pardon my language, ladies.' He stubbed out his cigarette in a Bakelite ashtray, which had "The King's Head" engraved on the side, and promptly lit another one, waving the packet in their direction. They all politely declined.

Alec explained, 'It basically says your father died of a heart attack. It sounds like he wasn't very well.' William nodded, looking at him with a frown of concentration. 'But it says nothing about burns or smoke inhalation.'

He stared ahead and whistled soundlessly, clearly shocked. 'Would you Adam and Eve it?' he said quietly, as if to himself.

Alec said, 'The evidence is clear.'

'Well … I don't rightly know what to say, Mr Medley. The copper told us he was burned to a crisp. I remember him saying that, 'cos my old mum always did her nut after that if we burnt the toast. But, what – I mean, I'm no fan of the coppers, but why would they tell porkies?'

Kate spoke up. 'Did you know the policemen who talked to you about it? How often did they come to see you?'

William's subdued manner had been replaced by a lively interest, and he answered her readily. 'It was just that sergeant Blunt. We didn't see no one else. Everyone knew him – this was his manor. He was a real stickler, always having a go at kids for playing football in the street. A right miserable bastard – sorry, ladies. We used to call him Blunt the—' He stopped abruptly, rubbing his hand over his face, and continued. 'He said it was the suffragettes. He had a bee in his bonnet about them, always going on as if they was devils. My mum didn't like that. She said women should have the vote. I can tell you, she was stronger and braver than any geezer I've known, bless her.' He reflected for a while. 'Now I think of it, there's a lot that never made no sense. Mum and I couldn't figure out why he was in the church. He hated that vicar and had a right run-in with him – it came to blows. Bit of a joke, really, 'cos the vicar arranged the funeral, seeing as we had no money.'

Alec asked, 'What happened with the police investigation? It seems they never did find who started the fire.' Kate shifted on the sofa next to him, but remained silent.

'Dunno. That's when the war started. I was hardly home the next four years. My mum wrote me to say she went down the nick a few weeks later and they said Blunt had retired. They didn't know nothing about my old man and she never did hear another squeak from the coppers. She said it was typical of them. Lazy bastards she used to call 'em. Pardon, ladies.' He suddenly seemed to remember Ellen and looked round at her. 'You all right there, missy?' His tone was genial and she smiled and nodded.

Kate asked in a carefully neutral tone, 'Did she know the sergeant was going to retire?'

'Nope. Mum said there was some sort of a bad smell about it. But everything was topsy-turvy with the war. I s'pose we didn't care that much. It's not like anything changed for us with his death.'

As he finished saying this, the door opened a crack and a boy of about ten, with the same square face and colouring, poked his head around. 'Please, Dad. Mum says if you don't come to eat your pudding she'll give it to the dog.'

'Oh, she will, will she?' William said with a laugh, which turned into a wheezy cough. He winked at his son. 'Tell her ladyship I'll be there in a sec.' The boy gave a cheeky smile and disappeared. William looked back at them, his eyes bright and friendly. 'Well, Mr Medley, I thank you kindly for telling me this. I must say, much as I disliked the old man, I'm glad he didn't die in the fire after all. I wouldn't like to think of any poor bugger dying like that, no matter who he is. I saw enough of it in the war.' For a second his voice faltered and he shuddered. He pointed at Alec's hand. 'Did you get that fighting?'

Alec nodded. 'Yes, in Amiens.'

William gave him a look of shared understanding. 'I was there an' all. You must know what I mean. If the old bastard dropped dead with a heart attack it's a better way to go. It sets my mind to rest.' He started getting up from his chair.

They stood up as well. Alec said, 'Here's my card, Mr Fawdon. Would you like to take this further? Find out why the police told you that story? There'll be no cost to you.'

William stood still to consider this, turning the card over in his meaty hands. 'It don't make no difference now, and I don't fancy stirring things up with the rozzers for no reason. You see, I went off the rails a bit when I came home from the war. I barely got a scratch, lucky eh?' He gave them a grin, which was both ironic and achingly sad. 'But all my mates died and I saw things … Well, I was in a mess, drinking and fighting. I got nicked and did time inside. Mum and Bessie stood by me, God bless 'em, and I sorted myself out.' He paused and the only sound was the ticking clock. 'I have a good life now. My kids mean everything to me and I have the best missus I could ask for. So, nope, I don't think so. But I'll talk it over with my Bessie and let you know if I change my mind. Well,' stretching his arms and smiling at them, 'best get my pudding before that dog gets any fatter.'

He walked with them to the front door. 'Thank you for taking the trouble to come out here and see me, Mr Medley, ladies. Good luck being a lady solicitor,' he added to Kate. 'Good night,' and then they were out on the front step. As he closed the door they could hear William calling out, 'I'm coming, Bessie!'

When they reached the corner, they stopped and looked at each other. 'Let's go back to your place and discuss what we do next,' Alec suggested.

They walked silently up to the bus stop, absorbed with their own thoughts. Kate appeared to be in a world of her own, barely aware of her surroundings. She stopped suddenly in the crowded street and a ferrety-looking man walked into the back of her.

'Watch out, you berk!' he shouted. She didn't react and he glared at her. 'Oy, you one of them Radclyffe Hall types? You know what you need—'

He scuttled off when Alec stepped in front of Kate and stared him down. Kate looked after the man with no apparent change in expression. Perhaps she hadn't even heard him.

'Here's the bus, Kate.' She looked at Ellen as if she were a stranger.

The bus was full. There was a steady ebb and flow of passengers as they headed back to Oxford Street: workers returning home being replaced by smartly dressed people going up to town, eager to have fun and full of ready laughter. Ellen kept glancing anxiously at Kate, several rows ahead. Alec, in a nearby seat, gave her comforting smiles.

By silent agreement, Ellen and Alec chatted lightly on the walk back to Jermyn Street. The animation started returning to Kate's face, and by the time they got to Jermyn Street she was joining in the conversation.

16

'Here you are! The warriors return,' Freddie exclaimed with a keen glance at their faces when they arrived in the sitting room. 'I've got drinks ready for you and you're going to have supper in a minute. Here, make yourselves comfy.' He got them seated, his hand lingering on Alec's shoulder. Ellen gave him a grateful look and took a gulp of her gin sling. Kate, sitting alongside her on the sofa, said, 'God, this drink tastes like heaven.' She smiled at Ellen, no longer pale and pinched.

Freddie settled himself on the floor near Alec in the armchair and commanded, 'Tell me all.'

There was a short silence. Ellen spoke first. 'I liked him. He's a decent man.'

Alec said, 'Yes, he's a good geezer,' and they laughed with a sudden release of tension, while Freddie looked enquiringly. Between them, they explained what had happened, clarifying and understanding better themselves as they talked it through.

'So, let me get this right,' Freddie summarised. They were on their second round of drinks by now. 'This Fawdon chap died of natural causes. The police told his family he died in the fire. They never saw his body and say he wouldn't have been in that church anyway. The police dropped the investigation, the sergeant mysteriously retired and the family heard nothing further. And it was never mentioned again in the newspapers. Well, it looks like the police lied from beginning to end, doesn't it?'

Alec agreed, 'It certainly appears that way.'

Kate spoke slowly, as if measuring her words. 'But – if Fawdon wasn't the man found in the church … I still don't understand what this means. Did anyone die in the fire? Why would the police make it up? Or is it a case, as Alec suggested, that it was someone else and he was either identified wrongly or … or there's some sort of cover-up? I feel stunned. Don't know what to think,' and she looked around, bewildered, at her friends.

Freddie suggested, 'Perhaps they had to hide the identity of the dead man. This was just days before the war started, remember. He might have been a German spy, or …'

'But in that case, why would they say they'd found a body at all? They'd hush it up completely,' Alec argued.

Freddie looked into his drink, then brightened and said, 'The newspapers might have found out there was a body, so the police had to produce an identity to stop them from investigating further.'

Alec gave a sort of groaning laugh. 'Perhaps … who knows? We seem to go round in circles on this. It's like one of those puzzles, where you open a box and find another box inside.'

Freddie nodded. 'Or like those dolls nested inside each other. I saw that in Selfridges once.'

Ellen suggested, 'Don't you think the answer is staring us in the face? There never was a body. Hilda said she'd checked the vestry and she couldn't see how anyone could have got in there before they started the fire. The whole thing is a lie.'

'Maybe I'm naive,' Alec replied, rubbing his hair. 'I can see the police covering up finding a body. That's certainly possible. But I just can't see an entire police force inventing a body, colluding in such a huge lie, and getting the newspapers to go along with it. Why? Only to discredit the suffragettes?' He shook his head, looking baffled.

Kate said, 'I feel – well, I don't know what to feel. Maybe I didn't kill anyone and I can be free of this bloody guilt. But I don't want to start feeling hopeful if that's wrong. It would be worse to have hope and then lose it again.'

Ellen responded, 'The important thing here is to find out the truth, and I feel we're still a long way from that. I don't think William Fawdon will want to take this any further, so Alec can't use him as the reason to investigate. Where do we go from here – that is, if you and Alec still want to continue?'

Kate's response was emphatic. 'God, yes. Whatever comes out now, if it was someone else killed in the fire, I need to know.'

Alec concurred. 'Count me in as well. I want to see this through to the end.' Freddie nodded to himself, then got up and went into the kitchen. 'As to where we go from here – I do have some further information. I asked my mother if she knew anything about this sergeant Blunt, without saying why I was interested, of course. She spoke to her friends who were active in the East End and rang me back today. It turns out he was well known for being hostile to the suffragettes. He had a reputation for using any excuse to rough them up. His speciality, apparently, was to put his hand up their skirts when he was arresting them.' He looked disgusted as he said this.

'Yes, we had personal experience of a few policemen like that. Or else they'd throw a suffragette into the crowd to be groped,' Ellen said bitterly, recalling the humiliation and shame she'd suffered, the time she'd found bruises all over her breasts after the police broke up a march.

Alec muttered under his breath. She caught the words, '… bloody pigs.' He composed himself and continued, 'The other thing is that I'm waiting on my contact to come up with the police file. He'll be in Bow tomorrow and hopes to locate it there. I'll ask him to find out more about this Blunt. It sounds to me he might be the key to all this.' He was going to say more, but Freddie emerged from the kitchen with a large plate loaded with slices of bubbling cheese on toast.

'Come along, my darlings, you look famished. All this sleuthing is hard work.' Freddie seemed euphoric, and Ellen knew it was because Alec was there. After handing around plates, he settled himself again on the floor, leaning against the armchair. A ray from the setting sun slanted in the window and highlighted his hair, which looked like flaming gossamer. Alec's fingers gently brushed the tendrils at the nape of Freddie's neck. 'How is it you can even make cheese on toast taste so good?'

Freddie smiled up at him. 'Ah, my dear, I use a secret ingredient.'

Perhaps as a reaction to the intensity of the previous hours, perhaps because of Freddie's drinks, but the atmosphere grew increasingly mellow. Bonhomie settled on them like a friendly embrace. Kate kicked off her shoes and curled up on the sofa, eating her third slice of toast, grinning contentedly at Ellen. Freddie came up with ever wilder suggestions for the identity of the corpse – a politician who was visiting his mistress; perhaps Houdini was not dead after all – which struck them as hilarious. Alec taught them Cockney rhyming slang. There was a gaiety in their laughter and also a sense of hope.

During a break in the conversation, Kate commented, 'Freddie, don't you have a birthday soon?'

'This Saturday,' he agreed. 'I'm turning thirty. Officially grown up.'

'We must do something special. It's good to have reasons to celebrate.'

'We could all go out to a restaurant. Or we could push the boat out and go to that champagne bar Oscar Wilde used to frequent.' Freddie was elated, as if he were drunk, although Ellen knew this was unlikely. Alec couldn't take his eyes off him.

Kate laughed. 'Ha! Did you know I drove ambulances with his niece, Dolly? She's a female version of Oscar, equally queer and witty.'

'I'm dying to hear your stories from those days. By the way, I've been admiring your dress. It's not French, is it?'

'You do have a good eye, don't you? You're quite right. I got it in Berlin last year.'

'There's just a difference in the cut. I don't know if I can explain it. That colour would look terrible on me or Ellen, but it goes very well with your complexion.'

'I disagree. Ellen would look beautiful in any colour or outfit. She could wear a sack and look fabulous.' Kate was looking at her and the air seemed to stand still in the room.

Freddie's eyes slid around to Ellen's face, but he went on in the same chatty tone, 'I have a hat that would suit your dress nicely.'

Kate said teasingly, 'Is this your polite way of saying my beret doesn't go?' Freddie shook his head smilingly, but Kate grinned at the others. 'Freddie must be in despair about our clothes. I suppose you'd love to dress Alec, wouldn't you?'

A dense silence followed. Ellen glanced over at Alec's downcast eyes and Freddie's red face. No, he'd like to do the opposite of that, she thought amused. Kate winked at her and she realised she'd made the remark quite deliberately.

She broke the silence in an attempt to ease her brother's discomfort. 'Freddie did find men's clothes quite boring in the end, didn't you? But if he gets the job to design ballet costumes he can be as creative as he likes.'

No one seemed to have heard Ellen. Freddie was studiously not looking at Alec, his eyes down instead on his hands. They were finely shaped, delicate hands, with fingers mildly greasy from the cheese.

'Take this,' Alec said, leaning forward to give him a handkerchief. They stared at each other. Freddie's look of love and longing was mirrored on Alec's face.

Ellen made a quick decision. 'Come on, Kate, I'll walk you home.' They grabbed their things and left, saying their goodbyes, not waiting for a response. She doubted Freddie and Alec had even heard them.

As they came out onto the street, they smiled at each other in complicity, which somehow transmuted into fits of gleeful laughter coming up from deep in their bodies. Ellen had to stop and wipe her eyes. How good it was to laugh like this.

Kate said, 'In German they call that *Sehnsucht*. I imagine they're already in each other's arms. I'm so happy for them.' They stood in the middle of the road, looking at each other.

'What would you like to do now? You could come up and see my photographs.' Kate's tone was conversational but she looked at Ellen from under her long eyelashes.

'I think you're in a mischievous mood this evening,' she replied, aware her heart was pounding.

Kate threw back her head and laughed. 'Oh, my Ellie. I feel so light-hearted. I feel ... free. I haven't felt like this in years.' Then she sobered. 'But I don't want to be too hopeful. Not yet. I think it's still the case that I killed someone. I want to find out who he was. And, this time, I'm going to deal with it, not run away. All I know is, you have very good instincts. You said something about this was wrong, and you were spot on ... Ellie, why are you doing all this for me?'

Ellen took a breath. 'Don't you know?'

Kate didn't immediately respond. Dusk was creeping along the street; it would soon be fully dark. When she did speak, it seemed a change of subject. 'Walk with me. I've found a pub in Shepherd Market where they'll accept my money.'

17

They retraced the steps they'd taken on Sunday evening, but this time Ellen crossed over Piccadilly with Kate. Wasn't there something in history, a story about a general crossing a river? she thought vaguely. She glanced back to Green Park, the London plane trees providing a wall of green, which confronted and diminished the buildings on the north side.

'I didn't know this particular corner of London very well before I moved here, but I've come to love it,' Kate commented. Ellen made as if to turn right into Half Moon Street, but Kate shook her head with a smile. They turned instead up the next lane, narrow and dark until at the end it broadened out into a small square, bright with the last of the gloaming and lights from the small shops clustered on the edges. 'Come,' Kate said, brushing her hand, and they crossed to a pub on the corner. 'My turn to get the drinks.'

Ellen squinted slightly at the bright interior after their walk, and claimed a small table in the corner. She looked around at the pub, which was half full. No one paid any attention to her. Her thoughts flickered to Freddie and Alec, but her focus was on one thing only. And here she was, crossing from the bar with two drinks and a smile that made Ellen feel she had come home.

As Kate sat down she was looking amused. 'I've just remembered something. Am I right? Did a man call me a "Radclyffe Hall type" before, in Shoreditch?' When Ellen nodded, she laughed. 'What a way to say it! Positively quaint. Did you read the book?'

'Uh-uh. It's banned here, of course.'

'It's in my bookshelf at home. I'll lend it to you. I bought it in Paris. But don't raise your hopes – it's pretty dire. Sad inverts leading lonely lives in the shadows, that sort of thing. If I'd read it when I was fifteen, I'd probably have slit my wrists at the prospect of such a life.' But she said this cheerfully enough. 'Do you still read a lot? You always had your nose in a book before.'

'Afraid so. I'm working my way through the London Library's collection. I get all sorts of comments. What, a working-class woman reading books? It makes me cross sometimes, people's assumptions. My parents had a solid education, even if they did have to go out to work when they were fourteen. Our house was filled with books. Mum loves to read potboilers, and my father makes his way through the collected plays of Shakespeare in the evenings.'

'Well, I've got a good collection myself at home, so you must borrow anything you want. Have you read *Orlando*? No? Oh, you must. It's a good antidote to the Radclyffe Hall horror.' They smiled at each other. Kate asked, 'Do your parents know?'

'They do and they don't, if you know what I mean.' Kate nodded with a look of instant comprehension. 'It's never been mentioned in so many words, but my mother told me she's glad Freddie and I have each other. She said recently she doesn't expect to have grandchildren. I think they're more aware about Freddie. They probably see me as some sort of sexless spinster.' She couldn't quite look at Kate as she said this. 'We went home last Easter for a couple of days. They're very dear to me, but I couldn't see myself living there again.' Kate made a gentle noise of understanding. 'What about you?'

'The same as you. I think my mother had an idea, but it was never discussed in so many words. She'd noticed I didn't show any interest in boys, and told me I must get a good education so I wouldn't need to depend on a man. Leaving wasn't an option for her. She had no employable skills, no money or family. That's why I stayed on at school, why I started at university. It was for her, really. I was desperate to earn money so I could get away … Anyway, you know all this. If she'd lived, I would have told her. I think – I hope she would have accepted me.' Before Ellen could respond, she added, 'But it was out of the question to tell my father. If he'd known, he might well have killed me, or at the very least thrown me out of home.' This was said in a matter-of-fact way.

Ellen had observed, before the war, how the angry presence of Kate's father brooded over the house like a sulphurous cloud. She knew about the beatings he doled out. The sons were inviolable; his violence was directed at the females in the household. Of course, he only did this behind closed doors. In public, he was the well-respected banker and family man. She'd once seen Kate's mother, a kind, anxious woman, with a black eye, but usually his blows landed on parts of the body not on open view. She asked sympathetically, 'Did the violence get worse?'

'Yes. It became unbearable in the last months before the war. How much I missed you then! I talked to Hilda about it, but it wasn't the same.'

'God, I'm so sorry, Kate. You didn't mention this when you visited me in Holloway. I wish you had.'

'The last thing you needed was to hear more misery, Ellie. But his drinking became impossible. He would rage around the house. It felt ... out of control. I used to lie awake at night, trying to work out how I might kill him and get away with it. Ironic, isn't it?' She made a failed attempt at a laugh. 'I ended up killing the wrong man.'

She stopped abruptly and looked down at her drink. Ellen placed her hand on top of hers. Kate went on, her words tumbling out now, 'One evening, he didn't like something my mother said so he started strangling her. My brothers weren't around – they never were. It took me several minutes to pull him off. I remember beating my fists on his back, feeling so helpless, realising how much stronger he was ... I took my mother into my bedroom for the night and put a chair against the handle so he couldn't get in. When I went out the next morning, I realised he'd stuck a knife in the door.'

'Oh, Kate.' Ellen gripped her hand. Her heart felt like breaking. 'When did that happen?'

'I think it was a week or so before the war started,' Kate replied, frowning at her memories.

'So, a few days before you and Hilda burned down the church?'

Kate nodded. 'I was barely home after that, just a few days here and there. I hated leaving my mother alone with him. I'd be sick with worry. But in fact, once Harry died, he was a different man. He seemed to shrink in on himself. He'd go hours without speaking. At least, my mother found him easier to manage.'

A group of people arrived in the pub, their noisy conversation washing over the two women. The men loudly discussed the merits of the new Greta Garbo talkie they'd just seen, their wives shrieking with laughter at their comments. Kate watched them with a cynical, almost hard, expression. After a few minutes they took their drinks to the other end of the pub, and Ellen and Kate's corner became peaceful again.

Ellen realised something. 'Are you not smoking?' They'd been so involved in their conversation they'd barely touched their drinks.

Kate's face relaxed into an embarrassed smile. 'No, I'm trying to give up. Disgusting thing to do, when you think about it.' She paused. 'I know what you used to think. I got involved in violent action because of my father. Because I was angry, or it was symbolic, or whatever. Am I right?'

'It may have been one reason why you took it up with such enthusiasm! God knows, you had every right to be angry. But no, it's never as simple as that, is it? And I can't talk. I smashed windows and I don't regret it for a minute. I think, for me, the part I was uneasy about was when it went to a level of violence where people could get hurt. Burning down houses, planting bombs – I felt very mixed about that. I know women argued we were suffering a form of violence from not having the vote, but for me it wasn't the same.'

'The end didn't justify the means, in other words.'

'Mm, something like that. I think …' and she hesitated.

Kate took a swallow of her drink, all the while watching her face. 'Take your time, my dear. We have all the time in the world.'

Ellen nodded, trying to get her thoughts into order. She usually had a clear, logical mind, but for several days now she'd felt overwhelmed by intense emotions, along with vivid memories from the past. It was as if the firm ground she was on had shifted under her feet. One day, when she could draw breath, she would make sense of this maelstrom happening to her.

'I'm lucky. My parents were always gentle and loving. But I'd see men down the pub, fighting each other when they got drunk, and I could never make sense of it as a child. What I saw from the war just confirmed it. Violence is ugly. It never creates, it only destroys. If someone attacks me, I'll hit back as much as needed, but that's different, that's self-defence. I just feel if we choose to use violence, it somehow, I don't know, lessens us as human beings.' She shrugged. 'Sorry, I haven't explained it very well.'

'You've explained it perfectly, Ellie. I don't disagree with what you say. I know I was angry, impatient. We'd spent decades asking nicely for the vote, and it got us nowhere. They only started to take us seriously when we moved to direct action. Deeds, not words, had more of an effect. But I started feeling uncomfortable with some of the actions, and I agonised over this question after that man, whoever he is, died in the church. I felt such deep remorse and it made me think: who has the right to decide if a cause is worth people's lives? And when does it become too much – at five lives, fifty, a hundred lives?' She frowned, shaking her head in perplexity. The noise in the pub had increased and the cinema group was engaged in a noisy discussion, but it didn't impinge on them. Ellen felt they were encased in a cocoon, intent on their conversation, with everything around them slightly misty or out of focus.

She remarked, 'The war changed everything, didn't it? I often wonder what would have happened if we hadn't gone to war. It seems bloody ironic that women did well out of it. We got to do jobs that had been blocked to us before, and we proved we could do them just as well as men. The arguments they used to deny us the vote just fell away.'

'*Après la pluie* ...' Kate murmured, as if to herself. Ellen's lack of understanding must have shown. 'Sorry, there's a French expression about this, similar to "every cloud has a silver lining". The war was hideous for so many, but yes, we got the vote, after a fashion. I don't count the 1918 change in the law, do you? For me, it only happened two years ago when we got the same full rights as men. Our victories are still so recent and fragile! We mustn't assume we'll never go back to those bad old days when we were shut up in our homes ... Tell me something, Ellie. Does this mean you think war is always wrong?'

Ellen was surprised, and took a minute to consider this. 'No, I can't say that absolutely. Isn't there an expression about a "just war"? I certainly don't think this war should have happened and I still don't understand why we got involved. But if we were threatened by a tyrant, or a country tried to invade us, then yes, we must fight back. That would be self-defence. But, hopefully, there won't be a war like that again.'

Kate was silent. She looked serious, even grim, and Ellen was suddenly gripped with dismay. 'Kate, don't think I'm saying this to criticise what you did. I would never judge you! I just open my mouth and talk sometimes without thinking how it affects others,' and she shook her head in exasperation at herself.

But Kate looked at her calmly. 'Ellie, you need never apologise or explain. I love that you say what you think. I love your integrity, your honesty. Please, never change. I can't tell you how good it is to talk to you like this.'

Ellen couldn't stop herself. 'And yet, you didn't want to see me because you thought I'd blame you for setting the fire?' The hurt she'd been repressing for days came bubbling up. 'So, tell me, Kate, why did you walk away from me? Why did you come back to London and not get in touch?'

She expected Kate to be defensive or angry, but to her surprise she put her head in her hands and audibly groaned. 'Oh, Ellie. Because I'm the biggest fool in the world. Do you think I haven't spent every day regretting this, cursing myself? I missed you so much. But I thought I didn't deserve to see you.'

Ellen gave an incredulous laugh. 'Am I so forbidding?'

Kate grabbed her hand again. 'Of course not. But your good opinion is very important to me. If I thought I'd lost that ...' Kate stared at her with such intensity, Ellen could not doubt it was from the heart. 'I promise you this, Ellen Fernsby. I'll never walk away from you again, unless you tell me to go.'

The landlord rang the bell and called last orders. A barmaid started collecting glasses from the tables and there was sudden movement in the pub. The spell was broken. Kate mentioned an early German class in the morning, and they finished their drinks.

As they stepped out of the pub and hovered uncertainly, Kate asked, 'What's the secret ingredient?'

Ellen knew immediately what she meant. 'Mustard. Freddie spreads it on the toast and puts the cheese on top.' People brushed past them in animated conversations.

'Well, I go this way,' Kate said, not quite looking at Ellen. 'You're coming for supper tomorrow night, aren't you?'

Ellen swallowed her disappointment. 'Of course, I'm looking forward to it. What shall I bring?'

'Only yourself. Come around seven thirty, I've got a private lesson before then. It's just up there on the left,' she said, pointing to Curzon Street which was at the end of the lane.

'Till tomorrow, then,' Ellen responded brightly.

They stepped forward at the same time to hug. Somehow, this changed and they were frankly holding each other. Ellen could feel Kate's arms around her with a tender strength, their cheeks gently brushing, their bodies fitting together like the missing pieces of a puzzle. Neither of them seemed to want to let go. 'Ladies, if you want a cuddle I'm available!' a passing man shouted merrily. They regretfully moved apart and smiled at each other.

'Sweet dreams, Ellie,' Kate said softly before turning away. Ellen watched her walk past the shops and under the building at the end of the lane. Turn around, she silently urged her, turn around. She needed a sign. Kate paused under the light and turned to look at Ellen, raising her hand.

The flat was quiet when she got back. A lamp was on in the sitting room and she could see Alec's jacket and briefcase there, along with the plates from their supper still scattered around. She quietly gathered up the plates, took them into the kitchen and washed them, leaving them in the rack to drain. She usually preferred to dry the dishes immediately, while Freddie would argue they dried equally well by themselves, with less effort. Perhaps he was right. She straightened up the cushions, hung Alec's jacket neatly on the back of a chair, smoothing out the wrinkles with her hands, and switched off the light.

All was in darkness when she came up to the top landing, just a sliver of light under Freddie's door at the back. She got into her pyjamas and turned down the cover on her bed, stopping to look at the picture of Kate. When she went into the bathroom to brush her teeth, she could dimly hear Freddie's voice talking and then an answering laugh. This time it will work, Ellen thought. They both know what they want. When she got into bed she hugged her happiness to herself.

18

Ellen rolled over to shut off the alarm and rubbed her eyes, trying to retain the wisp of a dream, which was rapidly retreating. Something about a swan flying into a pub and she was shouting at the men, 'No violence, let it be free!'

She could hear a murmur of hushed voices outside on the landing, then someone, presumably Alec, going down the stairs. After lying in bed with her mind drifting over the evening with Kate, she went to run her bath. Ah, the luxury of hot running water at the turn of a tap – she would never take it for granted. Back in her bedroom afterwards, she was in a dreamy mood, staring out of the window half-dressed, but snapped out of it when she saw the time. They had to open the shop in fifteen minutes.

Down in the kitchen, she filled up the kettle and put two eggs on to boil. With still no sign of Freddie, she called up to him and put the bread into the toaster. He eventually appeared in the kitchen, tousle-haired and still in his pyjamas, as she was halfway through her boiled egg.

'Good morning, sleepyhead!' she greeted him. He sat down at the table and stared at his egg, still three-quarters asleep. 'Here's some toast, and I've just poured your tea,' she said, knowing it was pointless to attempt a conversation with him in this state. All his life Freddie had awoken slowly from sleep, monosyllabic and abnormally sensitive to noise, seemingly in thrall to another level of consciousness. He sipped his tea, staring into the distance with a smile, lost in his world.

Ellen did a quick wash and rinse of her breakfast things. 'Right, I've got to finish getting dressed and open up the shop. I'll see you in a while,' dropping a kiss on his head as she passed by. She was emerging from her room when she heard Freddie start the bath, and laughed to herself as she started downstairs. But here was Hester coming up to the workroom, already talking, and she needed to focus on the day.

Freddie emerged in the shop half an hour later, dressed, abluted and fully awake. 'Sorry I'm late,' he offered with an apologetic smile. He stood in the middle of the shop with a jubilant expression.

'Are things well with you, little brother?' she asked him lovingly.

He replied, 'I'm the happiest man in the world.' Everything she needed to know was written on his face.

Before they could speak further, Hester came bustling down from the workroom. 'Good morning, Freddie!' she exclaimed with her eager grin. 'I thought you were unwell when I didn't see you first thing this morning. I feared you might have picked up this flu bug that's been going around. It sounds awfully nasty! My downstairs neighbour has been in bed all week, and I've been worried my poor mother might pick it up. But Ellen tells me you got to bed very late last night. Out on the town, were you, naughty boy?'

Freddie's eyebrows fluttered but he replied politely, 'No, I'm not ill. I was just – with a friend. In fact, I couldn't be better.' It was true – he bloomed like an advertisement for a magic tonic providing good health and happiness. The contrast from the wan, unhappy man of the previous week was palpable. Ellen noticed a flicker of uncertainty cross Hester's face and started talking about their plans for the day. Freddie had a fitting at eleven, and they agreed he would be in the shop all morning while Ellen did the books and Hester finished making up some orders.

The morning crawled along. Ellen found it difficult to concentrate on work, her thoughts floating away on another track. It sounded quiet in the shop, with only one walk-in apart from the fitting. She went through the last bank statement, balancing the books, and was pleased to see everything matched down to the last penny. She put in orders for material, started making out the quarterly bills for their regular customers and phoned Mrs Drummond to remind her a payment of thirty guineas was overdue. Perhaps Freddie's current state of beneficence towards the world had rubbed off on her, because Mrs Drummond, who could sometimes be difficult, declared she would put the cheque in the post. Ellen was uneasily aware of the threat posed to their shop by the growing popularity of the department stores – Harrods, Selfridges, Peter Robinson and the like. Not just in terms of attracting the sort of customers Fernsby Fashions needed, but also because they could offer seamstresses better working hours and pay. For now, business was good; but with the recent collapse in the economy, Ellen knew the future was less certain.

Hester worked away on the sewing machine with her usual efficiency and chatter, going down to the shop several times to consult Freddie about a pattern. Coming back into the workroom after one such trip, she stopped by Ellen's desk and observed, with a nervous giggle, 'I need to remember dropped waists are no longer in fashion, but Freddie assures me that's right. And we use up more material to make the longer skirts, but of course we must change with the times. Just as well Freddie knows all this! My goodness, he seems to be in an excellent mood today. I don't think he's stopped smiling! Anyone might think he was in love,' she added, darting a quick look at Ellen, who carefully returned a non-committal remark.

After another hour, Ellen stood up and stretched. 'Time for a cuppa, I think.' When she took Freddie's tea down to him he was absorbed in sketching, a few finished designs strewn nearby on the bench. She saw he was drawing a portrait of Alec and commented, 'That's lovely,' putting her hand on his shoulder. 'You've caught his likeness very well.' Freddie had a natural aptitude for drawing. She'd always been sad he hadn't had the opportunity to go to art school. Around the time he and Alec had their falling out, he'd started a mosaic with broken pieces of coloured glass and pottery, spending hours in the evenings working on it. 'Just something to keep me sane,' he'd said, but Ellen thought it was as beautiful as anything she'd seen in an art gallery.

A woman came into the shop and she went back up to the workroom to finish writing out the bills. When a nearby clock chimed the hour she suggested, 'Hester, why don't you go off now for your lunch break? Could you post these letters while you're out? Take as long as you like. The shop's quiet and it's a lovely day outside.'

'If you're sure, Ellen. I might just take the opportunity to pop to the butcher and buy sausages for tonight. My cousin is coming to supper.' She continued talking in her jolly way while she put on her hat and coat, but Ellen picked up a brittle anxiety behind the smiles. Her absence created a silence, which felt like a blessing. Ellen groaned at the ring of the telephone a few minutes later, but fortunately it was Alec.

'How nice to hear your voice,' she told him. 'I suppose you want Freddie?' but he replied, 'Actually, Ellen, it's you I want to speak to. Is it convenient to talk now?'

'Yes, of course. Is it – have you discovered something to do with the fire?'

'No, I'm still doing some research and waiting to hear from my police contact. I hope to have more news later this afternoon.' He hesitated. 'I wanted to speak to you privately, about Freddie.'

'Oh! That's fine, I'm on my own,' she replied, with a sudden grip of fear. Surely, he could not be about to say he regretted last night? Her mind skittered wildly, an image of Freddie, broken-hearted, devastated – but he was already talking.

'I'm aware he told you I was seeing someone. I just wanted to let you know, I told James last Sunday it was finished. As soon as I saw Freddie again, I knew nothing else mattered. I don't want you thinking I'm seeing someone else as well, that I'm playing around with Freddie. I'd never do that. I'd never do anything to hurt him.' His voice was serious, almost urgent. Relief thrummed through her body.

'Thank you for telling me, Alec, but really, it's none of my business. My meddling days are over, I hope! It's entirely between you and Freddie. I just know he's terribly happy.'

'I said this because I know how important you are for Freddie. And we are friends, too. I hope we always will be. Because I – well, Freddie means everything to me. I'm the happiest man on this earth.'

'Oh, my dear! Well, you might need to fight Freddie to claim that title, because he told me exactly the same thing a few hours ago.' Alec started giggling and she could no longer stop her laughter. For a few giddy seconds, waves of elation zapped and zinged along the telephone wires.

'May I ask you a favour?' he went on, once he got himself under control. 'I'd like to drive Freddie up to Yorkshire so he can visit Sam's grave. A friend is letting me use his cottage in Scarborough, so we could make a small holiday of it. I thought we could drive up on Thursday night next week, if it's possible to manage without him for those days? We'd be back on the Sunday night.'

'I'll be happy to mind the shop. Let me just check if he's got any appointments for Friday or Saturday.' She pulled the diary towards her and turned to the following week. 'Nope, you're lucky. They're both free. I think it's a wonderful idea. And you can have a little honeymoon.' He giggled some more.

'Thank you, Ellie. I'd like it to be a surprise for him. Could you not mention it? Now, on the investigation, I'll phone later this evening with an update. Freddie's coming over to my place tonight,' he said, his voice ringing with joy. 'Will you be at home or, um, at Kate's?'

'I'm going to Kate's for supper. Why don't you try there first?' After they ended the call she sat smiling to herself. She drew a line through the diary for the two days, writing "no appointments" with a flourish. But she could not settle again to her work. After daydreaming with her head propped on her hands, she went back down to the shop. 'Freddie, I'm going to grab something to eat and I need to pop out for a few minutes. Hester's at lunch. Do you want to have a break now?'

He shook his head, smiling beatifically. 'No, Ellie, I'm not hungry at all. You go ahead. I'll be fine. It's quiet here.' His sketch was almost finished.

She went up to the kitchen to eat some bread and cheese, then walked to a vintner's in St James's Street. The assistant confounded her by asking what sort of wine she wanted: red or white, dry or sweet – how would she know? Eventually she settled for a French burgundy he recommended.

Hester was in the workroom when she got back and related a long story about buying the sausages. Ellen muttered, 'Mm,' at appropriate moments, thinking she needed to give Freddie his break. When Hester had finished her tale she said, 'By the way, Hester, we mustn't make any appointments for Freddie on Friday and Saturday next week. He's going away with a friend for a few days.'

Hester did not respond. When she looked over a few minutes later, Ellen realised she was silently crying. 'Oh, Hester, what's wrong?' she asked with a sinking feeling. She shut the workroom door and went to sit next to Hester who was now sobbing noisily, her head on the worktable. After several minutes of inconsolable weeping, she started to calm down. Her mascara had run in dark streaks down her cheeks and her face was red and blotchy. It was only in romantic books or plays where the heroine cried perfect pearl tears down alabaster cheeks, Ellen mused distractedly. Hester blew her nose loudly into the handkerchief offered to her, leaving smears of her red lipstick.

Ellen's voice was gentle. 'Tell me what's troubling you.'

'Oh, Ellen, I know it's ridiculous. It's completely hopeless, but I do love him so much and I can see he's found someone. Of course, it was a fantasy. After all, why should Freddie look at me? He's so handsome and kind and clever and ... well, I know he's a little bit younger. But I could dream at least ...' and she hiccupped more sobs. Ellen waited, patting her shoulder. 'I feel so desperate, Ellen, so unhappy. I feel like screaming inside sometimes. When will I find a man to love me? I try to do all the right things. I look after my appearance, I smile and show interest when men talk, I laugh at their jokes. A man did walk out with me a few years ago and I hoped ... I want to make a home. I want a husband, I want children. I don't want to end my life on my own, living with my mother. What am I doing wrong? I feel such a failure,' and she wailed these last words before crumpling again into tears.

Ellen waited until she subsided. 'Hester, my dear, I hate to see you like this. You're not doing anything wrong. You're a lovely, warm woman. If men haven't had the sense to realise this, then more shame on them. You mustn't feel you're a failure – you're not! It's been such a success having you work with us. You're so efficient and quick. You have a fine brain. There's so much you can achieve in life.'

Hester sniffed, looking woebegone. 'But all I want is to be married and have children. Every girl dreams of going down the aisle in a beautiful white dress. Every woman wants children. It's the most important thing we can do. You're always cheerful, and I know you're younger – but you must feel it too.'

Ellen shook her head. 'I can honestly say I've never felt a desire to have children. I think they're nice and all that, but it's not for me.'

Hester stared at her open-mouthed, incomprehension written across her face. 'Maybe you think that now, but it will change. If – when Freddie marries his sweetheart and you're left alone …'

Ellen sighed inwardly. 'He's not really the marrying kind, Hester,' she said as gently as she could. 'Yes, one day he'll move into his own home with – with a friend, but that changes nothing. You can't go through life looking to others to make you happy. It needs to come from inside. You have a good life, and it sounds like you have good friends.'

Hester was doubtful. 'But they're just women. I want to find a man to love me.' The telephone started ringing. Hester glanced at it, stricken, but Ellen shook her head saying, 'Bugger the phone, let it ring.' Hester looked shocked, then sniggered.

'Listen, my dear. Right now you feel upset, but there's no reason why you won't find someone. You're still young. Perhaps it will come when you least expect it. You'll be at the butcher's buying mince, thinking about your supper, and a man will start chatting to you, something like that.' Hester gave a watery smile. 'Why don't you leave early today? It's very quiet, after all. Go and get yourself a cuppa and a nice cake in the Lyons Corner House and treat yourself. You deserve it.'

'Are you sure, Ellen? Well, perhaps I will … I promise I'll be fine tomorrow and I'll work ever so hard. I've just got one order left to finish. You – you won't say anything to Freddie, will you?'

Ellen shook her head. 'Of course not, Hester. This is just between us. Go and wash your face and forget about everything.'

After she had walked Hester out, she went into the shop where Freddie looked half-asleep. 'Freddie, I'm so sorry. You must be ravenous! Go and take a long break now and I'll be here. Hester's not well, so I've sent her home early.'

'I'm sorry to hear that. I wondered if she was all right. She seemed a little ... strange. I'll just grab a sandwich. Shout up if you need help.' He gave her a hug as he went out.

19

Three more hours before closing time. Ellen thought, God, this day is dragging. But in fact, customers started coming in and she was kept busy for the remaining time. She even had a triumph, selling two hats to a woman who had come in to look at a blouse. Freddie didn't reappear and it was silent upstairs. After she finally put the "Closed" sign on the door, she found him fast asleep on the sofa, his arms bent above his head in relaxed abandon. The wireless was playing quietly and a cold cup of tea and half-eaten sandwich were on the floor nearby.

She stood looking down at him. She was two and a half when he was born, and had fiercely loved her little brother from the first day. Growing up, they'd been the best of playmates and friends. Realising they were both queer had brought them even closer. After he was conscripted, she had woken every morning dreading that would be the day she'd hear of his death. Her relief had been overwhelming when he'd arrived home at war's end, seemingly safe. But the worst was yet to come – he was not the same boy who'd gone off to war. He was physically drained, his lungs excoriated, his mind overwhelmed by the atrocities he'd witnessed, his heart broken over Sam. She'd cared for him as if he were a helpless infant: spooning food into his mouth, reading aloud to him or just sitting with him, silently cheering, as he slowly emerged from his dark place. She had feared he was too sensitive to recover from life's cruelties, but he'd shown a resolute will to survive. He had recovered and got on with his life. After that, their bond was unbreakable. And now … how far they'd come from those bad days.

Perversely, when she switched off the wireless he woke up, stretching and smiling at her sleepily. She went to the kitchen to make a fresh cup of tea and took it to him on the sofa, where he was now in a sitting position, looking around in a vague way.

'Drink this, Freddie. I'm sorry you had to spend nearly all day in the shop on your own.'

He yawned. 'I didn't mean to fall asleep. What time is it?'

'It's nearly seven. I didn't know when you needed to be at Alec's.'

'He's got his choir practice until eight thirty, so I have time.' He took a gulp of tea and picked up his sandwich from the plate. 'Crikey, I'm hungry! Thanks for this, Ellie.'

'Alec certainly tired you out last night,' she remarked slyly, settling on the sofa next to him. He laughed, his eyes misting over at a private memory.

'He is … magnificent. But, Ellie, my God!' He shook his head, suddenly serious. 'I can't believe how fucking stupid I've been. Why did I try to wreck it before? It was madness. I never told him about Sam. I never gave him a chance to understand why I got so scared – well, I didn't understand it myself. But it feels so different this time.'

'What's changed for you both?' Ellen was genuinely curious, aware of certain parallels with her own situation.

'Now we really trust each other. We've done a lot of talking these last few days. I had to explain why I played such a cheap trick on him, and it forced me to confront myself. As unhappy as these past weeks have been, I think I needed it to shock me into my senses …' He sighed deeply and went on. 'Life has been so generous, giving me a second chance with Alec. This time I won't do anything to ruin it. I can't go on being controlled by things that happened to me years ago. It's time to grow up and let go. I feel – I don't know how to explain it – but somehow, I'm free of the past. It's still there, but now I care only about my present and my future with him.' He spoke with conviction, a look of peace on his face. 'And it's all thanks to you, sis. You broke the stupid deadlock between us. Alec and I know we owe you everything. We'll never forget it.'

Ellen grinned at him. It was obviously her day to be the recipient of emotional outpourings, but this time she treasured every word. 'To see you both so happy is all the thanks I want.'

He continued looking at her and remarked, 'Which reminds me. I thought you might not come home last night. How are things between you and Kate?'

A reasonable enquiry, and one she wished she could answer. But his question had reminded her. 'Bloody hell! I've got to be at her place at seven thirty! I'd better get changed.' She jumped off the sofa in a fluster.

Freddie laughed. 'Go and get your glad rags on, Ellie. I'll walk with you.'

*

'What do you think?' Ellen gave a twirl. She'd changed into her favourite trousers and a grey blouse with a tie at the neck, both designed and sewn by Freddie. 'Am I a good advertisement for Fernsby Fashions?'

Freddie, who had also changed out of his work clothes, replied, 'The best! You look fantabulosa, darling. How could anyone resist you?'

Ellen smiled but did not respond.

Grabbing their jackets, and the bottle of wine from the table, they went out to the street, chatting about work things. Freddie insisted they have a look in the Fortnum & Mason window display and described a new design, for a woman's top with a cowl neck, he'd sketched that day. Ellen told him about her success with Mrs Drummond and the customer buying two hats. They agreed there was no food in the flat and Ellen suggested she duck out to do some shopping in the morning.

But, as they waited to cross over Piccadilly, busy with evening traffic, Freddie returned obliquely to their earlier conversation. 'I've seen quite a change in Kate since last Saturday. She looks happier, less haunted, somehow. Whatever comes out of this investigation, it's helped her come to terms with what happened.'

Ellen glanced at him as they started to cross. 'What do you think we'll find out?'

'I think they used that man – what's his name? Fawdon, yes. They used his identity to cover up for the real person. Mark my words, there's something political going on.' He saw her bleak expression and added, 'I may well be wrong, Ellie. But, even so, I can see how positive it's been for Kate. Whatever the truth, she'll cope with it, don't worry. She's a strong woman.

It's just that she's been through a hard time. Her family are all dead, you said?'

'It's more than that.' She told him about Kate's father and her experiences in Paris. He listened with his usual ready sympathy.

'Poor Kate! I'm not surprised she had a breakdown. That woman sounds all wrong for her. She needs someone calm and balanced, not a moody drug user. I imagine it must be hard for her to trust people. Do you realise she's been all alone in the world?' She nodded. 'Not any more. She's got you, and me and Alec as well.' Ellen turned his comments over in her mind without replying. Freddie had always been a perceptive reader of other people.

They turned up the lane towards Shepherd Market, but all at once he stopped dead and looked at her with a slight frown. 'Ellie, hold on – how did you know I was going to Alec's this evening?'

'Oh, we had a chat on the phone today.'

His eyes shone. 'Really? What did he say? Anything about me?'

She shook her head, laughing, and they continued walking. 'Alec and I can have a private conversation, you know. But you needn't worry. I think he's floating on the same cloud as you.'

They were coming up to the pub she and Kate had been in the previous evening. A group of men stood outside in the evening sunshine, drinking beer and chatting. Freddie looked around with interest, commenting, 'It's quite a while since I've been here.' It was busier than the previous night, with a few shops still open and people passing through on the journey home from work. Freddie's attention was caught by a shop on the other side of the square, and he went over to look in the window. When she joined him, he was staring at a delicate marcasite tie pin. 'It's rather lovely, isn't it? I'm thinking about Alec's birthday in August.' Ellen's eye was caught by a necklace in the same jewellery display, a simple chain with a round tiger's eye pendant surrounded by a thin silver band. It would look beautiful on Kate. For a moment, she and Freddie stood there, caught up in similar dreamy imaginings.

They resumed walking through the square and on to Curzon Street. Ellen checked the numbers as they walked along. When they came to Kate's apartment block, they stood appraising it. There were intricate stone carvings, with a vaguely Egyptian flavour, all around the entrance, while iron scrolls surrounded the street number set in a window above the solid oak doors.

'Nice,' Freddie said approvingly. 'Quite modern – just before the war, I'd say. This is a posh area, you know. Beau Brummell used to live around the corner. What floor is she on?'

'She said the fifth floor,' Ellen said, craning her neck to look up the front of the red-brick building. 'Alec won't be back yet. Do you want to come up for a while?'

'Another time, sis. I've got a key to his place. Right, I'm heading off this way,' Freddie said, indicating with a tilt of his head the direction of Berkeley Square. He was ablaze with a barely suppressed excitement. 'Have a lovely evening. See you in the morning. Promise I won't be late.' He strode off with a cheery wave. Ellen pressed the button for Kate's flat and was buzzed inside.

20

The lobby was smartly turned out, with marble tiles and an impressive fireplace. Ellen walked past the empty porter's desk into a small hallway, where she was presented with two lifts. She usually preferred to take the stairs, but right now she didn't fancy arriving at Kate's door in a breathless state. Her heart already seemed to be banging away unnaturally. When she pulled back the iron gates and stepped out on the fifth floor, Kate's flat was on the left. She rang the bell, composing her face into a portrait of placid friendship. But her nervousness was forgotten when Kate quickly opened the door with a warm smile and a hug. 'Welcome to my home!' she announced gaily.

Ellen's first impression, when she stepped inside, was of light and space. Kate's flat was on the south side of the building, away from the street. The sitting room was large and simply furnished with a pale carpet, sofa, two armchairs, a table in the corner. One wall was taken up by shelves filled with books. There were a few framed photographs on the walls. But she couldn't stop herself from walking directly to the window and exclaiming, 'Oh, Kate, what a magnificent view!' She was looking back down onto Piccadilly and beyond to Green Park, an oasis of trees, and Buckingham Palace with its own substantial gardens. If she squinted her eyes, she could make out Jermyn Street. To the west, the beginnings of Hyde Park. Traffic crawled around Hyde Park Corner, the goddess of victory looking down disdainfully.

Kate stood next to her. 'I never get tired of it,' she said, resting her hand on Ellen's shoulder. 'There's always something to see – the light at different times of the day, or the change of the seasons. I've seen some fabulous sunsets, and the sun pours in here in the morning. Sometimes I curl up in the armchair and bask like a lizard.'

'If you had binoculars you could probably see our place.' Ellen gazed at the panorama laid out before her like a patchwork.

But Kate had just spotted the wine. 'Ellie, I told you not to bring anything! It's a good choice, though. It goes well with the meal.' Ellen tried to look as if she'd planned it. 'Sorry, I'm a terrible hostess. Give me your coat and hat,' and she hung them on a stand by the door. 'You look wonderful. I love that blouse. Is it one of Freddie's designs? Here, I'll open the wine.'

Ellen handed the bottle to Kate and followed her to the kitchen, which had a door to a narrow balcony. It contained every modern appliance, including the latest style of cooker and – 'Blimey, Kate, you have a refrigerator!' She stared, impressed, at the oblong object humming in the corner. 'What luxury!'

'Isn't it? It seems decadent, but I couldn't do without it now. I can keep food fresh for ages, which suits me fine. I got very bored having to shop every day. Life's too short.' She opened the bottle of wine and put it on the bench. Noticing Ellen's look, she explained, 'Red wine has to breathe.'

Ellen couldn't help retorting, 'What, like a wounded animal?'

Kate laughed. 'Very witty. Right, shall I give you a tour?' She took Ellen back through the sitting room and into a corridor. 'Bathroom,' she announced unnecessarily as they passed by. 'My bedroom.' Ellen glanced curiously at the double bed and large window framed by deep blue curtains. 'And this is the second bedroom, which I'm using as a sort of photography studio.'

Ellen stopped at the doorway to take it all in. There was a bed in the corner, but otherwise it appeared to function as an office, with a filing cabinet, camera equipment, tripods, lights and piles of photographs on a large desk. She went over to look, becoming so absorbed she forgot Kate was standing next to her. The photographs showed life in the street: East End children playing football or hide and seek, puffed up with swagger. A weary mother with a crying baby. Old men playing draughts in the park. A pair of lovers in a crowd, lost in their world. A man in a bowler hat standing still while commuters streamed past him on London Bridge. After a while she looked up at Kate, her eyes shining. 'Kate, I had no idea – I thought it was a hobby. But these are absolutely marvellous!'

'Do you think so?' Kate asked, looking pleased. 'I value your opinion, Ellie. I'd love to make some sort of a career from this. At the moment I'm putting together a portfolio of portraits for a studio in Dover Street. I wondered ... could I take pictures of you for my file?'

Ellen blushed. 'Of course, I'm glad to do anything to help you, but I'm no one important.'

Kate's expression was unreadable. 'On the contrary, my dear. But you needn't worry. It's just to show the studio what I can do, and the camera will like your face. I want to start making contacts and getting my name known. There's a certain amount of jobbing work I can try to pick up – portraits, weddings, advertising and the like – although it doesn't particularly excite me. My passion is for street photography.'

'When did you get into this?' Ellen had moved onto a second pile, which contained portraits of individuals, each photograph telling a different story. One caught her attention. An older woman with white hair looked at the camera with a proud smile, but Kate had caught the sadness in her eyes.

'I met several women photographers in Paris and basically learned the trade from them. They were very helpful, they let me follow them around and ask endless questions. Have you heard of Germaine Krull? No? She was the one who really taught me photography.' Kate started explaining how she framed the pictures, tricks she used with light or shade. Ellen was reminded of how Freddie lit up when he was talking about design. It doesn't matter what job you do, she reflected, the thing is to be passionate about it and do it to the best of your ability.

'It all looks so professional. How many cameras do you have?'

'I've got two. This Leica is for street photography – you need something portable and not too obvious. I use the Rolleiflex, the larger one, mostly to take portraits. The rest is the equipment I need to develop the photographs.'

'You do that yourself?' Ellen asked, increasingly impressed.

'Yes, I use the bathroom. It's ideal because it has no external window, although it does mean the room smells permanently of chemicals,' she added with a shrug. 'I've just moved to silver-bromide paper to develop the photographs and …' She came to a halt and gave an embarrassed laugh. 'Sorry, I've been nattering on like a great bore.'

'Not at all, Kate. It's fascinating. I'd love to hear more.'

Kate looked almost bashful and said, 'Well, I'd better check the oven. It should be nearly done.'

They went back to the sitting room and Kate disappeared into the kitchen. Ellen wandered around looking at Kate's things, trailing a finger over the sofa and armchairs. A wireless was softly playing swing music. One of the photographs on the wall was a street scene by Kate, obviously in Paris as the Eiffel Tower soared in the background. A woman, head down, walked along an empty street with dramatic dark clouds above her. It gave a sense of melancholy and loneliness. Next to it was a studio portrait of Kate's mother when she was a young woman, probably on her wedding day as she was in smart clothes and holding a bouquet. Ellen studied it for some time, spotting a resemblance to Kate in the long nose and generous mouth. When she turned to the final photograph, she realised it was identical to the one in her own bedroom, showing the two of them at Emily Wilding Davison's funeral procession.

For a moment, she had to blink back tears. She felt emotional and brilliantly alive, as if her blood were fizzing in her veins. Now she realised why Kate had spoken to her of one's first love. Everything was falling into place.

When Kate returned a few minutes later, Ellen was browsing through the bookcase. Kate handed her a glass of wine and said, 'Remind me to get out those books for you.' They clinked glasses. Ellen took a cautious sip of the wine and was pleasantly surprised. The vintner had known what he was talking about.

She commented, 'This collection would keep you busy for a while. Did you have all the books and furniture sent over from Paris?'

'God, no! About half the books are from Paris, the rest are from my old home. It took me until the end of the winter to sort out everything left in the house. I gave most of it to charities and kept just minimal furniture for here. The only important things were my mother's possessions and my stuff, or what was left of it. My father destroyed most of my things.' She said this in a neutral tone but Ellen noticed a passing shadow in her eyes. 'Supper should be ready in a few minutes. I've barely used this cooker. I'm still getting used to it. I'm afraid there's no starter – I'm not as organised as Freddie.'

'What are we having?'

'*Coq au vin*, only it's chicken in wine rather than the rooster the recipe calls for.' She smiled to herself at some private joke.

'Very accomplished! I don't think I've ever eaten that before.'

'Don't be too impressed. You'll soon learn I have two recipes: this, and a fish pie. Otherwise, it's toast or boiled egg. Unfortunately, French cuisine was something I didn't manage to pick up. You'll get sick of my *coq au vin* before too long, believe me.'

Ellen couldn't help noticing Kate's remark assumed they would be seeing a lot of each other. 'Kate, I love your flat,' she said impulsively.

'I'm glad you like it. I do, too. I think this place is one thing I managed to get right. Well, it should be done now,' and she went back to the kitchen. Ellen continued to browse the bookshelves, noting several novels she'd like to read, before taking out a slim book. She'd never got the point of poetry before, but it was unusual to find published poems by a woman. When Kate returned a few minutes later to put plates on the table, she was in another world. She had just realised how poetry could speak to you directly with a piercing truth.

'Were you called a bookworm as a child?' Kate asked with a laugh. 'What have you got there?' Ellen wordlessly held it up. 'Oh, Edna St Vincent Millay. I didn't know you liked poetry. If you haven't already read the war poets, you must. Powerful and devastating.' Then she looked at Ellen more closely. 'What is it?'

'Oh,' Ellen hesitated, 'this poem I'm reading.'

'Which one? What does it say?'

Ellen looked back at the page and slowly read out:

Over these things I could not see;
These were the things that bounded me.

Kate nodded. Ellen could read a mixture of regret and self-acknowledgement on her face. 'Yes, Ellie. That's me.'

'Not just you, Kate. Not just you,' Ellen replied.

Then Kate lifted her head and added proudly, 'Or rather, that was me. I lost myself for a while. Not now. And never again.' They looked at each other. 'Well, supper's ready. Let's eat.'

21

The meal was pronounced a great success. Kate insisted on putting a second helping onto Ellen's plate. 'I can't have you going hungry,' she said, when Ellen protested. Kate had placed two tall candles, set in silver filigree holders, on the table, which Ellen supposed must be the French fashion. Her memories of growing up without electricity had not yet faded; perhaps she was too pragmatic, but she still welcomed the gift of light at the flick of a switch.

Despite a mood of restless anticipation, their conversation flowed easily. Kate asked about Ellen's nursing experiences, and her lively anecdotes kept them entertained for some time. Chin propped on her hand, Kate asked questions and laughed at the right moments. Ellen chose to focus on the lighter aspects of her work and to leave out the war years – the wretched echoes of that time had been too much in their minds lately. Once or twice she mentioned Beth as she talked, and part of her brain noticed the feeling of calm acceptance that accompanied her former lover's memory. She filed the thought away to examine at another, more private time.

'Do you miss nursing?' Kate asked, after Ellen had finished telling her the story of the Royal Visit and the Lost Pyjamas.

Ellen wrinkled her forehead thoughtfully. 'Not really. I liked parts of it, but too often I was just a glorified skivvy. It did come in handy when Hilda became ill.'

'Oh, yes … poor Hilda. I was planning to visit her when I heard she'd died. I do regret not seeing her when I had the chance.'

Ellen said seriously, 'Don't be sorry, Kate. She wasn't herself this last year. Better to remember how she was. I know nursing is an option if – well, everyone's saying the economy will get a lot worse. If we can't make a living from the shop, it could be something to consider again. But, for now, I prefer what I'm doing with Freddie. It's been a lot of fun.'

'That reminds me – how could it have slipped my mind? Do you have any news on the Freddie and Alec front?' Kate asked, regaining her smile.

'Of course, I forgot you didn't know. Yes, they're lovers again. All is well,' and they grinned with relief at each other. 'They separately told me they're the happiest men in the world.'

'Ha! I'm delighted for them. This seems to be a momentous week for all of us. Leaving the past where it belongs, making crucial decisions.' Kate gazed at Ellen, who busied herself taking a sip from the glass. She was conscious her face was flushed from the red wine. Gin never had that effect. Kate's sitting room felt warm, even though she'd opened a window.

'It's a shame they had to go through such unhappiness, but I wonder if it might have served a purpose. I think they've both learned something. Freddie told me it's time he grew up and stopped being ruled by the past. You see, Kate, he's very gentle, too much so, really. I've often worried that other people could take advantage of him. He needs to be tougher to survive in this world. Alec will be so good for Freddie in that and in every other way.' Stop gabbling, she told herself. But Kate just nodded.

'I agree, Alec is perfect for him. They deserve this happiness. God knows, it can be hard in this society if you love your own sex. Finding the right person to share your life with – it's so precious. You must guard it with your life.' Kate said this quietly, almost as if talking to herself. Ellen held her breath as they looked at each other. Kate went on, in a more conversational tone, 'And I don't dispute that we all need a certain toughness to get by. But you underestimate Freddie. He's more resilient than you think. He survived those horrific experiences in the war – that took real courage. I can see you're very protective of your brother, but you need to think of yourself more. You're a strong woman, Ellie, we all know that, but sometimes you can let someone else look after you as well.' She didn't wait for a response, instead standing up and clearing the plates from the table. 'Ready for the dessert, I think.'

She was in the kitchen for several minutes, giving Ellen time to mull over her words. One of the candles flickered, as if caught in a draught, but the flame soon steadied. Ellen suddenly realised why the candle holders looked familiar: they had belonged to Kate's mother. Being able to use them must give Kate a measure of comfort. In any event, Ellen was already less sceptical about dining by candlelight. There was a certain romance to it, after all.

When Kate came back, she was carrying two bowls of strawberries with cream. 'I thought we could finish our dessert from the other day,' she announced with a mischievous look.

They ate silently for a few minutes. Kate remarked, 'There's something about Kent strawberries. They have a particular taste you don't get anywhere else. The strawberries I had in Paris a few weeks back were nowhere near as good as these.'

'I didn't know you'd been back to Paris.'

'Oh, I've been back and forth a few times, mostly last winter, when I was feeling a bit lost. I've got a couple of good friends there who kept me going.'

'Tell me about them.' Ellen felt oddly unsettled.

'Marie is my oldest friend – I know her from the ambulance service. She lives with Agathe, who's a teacher. They're in their forties. I suppose I see them as older sisters or something. Marie was the one who looked after me when I – when I had the breakdown. And I met Philippe through Simone. The only good thing to come out of that,' she added, briefly compressing her lips. 'I must say, Alec reminds me a little of him. That's why I went back at the beginning of the month. It was Philippe's thirty-eighth birthday.'

'They sound nice,' Ellen said.

'You'll like them. I got letters today and they're dying to meet you. Marie's practising her English especially.'

'Oh.' Say something, she urged herself.

'Ellie.'

'Yes?'

'You know what's happening here, don't you?'

Ellen's heart was thudding and the colour came to her face, but she maintained eye contact. 'Yes, Kate, I know.'

Kate leaned forward and took Ellen's hand in hers. 'Are you—?'

Before she could continue, the telephone shrilled. They both jumped and looked over at it. 'Just ignore it,' Kate said, but Ellen gave her an apologetic smile.

'It might be Alec. He told me he'd ring this evening.' All at once, the shadow of the past was on them again.

'All right, I'd better get it.' She gave Ellen an almost flirtatious look, saying, 'Don't go away,' crossed to the small table next to the sofa and picked up the receiver. Ellen glanced at her watch. It was after ten. She looked out the window and saw that night had silently arrived. After a few words, Kate said, 'Come and listen in, Ellie.' She walked over and sat on the sofa next to Kate who held the telephone on her lap and put the earpiece between them, their faces close together. 'Right, Alec, we're both here, talk away.'

Alec's voice sounded tinny but clear. 'Hello, Ellen, sorry to disturb your evening. I hope you two weren't in the middle of your meal?'

'Well, we were halfway through the strawberries, but I almost expected to be interrupted,' Kate said.

'What? Oh, sorry, Freddie's asking me what you had for supper.'

Ellen leaned over to the mouthpiece. 'Tell him Kate prepared chicken in wine, a French recipe, and it was delicious.'

They could hear a muffled conversation from the other side, then Alec said, 'Freddie's jealous – he wants you to make it for him. I'm afraid he didn't get much of a supper off me this evening.'

Kate laughed. 'I promise I will, and I'll teach you the recipe so you can cook it for him.'

'All right, we'd better get down to business. The first thing is that William Fawdon rang me when I was about to leave work. As we expected, he doesn't want to take this any further. But he said he was glad he found out his father didn't die in the fire and feels more at peace now, which is nice, don't you think? He sent his regards to both of you.'

Kate said, 'That's fine. We agreed we'd go ahead anyway.'

'Yep. Well, I've had some very interesting information from my contact. The file for the police investigation into the fire is missing. He said there's a ledger listing all the files in numerical order. All the other files are there, including those numbered immediately before and after this particular one. It looked like it was removed for a reason, so he asked around. No one knew anything about the file, but he did find a police-man who knew this sergeant Blunt. All the others who were there in 1914 have either retired, transferred elsewhere or died in the war. This particular chap was a rookie constable at the time and remembers the fire, although he wasn't involved in the investigation. He knew they thought it was the suffragettes but didn't seem to have any leads. Anyway, he said there was some sort of a scandal attached to Blunt. Apparently, he was shut up for hours in the Chief Inspector's office along with a bigwig from Scotland Yard. At the end of the day, they were all called together and told Blunt was retiring with immediate effect, due to ill health. This chap was surprised, because Blunt was never off sick. He remembers all this clearly, because it was the day war was declared.'

Kate appeared deep in thought. Ellen asked, 'Did he see Blunt again?'

'There was a retirement party, which he said was awk-ward. Blunt got drunk and was angrily mouthing off, something about being treated badly after all he'd done. The final thing this policeman said, is that he asked a week or so later about the investigation into the arson, and was told it was closed.' They were both silent, digesting this. 'Hello, are you there?'

Ellen cleared her throat and leaned over to say, 'Yes, we're here, Alec. It sounds as if he was forced to retire and it's directly related to the fire.' Kate was staring ahead with a frown. By this stage of the phone conversation, they were nestled close together on the sofa.

'It certainly looks that way, but we need to be careful not to jump to conclusions. He might have been forced to retire for some other reason. Incompetence, or he had his hand in the till, for example,' Alec replied. For a second Ellen got a sense of his work persona: incisive, intelligent, cautious.

Kate suddenly spoke up. 'Is Blunt still alive? Can we go and see him?'

'That was going to be my suggestion. We can speculate all we like, but this man seems to be our best way to find any answers. He'll probably refuse to talk to us, of course, but we can at least try.'

Ellen interjected, 'What's to stop him from calling the police, or arresting Kate himself if we confront him? Could this make things worse?' She was torn between her desire to find the answer and her terror that Kate could be plunged into an even worse situation.

But Kate replied immediately, speaking into the mouthpiece while looking at Ellen, 'I don't care. I want to do this. I need the truth.' They looked silently into each other's eyes. After a few seconds they realised Alec was speaking.

'I can use my mother's car to drive us down there sometime,' he was saying. 'I suggest we don't contact him to make an appointment. We should just turn up at his door. Don't give him time to prepare or speak to anyone else.'

'Sorry, Alec, did you say you know where Blunt lives?' Kate asked, still looking at Ellen.

173

'Yes, did you miss that? He lives in Croydon. I've got his full address. He'd be in his seventies now. I rang him at home today, pretending it was a wrong number, so I know he's there.'

'Let's do it tomorrow,' Kate said abruptly. 'I'd like to get this finished as soon as possible. Would that be a problem for you?'

'Hold on.' Alec had a muffled conversation with Freddie, coming back to confirm, 'Yes, I can do that. There's no reason to wait. In fact, it might be better to do this quickly in case someone tells him that questions were being asked. Mm ... why don't we meet at the shop tomorrow after work and drive down to Croydon? I could be there at seven with the car.'

'It's a deal,' Kate agreed. 'Alec, we couldn't have done this without you—', but he broke in.

'This has become very important to me as well. I love to feel I'm helping you and righting an injustice. What? Oh, Freddie sends his love,' his voice softening. 'And the same from me. Don't worry. See you both tomorrow,' and he rang off.

Kate reached over to put the telephone back on the side table. They remained sitting close together on the sofa. The call had sobered them; the earlier gaiety and promise had been checked. 'Well, perhaps this time tomorrow I'll know what happened in the fire,' Kate said. Her casual tone was belied by the tension on her face.

'You know you can stop this at any moment,' Ellen began, but Kate was shaking her head.

'You mustn't feel guilty or responsible. I think this is one of the best things I've done. I only wish I'd done it years ago.' Her voice faltered before she put her hand softly up to Ellen's face. 'Ellie, we started talking about the two of us. I want to continue that conversation, but – can we come back to it after tomorrow night? I need to get this thing resolved first. I can't explain it, but somehow, it's important. Something to do with having a clean slate, if that makes sense,' she concluded with a helpless shrug.

'Yes, of course, Kate. I understand.' Ellen sensed a vulnerability in Kate that had not been there before. She pressed Kate's hand and stood up. 'Right, shall I help you with the dishes?'

'I wouldn't dream of it, silly. Will you be all right walking home?' Kate stood up as well.

'Of course! Well, I think I'll head off now. Come to the shop tomorrow any time you like. I'm sure Freddie is dying to try his designs on you.' Ellen was determined to keep the mood light.

Kate walked with her to the door. 'Well,' she said and took Ellen in her arms. They stood there holding each other, imperceptibly relaxing into the embrace.

Ellen's cheek was next to Kate's. 'I like your perfume. What is it?' she asked inconsequentially.

Kate laughed. 'Some French thing.'

They looked into each other's eyes, their faces close together. Afterwards, Ellen could never remember who made the next move, but their lips brushed and then they were kissing. Kate's lips were soft and warm. She tasted of wine and strawberries. Ellen had been imagining this for days, wondering if it might feel strange, as if she were kissing a sister or an old family friend. But it simply felt wonderful and entirely natural, as if she had been born for this. They held each other tighter, kissing deeply, breast to breast, thigh to thigh. Any conscious thought ceased. After a few minutes, they pulled apart slightly, their breath coming quickly, laughing in mutual delight. But

Ellen knew the following day's confrontation hung over them like a spectre at a party. Better they should come to this with no shadow between them. She said softly, 'To be continued.' Kate nodded. They hugged some more and broke apart. 'See you tomorrow.' Ellen took her coat and hat and left quickly before she could change her mind.

The two men were only a few yards away when Ellen realised the danger. Usually, she had finely tuned antennae for men when she was out at night. Experience had taught her to trust her instincts, always to walk purposefully and watch out for potential signs of trouble: drunken groups, pubs at closing time, empty train carriages, footsteps behind her in a quiet street. But her heart and mind had been so full of Kate, she had dawdled back from Curzon Street without noticing her surroundings. And now, just as she turned into Jermyn Street and home, it seemed she would pay for her lack of attention. The taller man, dressed in a pinstriped suit, said loudly with a toff's accent, 'Here's a pretty redhead all on her own. Don't worry, darling, we'll keep you company.'

His companion, a smaller chip off the same block but wearing Oxford bags, brayed with laughter. They were young, perhaps only in their early twenties, but a sense of entitlement already oozed out of them. Ellen started walking quickly past with her head down, but he put his arm around her shoulder and breathed alcoholic fumes over her face, slurring, 'Let's have fun.' Ellen was above middle height, but he had a considerable advantage on her in height and weight.

'Leave me alone,' she said, trying to keep the anger from her voice. She had learned, the hard way, these situations quickly degenerated if she displayed her true reaction.

'Don't be like that! I need a kiss.' Suddenly he was pawing at her breasts while his friend shouted encouragement.

Ellen shoved him away, saying, 'No, piss off,' but he slammed her against the wall, anger on his face.

'Why, you little cunt, think you can push me?'

Instinct and training took over. As he came towards her again, Ellen brought her knee up hard in his groin. Luckily, she hit the right spot. He gave a yelp of pain and doubled over. Just as she was making her escape, his friend made a drunken rush at her. She grabbed his arm and, stooping down, used his momentum and her other arm to flip him over her back. She didn't wait to see the outcome, instead running back up to Piccadilly where there would be cars and people.

After a few minutes, her breathing returned to normal. That was close, she told herself. She walked along among the crowds, looking behind her, but couldn't see the men. When she came to the church she lingered, watching the people passing by, glancing down the lane to Jermyn Street, which appeared still and quiet. Taking her key out of her pocket, she walked down the lane and into her street, checking carefully, but there was no sign of them. She crossed quickly to her door and let herself in, her breath sagging out with relief. As she came in, she heard the telephone in the workroom cease its ringing.

The adrenaline rush had passed. Ellen went wearily up the stairs, aware her knee was sore. Not as sore as his balls, she hoped with grim humour. The flat was in darkness. She turned on the light in the sitting room and looked around, undecided whether to have a cup of tea or go straight to bed. The encounter in the street was not so unusual; what made her angry was the way it had interrupted her reveries about

Kate. The phone started ringing again and she ran down to the workroom.

Kate's voice came clearly down the line. 'Ellie, you're home. I rang a couple of times to check. I thought you would have been back earlier.'

At the sound of her voice, Ellen laughed aloud. 'How good to hear your voice! Actually, I did have a bit of a problem coming home. A couple of drunk men thought I wanted their company. That's why I wasn't back earlier. I had to hang around in Piccadilly for a while to make sure they'd gone.'

'What happened? Are you all right?' Kate asked, alarm sounding in her voice.

'I'm fine. Thank God I learned jujitsu! I kneed one in the balls, threw the other over my back, and got the hell out. Do you remember flipping the policeman in Glasgow?' She fiddled with the telephone cord, picturing Kate sitting on the sofa in her flat as they talked.

But there was anger in Kate's voice as she said, 'Yes, the things we learned as suffragettes will always be with us. What bastards! Do you want me to come over?'

'I'm fine. Don't worry,' Ellen said firmly. 'I'll see you tomorrow. And thank you for a lovely evening.'

'Ellie ...' They were both silent for a while, listening to each other's breathing. Then Kate said softly, 'Good night. Sweet dreams, my lovely.'

'You too, Kate.' She was still smiling to herself when she fell asleep.

22

Ellen was starting her breakfast when she heard Freddie come in from the street. She'd already been down at eight to bring in the milk and Gladys. The roar of the hoover was seeping up faintly through the floorboards from the workroom. Freddie stuck his head around the door with a lively look, said, 'Give me five minutes,' and ran up to the top floor.

When he came back in his work clothes, his unruly hair combed, Ellen wordlessly pushed tea and toast towards him, but he'd woken up on the walk back from Alec's and was in a chatty mood. In response to his enquiries, she described Kate's flat and her photographs, as well as her spot of trouble on the walk home. He showed interest and concern at all the right points, but refrained from asking about more personal aspects of the evening, although she could see the questions crowding onto his face, like impatient customers jumping the queue. He even, at one point, bit his lip in a comic show of restraint, gazing at her with limpid eyes. She suspected Alec was the cause of his unusual discretion. Whatever the reason, she was grateful. They'd always told each other everything, but she didn't yet feel she could discuss what was happening between her and Kate. The forthcoming encounter in Croydon was looming over her, putting a murky shade on all her thoughts.

As they put away the breakfast things, Freddie said, 'This time last week, you were getting ready to go to Hilda's funeral. Isn't that amazing? It seems such a long time ago. So much has happened.'

Ellen nodded pensively. It was true. The previous week, Freddie had been unhappy, yearning for Alec, lamenting his mistake – and Kate hadn't come back into her life. What a difference that encounter had made! Her world had turned on its axis. If Kate hadn't gone to the funeral … She sighed, thinking how fragile life was, with so much happiness and despair turning on chance. But then, she reflected, Hilda always did say you made your own luck.

Freddie had a dreamy expression. 'I think this has been my best week ever. Not just for what has happened, but because I know my life has changed permanently. Now I have the essentials – Alec, you and Kate, my health, work. I'll fight to keep this. I'll never take it for granted.' Then he laughed. 'Look at me, such profound thoughts at breakfast!'

Gladys appeared in the sitting room, a stout woman who took pride in her work and had a soft spot for Freddie. 'All right, me old china?' she greeted him now with a toothy grin.

The shop was much busier than the previous day, which helped. Hester was initially self-conscious, but Ellen's unchanged manner, and Freddie's obvious lack of awareness, helped her relax. The cheerful facade, the jolly shopfront, was back in business; the shutters had been brought down on the glimpse of her despair. Soon, she was chatting away about her evening with her cousin and their planned trip to the Lakes in August, when the shop would be closed for the summer holidays.

After the postman had delivered Mrs Drummond's cheque, along with a couple of others, Ellen suggested to Freddie, 'How about I slip out now, while it's still quiet? I can deposit these cheques and our takings in the bank, and do the food shopping.'

'Of course, Ellie. Hester and I are fine, aren't we?' Ellen saw Hester gulp with a quick look of misery and then nod brightly. As she went upstairs to fetch her coat and purse, Ellen knew it would be all right. He had not guessed Hester's feelings, and she would not tell him, but Freddie's kindness was the bedrock to his character. She'd once seen him apologise to a cat, hissing in alarm, which he had accidentally startled as he passed by. Hester had no thoughtless insensitivity to fear.

It was a beautiful day, the sort of balmy sun which bathed London in its reflected glory and made you glad you were alive. The buildings appeared less grubby in the golden light and people smiled at each other in the street. Ellen lingered, watching a shepherd driving his flock of sheep down Piccadilly in the direction of the parks, heading past a sign claiming that "Life seems brighter after Guinness". A lamb tried to make a break for freedom, running across the road before the shepherd used his crook to return it to the group. Cars and buses crawled along behind the flock in varying states of patience. It always amused her to find sheep in the heart of the city, one of the old traditions which still persisted. A few animals tossed their necks and jumped skittishly, as if to illustrate the glories of spring.

When she came out of the bank, she stood for a minute with the sun on her face, her eyes closed, her mind still. She imagined Kate curled up in her armchair like a cat, enjoying the sun. That led to the thought of the meeting with Blunt, never far from her mind, and her apprehension returned. She strode off to do the shopping.

When she got back to the flat an hour later, they had enough food for a week, along with clean clothes from the laundry. Kate's roses were starting to wilt and would need to go soon, but for now she cut the stems and refreshed the water. She paid Gladys, who was just finishing up, and nodded sympathetically at the usual complaints about her good-for-nothing husband. Entering the shop where Freddie and Hester were bent over the latest *Vogue*, she announced, 'Right, I've done all the boring household things. At least now we've got food to eat.'

'Thank you, Ellie! I ran up a top while you were out. Could you try it on for me? It's the new cowl neckline design. Hester thinks it should be popular. It's up in the workroom,' and Freddie led the way. Ellen took off her blouse and put on the cobalt blue top he was holding out.

'You used that material we bought last week from the new suppliers,' she observed.

'Yes,' he admitted with a sheepish look. 'I decided I should embrace man-made fabrics more often. Rayon material can be so cheap and nasty, but this looks almost as good as silk.'

'Anything but serge, hmm?' and they smiled at each other in understanding.

'The colour is gorgeous. It goes well with you.' He got her to turn around and walk up and down, finally declaring,

'Yes, I'm pleased with it. It suits you and the style is flattering. But it's practical too – women can wear it with skirts or trousers. I think the sleeves are a bit long. They're meant to be three-quarter length.' He put in some pins, frowning in concentration. 'I'll fix that later, unless you want to wear it now.' Ellen shook her head and put her blouse back on.

When they went back down to the shop, Freddie suggested, 'What do you say, Hester, to running up a few tops today? We could do some with short sleeves and some sleeveless, in a range of colours, and I'll make up a window display. You could use the new printed rayon crepe we got in. But I'll leave it to you to choose. You have a good eye for that sort of thing.' Hester departed for the workroom, pink and beaming. Ellen reflected that his honest praise of her dressmaking and fashion skills would make all the difference to her wounded pride.

She sent Freddie off for an early lunch and dealt with a few passing customers. Unlike many fashion shops, Ellen disliked doing a hard sell on customers, preferring to leave them to browse at their own pace and ask for help if they needed it. When the bell on the door tinkled again, she glanced up to greet the incoming customer and found herself being appraised by Myra, standing in the doorway. 'Oh! Hello,' she said, taken aback.

'Hmm. There's some expression about the mountain having to go to the prophet. No idea where it comes from, but I'm sure you know what I mean. I've been ringing you for the last two nights,' Myra said in a caustic drawl. Her peroxided hair waved in the latest style, she looked chic in a silk chiffon dress with black and white geometric patterns and matching bolero jacket. Even as Ellen scrabbled for something to say, part of her brain was thinking: that must have cost at least twenty guineas. Scarlet lipstick, and eyes elongated with kohl, completed the picture. Myra went on, 'There's a sweet slouch hat in the window. Is it one of your brother's designs?'

Ellen nodded and said only, 'I suppose you got my letter.'

'Oh, yes.' Her voice was coolly amused, but Ellen thought she spotted a flare of sadness in her eyes.

Before she could respond, Freddie returned. 'Hello, Myra,' he said, with a quick glance at Ellen. 'I hope you're well?'

'Can't complain. I must say, Freddie, you're looking jolly well. By the way, I adore that hat – it's in the Garbo style, isn't it? Would you make one up for me in black?'

'Of course! I'll give you a good rate,' he replied. 'Ellie, I'm here now. Why don't you go and have a cuppa with Myra?'

Ellen smiled at him gratefully and said to Myra, 'Come upstairs.' She led the way up to their flat, discomfited, trying to remember exactly what she'd said in her letter. When they got to the sitting room, Myra stared at the roses but made no comment.

'I've got Earl Grey. I know you like that. Take a seat.' She walked into their small kitchen. It was silent while the kettle boiled. When she emerged with tea and biscuits on a tray, Myra was standing at the window looking out, in much the same spot Ellen favoured.

They sat down and she poured the tea. Myra's previous brittle gaiety had been replaced by a more sombre mood. After sipping her tea and fiddling with a pleat on her dress, she said, 'You put nice things in your letter, but it's clear you've tired of me. I knew that would happen at some point, but I'd hoped it would last a bit longer. We were having fun, weren't we?'

'Yes, Myra, we had fun. But you always fitted me in around your husband. There was never any question of a serious relationship,' Ellen replied calmly, although she was taken aback. Myra had always adopted the air of a cynical socialite, who thought only about going to parties and revelling in the comfort and prestige provided by her husband. It hadn't occurred to Ellen she might have cared.

Myra examined her, pursing her lips. 'You've found someone, haven't you? I noticed you seemed different when we went to the theatre last Friday. Well, go on, tell me all about her. What's her name?'

'Well, I ...' Ellen felt exquisitely uncomfortable. If she hadn't felt ready to talk to Freddie about her feelings, she certainly didn't want to discuss them with the woman sitting opposite.

But Myra persisted. 'Is she married?'

'God, no,' was Ellen's spontaneous response. She gave a small, irritated shake of her head, realising she'd given herself away.

Myra regarded her for a moment. 'I won't press you, Ellen. The answer's clear on your face. You're in love, aren't you? She's not married, so I guess she's someone like you and you can see a future with her.' Ellen was silent, but Myra must have seen enough on her face. She started speaking simply, her usual drawling manner absent.

'I know I've teased you about this, but I do think you're terrifically brave, being openly ... queer. I can't do that. I couldn't face the hatred, the ridicule. Knowing people disapproved or found me disgusting, being blacklisted from certain circles. Being different, facing comments on the street, or worse. Feeling a failure because I wasn't married.' She gave a tight smile. 'I suppose I'm a coward. I need to have the security of a man's protection, even if I don't love him. Oh, Frank and I get on well enough, but it's all on his terms. I know I'll never feel the love and passion for him that I do for … for other women. I did become quite fond of you, you know,' she added, glancing at Ellen with a regretful expression.

'Oh, my dear! But you'll soon find someone else. You'd do better with someone more like you, a woman who moves in your world. You and I are too different. We can still see each other as friends,' Ellen offered, stricken with an unexpected sadness. But Myra shook her head.

'No, Ellen, I don't think so. I have tons of friends. I don't need more, and it would be hard to see you in that way. It was very nice making love with you … so, no. I'll miss you, but life goes on,' she added, with a sudden return of her drawl. She put the cup back in the saucer and stood up, looking down at Ellen.

'I wish you the best in life,' she said, before turning and going down the stairs. She didn't look back.

23

Ellen looked over at the clock again. Was it really only a few minutes since she last checked the time? Her father had once told her a dog year was equivalent to several human years; perhaps she'd entered some strange time warp where ten minutes took an hour to pass. Thinking of this, she recalled her childhood, when the summer holidays had seemed to last forever. If they weren't needed in the shop, she and Freddie would spend the day outdoors rambling around, swimming in the river or sea, exploring and talking. It felt as if a week had passed by the time they traipsed home, muddy and hungry. But this was different. She drummed her fingers with an edge of nervous anticipation, of fear and hope that, today, they would get the answer. Would Kate be delivered from her guilt, or would she be plunged into fresh remorse – or worse?

Hester had just finished the last top. 'Gosh, it's past five o'clock! Today has flown by!' she exclaimed. Standing up from the sewing machine, she came over to the desk. 'Ellen, I wanted to thank you for your kindness yesterday. I feel so foolish. I assure you it won't happen again,' she added with a touch of anxiety.

Ellen gave her a reassuring smile. 'My dear, you don't need to worry. I was just concerned to see you so unhappy. I hope you feel better today.'

'Yes … it was a silly fantasy, I do realise that. It helped that I had such a nice time with Betty last night. She's my cousin, you know. She was telling me about the people we'll be staying with in August. It sounds as if there are lots of jolly men there! She said they get up to all sorts of fun. Every night they play charades, or dress up. Last year they went for a midnight swim!' Ellen knew her prattle was forced, but was disinclined to probe – she had enough of her own worries. Hester's mention of fun brought a reminder of the earlier conversation with Myra, which had been replaying in her mind. She suggested, 'Shall we take these tops down to Freddie?'

They were discussing the window display when Kate entered the shop, stopping as they looked over at her. Freddie stepped forward to give her a kiss on the cheek. 'Welcome to Fernsby Fashions, Kate.'

Hester, next to her, stiffened. Ellen realised she had jumped to the wrong conclusion. But she couldn't worry about that right now. Seeing Kate, she had a sudden awareness of how changed she was from the tense, wary person she'd met at Hilda's funeral; but mostly she was overwhelmed by a conviction she could no longer deny. She wanted to spend the rest of her life with this woman. For a few heartbeats she luxuriated in the certainty, before her nerves about the forthcoming interview broke through. Freddie introduced Hester, who was unusually quiet, and showed Kate around the shop. Ellen just stood smiling at Kate, who looked back with understanding in her eyes. I know, they seemed to be saying.

They often had a rush of business in the last hour. Unlike their daytime customers, these tended to be working women who looked for value and, usually, ready-made clothes. Freddie was less required for fittings or design advice, so he took Kate upstairs. When Ellen came into the sitting room after closing the shop, Kate said to her, 'I didn't like to leave you working hard in the shop, but Freddie thought it was best not to get in your way.'

She laughed. 'Oh, heavens, I don't mind at all. It was probably best not to be distracted.'

Freddie patted the sofa. 'Come and take the weight off your feet, Ellie. I've made up cold meat sandwiches. You need to eat something before you set off.' Ellen sat down thankfully next to Kate. Freddie pushed a plate towards her, along with a coffee he'd just poured. 'I'm having an argument with Kate, because she'd like one of our new cowl neckline tops but insists on paying me, and I refuse to take money from a friend.' From his grin at Kate, it was obviously a friendly dispute.

Ellen suggested through a mouthful, 'Why don't you do a barter of some sort? You make the top for Kate and she can do something for you.' They looked at her, their faces intrigued.

'Such as?' Freddie asked.

'Well, Kate's an excellent photographer and I've been thinking we should advertise our business a bit more. She could take a picture of one of our outfits, and we use it to run an advertisement in fashion magazines.'

'What a brilliant idea,' Kate declared. 'You clever thing! Publicity for you, and it won't hurt me either to get one of my photographs published. But on one condition – you have to be the model, Ellie.' They started discussing the details. Freddie was suggesting he make up Kate's top in burnt-orange silk, when the doorbell rang. 'Oh, he's early,' he exclaimed, and jumped up.

Left alone, Ellen and Kate smiled at each other. 'How are you, Ellie?' Kate asked, taking her hand.

'I'm very well … but I'm rather anxious about this confrontation.'

'Me too,' Kate confessed. 'But I'm ready for it. Whatever happens, remember that. This is the right thing to do.'

Ellen was about to respond when Freddie reappeared with Alec. She hadn't seen them together since Wednesday night, but everything she needed to know was instantly apparent, along with a tranquil solidity, which was new. Freddie supplied Alec with food and drink before their "expedition" and they chatted about their day. But, after a while, the conversation dried up as the air of tense expectancy grew.

Alec glanced around at the others. 'We may as well go now.' There was an unspoken enquiry in his look at Kate, who nodded in response.

'I'm coming with you,' Freddie announced. 'Don't worry, I'll wait in the car. I realise the four of us turning up at this man's door will be too much. But I want to come.' He tried to sound nonchalant, but Ellen realised he was equally worried and wanted to be there in case something went wrong.

Alec smiled at him. 'Well, in that case you can be our navigator. I know the way to Croydon, but I'll need help with getting to his particular street.'

In spite of her nervousness, Ellen couldn't help a wry amusement, knowing how often Freddie got his left mixed up with his right. She suggested, 'We've got a Bartholomew's Atlas here. Why don't we have a quick look before we set off?' They stood around looking at it on the table while Alec showed the section of the journey where he needed help. Then they put on their coats and hats and went silently down to the street.

'I've parked around in St James's Square,' Alec said. It was a still, warm evening. As they walked past the pub, busy with Friday night drinkers spilling onto the street, Ellen glanced at the table where they'd sat the other evening. She saw Kate was doing the same. When they got to the square, Alec stopped in front of a white saloon with black trimmings and roof.

'Mm, nice automobile,' Kate said.

Alec grinned. 'It's an Austin 7 Swallow. My mother bombs all around the country in it, driving much too fast and causing general mayhem.'

'She has good taste. Do you remember those uncomfortable beasts we used to drive in the war?' The two of them discussed cars for a minute, standing in the street. Freddie raised an eyebrow at Ellen, the talk of pistons and side-valve engines going over their heads. The conversation came to a halt.

'Right, let's go. Time to beard the lion in his den,' Kate said with a look of decision.

It was still quite a novelty for Ellen to travel by car. Her parents had never owned one, of course, and she walked or used public transport to get around London. All life seemed to be out on the streets at that hour. Women were selling bunches of spring flowers. Boot-black lads polished the shoes of men in top hats. As they came up to Trafalgar Square, a boy dressed in smart hotel livery dashed in front of the car. Alec braked sharply. For a second, he looked at them, his freckled face alive with a cheeky grin, his pillbox hat at a jaunty angle, before melting into the crowds. He looked no more than twelve, Ellen thought, he should still be at school.

They inched their way down Whitehall in heavy traffic. Freddie and Alec chatted quietly while Kate, beside her in the back seat, was silent. Ellen looked out at the stone buildings on Whitehall, implacable keepers of government business. Men were selling the evening paper, shouting out, 'Final!' She remembered how she and Kate would stand there selling *Votes for Women* to harried civil servants and functionaries. They passed Downing Street, where she'd once gone with a delegation to present a petition, snatched from their hands by a surly policeman. Turning left past Parliament Square brought more memories of the marches and brawls outside Parliament, the rough hands of the police and jeers of the crowd. Were her suffragette memories destined to lie heavily on her every thought? She shifted impatiently, and Kate, still not speaking, took her hand. Her spirits lifted as they crossed Westminster Bridge, with the sky expanding over them and the river looking almost blue in the evening sunshine.

Alec glanced over his shoulder. 'By the way, my mother sends you both her greetings. She said she'd love to have you to tea.'

Kate looked surprised. 'Surely she doesn't remember me? I was just an insignificant cog in the wheel.'

'Well, she does! She said everyone used to call you two "the inseparables". She remembers you speaking at a meeting and dealing very smartly with a heckler.' Ellen and Kate gave each other a reminiscent smile.

Ellen said, 'It's generous of your mother to lend you her car.'

'Yes, she's a nice mother.' Alec was about to say more when a car sped past them on the left-hand side and his attention was forced back to the road. 'You'd never think there's supposed to be a speed limit of twenty miles an hour,' he grumbled. 'Everyone ignores it.'

The traffic eased as they drove further south. Ellen gazed back out the window at a tradesman working on the pavement mending chairs. On the next corner, an olive-skinned man with a splendid moustache was selling ice cream from a box set on a tricycle. A queue of children waited, a sign that summer was nearly here. Why did all the ice cream sellers seem to be Italian? All these people, going about their lives, their livelihoods, all caught up in their own concerns and worries, their hopes and fears. How many were loved, secure, looking to their future with optimism? Or did they lead lives of quiet desperation, just scraping by, teetering on a cliff-edge?

'I'm coming up to a junction, Freddie, can you tell me what I should do?'

'Um … you turn left.'

'Left? Are you sure?' Alec asked.

Ellen hastily said, 'No, he means right.'

'Ah.' Alec made the turn and said, 'Yes, this looks correct. We're not far now.' He stopped to let a trolleybus lumber past. They heard a roaring noise and turned in time to see a plane taking off in the near distance.

'Oh, that's the airport,' Freddie commented. 'I didn't realise we'd pass so close to it. I know someone who took his family there for the day to watch the aeroplanes. Can you imagine? I'd prefer a trip to a gallery or museum, myself.'

'I think this is where Amy Johnson started her flight, isn't it?' Ellen asked, watching the plane grow smaller in the sky and wondering if she would ever be lucky enough to travel on a plane.

'That's right. I've gone to Paris from here a few times,' Kate said. They were chatting calmly, as if they were on a pleasant outing, Ellen thought.

After they'd moved off again, Alec said, 'This is the bit I don't know. What do I do next?'

Freddie frowned over the Bartholomew's. 'Are we coming up to the roundabout?'

'No, we passed it some time back,' Alec replied, a touch of impatience in his voice.

'Shall I have a look?' Ellen offered, and Freddie passed the atlas back to her with a grateful look. 'You take the third street on the right, and then it's second left.'

'I'm afraid I'm not a very good navigator,' Freddie confessed. 'I've come under false pretences.'

Alec said quietly, 'Nothing false about you, darling. I love to have you here.' Freddie put a hand on his knee.

They were in quiet residential streets now. There was silence in the car for the last few minutes of the drive. Alec slowed down, peering to his left at a terraced row, and said, 'That's the house,' but kept on driving. 'I'm going to park around the corner.' This was done casually, but Ellen guessed he was anticipating trouble.

He turned down the next road, a cul-de-sac with a small park on one side, and stopped the engine, pulling up the handbrake and turning around in his seat to Ellen and Kate. Now, he was the solicitor about to visit a difficult client, his tone businesslike. 'Shall we do the same as before? Ellen, you pretend to be my assistant, and Kate, you're a solicitor.' They nodded. 'Look, we don't know how he's going to react, so I'm going to play a lot of this by ear. Don't be – try not to look surprised, whatever I say. Are you all right with this, Kate?'

She was pale, but responded immediately. 'Yes. Let's just do it.'

'I'll wait here,' Freddie said. He got out and waited as they emerged from the back, gripping both their shoulders for an instant. 'Good luck.' He was unable to keep the anxiety from his voice.

24

They walked around the corner and down the street, which was narrow and bare: no trees or people, apparently devoid of life. Everyone must be safely inside – children put to bed, husbands fed and relaxing in their armchairs, wives in the kitchen cleaning up. The unvarying, stifling routine. A row of terraced houses opposed each other in a belligerent face-off. Each house looked identical: two-storey brick dwellings built not long after the war, bay windows screened by lace curtains and a small garden at the front. Most of the gardens were bare earth, or held straggly flowers. Here and there a child's tricycle or ball lay abandoned. A couple of houses had freshly painted doors or little signs: "Dunroaming" or "Beware of the Dog"; one had put up a hanging plant. But it felt dreary in the sunshine – what must it be like on a grey day? Ellen supposed the housewives living here must feel they were in a sort of prison. She shuddered, thinking of the endlessly interesting life on the streets around her home.

They stopped outside Blunt's house. No effort had been made here to brighten up the exterior. It was blank, impassive, an absence of character.

'Here we go,' said Alec.

They walked up the small path and he rang the bell. Somewhere at the back of the house a dog started barking, before this was muffled by the sound of a door being shut. Ellen's heart was pounding. She felt a hand briefly clasp hers, and looked up to see Alec give her an encouraging smile. Kate stared at the door.

The lace curtain in the front room twitched. A moment later the door opened, revealing a thin woman in her sixties or early seventies, grey hair permed into tight frizzy curls. Ellen supposed the woman's eyes must once have been blue. Now, they seemed colourless – washed out and defeated. They peered out dully from behind round spectacles, an expression of hesitant surprise settling onto her face. She was much the same height as Ellen and Kate but appeared shorter due to a permanent stoop, which made her look almost as if she were cowering. 'Can I help you?' Her voice was rusty, as if she hadn't spoken for some time. Already Ellen had picked up a certain submissiveness in the tone. This was a woman who lived in the background, who was used to being ignored or overlooked.

Alec's tone was courteous. 'Good evening. Are you Mrs Blunt? I hope we're not disturbing you. Is Mr Blunt available?'

'Is he expecting you?' the woman asked doubtfully. She eyed them as if they were exotic animals in a zoo, then peered past them into the street, as if to check whether there were more strange beasts wanting to gain entry. It was clear this was not a usual occurrence. This house did not get visitors after supper.

'No, he's not, but we won't take up much of his time. I'm a solicitor. My name is Alexander Medley.'

The woman's reaction was unexpected. An expression of sly interest crossed her face, gone almost before it registered, and she drew herself up as if suddenly energised. 'Come in,' she said, standing aside for them to enter the dim hallway. 'He's down here.' She led the way down the hall.

They could see into the first room as they passed, a parlour with the lace curtains from behind which Mrs Blunt had observed them, a profusion of lace antimacassars on the sofa, magazines and knitting lying on a chair. When she opened the door to the second room, a small, rather portly dog scampered up to them, yapping enthusiastically. 'Shut it!' a man's voice ordered and the dog obediently stopped, sniffing their shoes. Ellen had a confused impression of heavy, dark furniture and carpet, busy wallpaper and a strong odour of pipe smoke. This was clearly the male preserve and she guessed Mrs Blunt spent her time in the parlour. But there was no time for speculation, because a man was hauling himself to his feet from an armchair and demanding, 'Who the hell are these people?'

'They've come to see you, Percy. I'll make some tea,' Mrs Blunt said in a timid voice.

'Don't make them any bloody tea, woman!' Blunt roared but it was too late – she'd disappeared to the back of the house.

He glared at them. Ellen's first thought was that, somehow, he looked familiar. Watery, pale-blue eyes were set over a bulbous nose and a ruddy face, which suggested not health, but rather high blood pressure. His dark, bushy eyebrows contrasted bizarrely with sparse white hair combed over from the left ear, a pink scalp showing through. He leaned on his stick, gripping it with gnarled hands. 'Well, what do you want? Speak up!'

Alec held out his card. 'Good evening, Mr Blunt. My name is Alexander Medley. I'm a solicitor. This is my colleague Miss Shergold and my assistant Miss Fernsby. I'd like to take up just a few minutes of your time to ask some questions.'

Blunt frowned at the card and then back up at Alec through narrowed eyes. 'What sort of questions? If it's anything to do with my neighbour and her bloody cat, you can leave now. I told that stupid woman what I'd do if the cat came into my garden—'

'No, no, Mr Blunt, it's nothing to do with your neighbour. My questions relate to a case you worked on some years back, when you were in the police.'

'Oh!' Blunt looked surprised. 'Well, I was in the police a long time. I worked on a lot of investigations. Jack the Ripper was my first big case. I could tell you lots – we didn't let the public know the half of it. Is it to do with them murders?'

'No, but it sounds as if you've had a fascinating career.' Alec's polished manner seemed to do the trick. Blunt visibly puffed up with importance.

'You'd better take a seat then,' he said grudgingly. Up to this point he had ignored the two women, but as Alec and Kate sat on the two facing chairs, Ellen perching on a low stool nearby, he shot her a sharp look, which lingered. The dog settled on the floor near Blunt with a resigned grunt. He absent-mindedly scratched its ears.

'How did you get my address, Mr … ah, Medley?' Blunt's manner was less hostile but he still regarded them suspiciously. He held Alec's card out in front of him, frowning at it as if the paper might erupt into flames at any moment.

'From a contact in Bow police station. I understand you retired in 1914?'

'Not so quick, I'm asking the questions here, young man. Who are you working for? I presume you're acting for someone? Or are you with a newspaper and just pretending to be a solicitor?' Blunt had an odd way of talking: a mixture of flat estuary vowels and a strangled posh veneer. Within the same sentence he veered from the home counties to geezer and back again.

'I can assure you, Mr Blunt, I am indeed a solicitor. My client has asked for confidentiality, but he's related to someone whose death you investigated.' Alec's manner was composed. He might have been talking about a routine legal matter.

Blunt appeared mollified. 'All right. I did have quite a few murder cases. You asked if I retired in 1914, Mr Medley. That's right. Just before the war, as it happened. I still had a few years left officially, but my dodgy knee was giving me problems. I decided to go, even though my boss begged me to stay. And then I lost my only son fighting in the war, so my plan to live with him went out the window. I moved down here for a quiet life. Did you fight, or were you too young? You weren't one of them bloody conchies, I hope?' He fixed Alec with his rheumy eyes, prepared at any moment to be scandalised.

'I fought in the last year of the war. I'm sorry to hear about your son. Was he in France?' Ellen made herself sit still but hummed with impatience. Why this meaningless chatter – why didn't Alec just get to the point?

'Oh, he was all over,' Blunt replied with a vague wave of his hand. He turned to Ellen, who was sitting on his right. 'Don't I know you from somewhere?'

Startled, she adopted a demure facade. 'No, I don't think so, Mr Blunt.'

'I've seen you before. Do you live around here?'

She shook her head. 'No, this is the first time I've been to Croydon.'

He continued looking at her. 'Is that a Norfolk accent I hear?'

Ellen nodded, dropping her eyes to her notebook. She knew he would interpret this as a sign of modesty or weakness, but hadn't wanted him to see the sudden recognition in her eyes. She pretended to write in her notebook, a wave of panic washing over her.

She realised where she'd seen him before: at Bow in October 1913, when the police attempted to arrest Sylvia Pankhurst during a meeting. A few women had managed to hustle Sylvia away – Hilda said afterwards she'd put on someone else's coat and hat as a disguise and made her escape. This had been Ellen's first brush with the Bow police and their brutality had shocked her. They'd waded into the crowd with truncheons, beating women unconscious, breaking arms and heads. Separated from Kate in the fracas, Ellen had found herself in front of a policeman, his club raised. They stared at each other, inches apart, before she ducked to escape his blow. He had grabbed her, painfully squeezing her breasts, his breath hot on her cheek, before she wriggled free and bolted into the crowd.

And now she was sitting opposite that policeman, hoping he would give them the information to free Kate from her bonds of remorse.

Alec was speaking. 'I'm sure you must have met so many people in the course of your work, Mr Blunt. Criminals, victims and their families, members of the public. You must have many stories to tell.'

His distraction appeared to work. Blunt launched into a boastful discourse about his brilliant career. Alec nodded and made encouraging noises, after a while shooting a glance at Ellen, his eyes questioning. She'd had time to quickly review her options. If she made an excuse and left, it would only increase his suspicions. This was Kate's opportunity to find out the truth. She must stay and brazen it out. Surely, he wouldn't recognise her after all this time. Kate was also looking over at her. Ellen gave them both a reassuring smile.

Alec waited for a gap in Blunt's monologue. 'You've been generous with your time, Mr Blunt, and I won't impose on you much longer. I'd like to come to the reason I'm here. I understand you were in charge of investigating an arson attack on a church in Shoreditch, in July 1914. The newspapers reported a man's body was found in the ruins. Can you tell me about that case?'

The impact of his words on Blunt was dramatic. His mouth fell open and he gaped at Alec for a full minute, his face flushing an even deeper red. He opened and closed his mouth a few times, convulsively squeezing his stick. Alec waited, and then prompted him. 'Do you remember the fire?'

Blunt finally found his voice. 'Them suffragettes were a disgrace to their sex! Burning down buildings, setting bombs, acting like common criminals. No bloody shame! They were happy to attack property, but they couldn't take it if they got the same treatment. I had a good time teaching them a lesson. We had some proper brawls with them in the East End. No more than they deserved. Prison was too good for them!'

He continued for several minutes, spittle dotting his lips, escalating to claims that the suffragettes were responsible for the collapse of morality in society. But his outrage held a false note. The earlier cocky bravado had vanished. He sounded uneasy, his eyes skidding around the room before resting on Ellen. His rant came to an abrupt halt.

'I know where I seen you!' he exclaimed. 'I never forget a face. I nearly arrested you but you got away. You were one of them bloody suffragettes. Admit it!'

Alec interrupted, raising his voice. 'This is completely irrelevant, Mr Blunt. I'd like you to answer my question.'

But Blunt, triumphant now in his discovery, shouted him down. 'I know what this is about! You're here because of her!' He stabbed his finger at Ellen. 'She set the fire, didn't she? She's the arsonist! That's why you came. You wanted to find out what I knew about it. Well, you weren't clever enough!'

And then he was on his feet in front of Ellen, pulling her up by her arm, grabbing and twisting her wrist painfully. 'Now you'll pay for your crime! I've got you, you suffragette bitch!'

25

The next few seconds were a chaotic blur. Kate flew out of her chair at Blunt, shouting, 'Leave her alone!' The dog started a frenzied barking, jumping up and down on the spot as if on springs. Alec, on his feet next to Blunt, ordered in a commanding tone, 'Take your hands off her at once!' Ellen hadn't seen him like that before. He'd never spoken of the war, but Freddie had told her he'd been made a captain, in spite of his youth. She could see now why he'd been given that responsibility. The authority in his voice was impressive, and had an immediate response. Blunt dropped Ellen's wrist and the dog stopped barking. They both gaped at Alec.

'I think it's time for a nice cup of tea.'

They all turned and stared at Mrs Blunt, as if in a dream. Ellen had read recently about a French film that made no sense: ants coming out of a man's hand, dead donkeys in pianos. She felt as if they'd all stepped into a surreal production like that. Any moment now, the director would appear and call, 'Cut!' Mrs Blunt was smiling in her effacing way and placing a tray on a low table. Her apparent lack of awareness of the scene would seem bizarre if Ellen hadn't seen the expression on her face, quickly wiped off. She had looked pleased, almost gleeful.

'You mustn't get yourself excited, Percy. You know you have a bad heart,' she said in a mild voice. What is that about? Ellen speculated, as she rubbed her left wrist. Kate stood close to her, glaring at Blunt.

After a stunned pause, Alec turned back to Blunt. 'How dare you lay your hands on her! I could have you arrested right now for assault.' Ellen wasn't sure how much of his anger was genuine, and how much a ploy, but it proved effective.

Blunt insisted in a whining tone, 'Don't tell me she wasn't a suffragette.'

Ellen was fed up with people talking about her as if she weren't there. 'Yes, I was a suffragette,' she declared to Blunt. 'I've never tried to hide it. I'm proud of it. But I had nothing to do with burning down the church and I can prove it.'

'How?'

He was still standing too close. His breath was foul but she refused to turn her head away. She noticed Kate opening her mouth to speak and said hastily, 'Because I was in prison at the time,' giving a slight shake of her head to Kate.

'Well, you'll have to explain that to the police when I call them,' he blustered, but Ellen saw the first signs of uneasiness in his eyes.

'If you call the police, I'll tell them about your attack on Miss Fernsby,' Alec said immediately. The three of them stood close together, facing Blunt in an apparent stalemate.

'Now, why don't you all sit down and take a few moments to drink your tea? You'll feel much better after that.' Mrs Blunt might have been speaking to recalcitrant children. Somehow, they accepted the cups from her and sat back down, this time with Kate a protective presence next to Ellen. The tea was milkier and sweeter than Ellen usually liked, but it was exactly what she needed. She greedily drank it down.

'Are you all right?' Kate asked her, Alec looking on, and she nodded. The confrontation had been unpleasant, her wrist ached – but she had a sudden intuition it might work out in their favour.

Alec turned back to Blunt, his face stern, and said, 'I'd like you to apologise to Miss Fernsby before we go any further.'

To her surprise, Blunt squirmed in his chair like a sulky schoolboy, and muttered, 'Sorry.'

Mrs Blunt reminded him, 'Drink your tea before it gets cold, Percy.' Docile now, he followed her instruction. She smiled around at them, the polite hostess. 'Who would like a biscuit with their tea? I've got shortbread or ginger.'

There was silence as they drank the tea. Whatever next? Ellen wondered in astonishment. Would the dog stand on its hind legs and start reciting poetry? She felt a slight hysteria bubbling inside. But then she looked up to see Mrs Blunt watching her husband with sharp eyes, and sobered. Blunt must have felt her gaze, because he looked over at his wife and half shouted, 'What are you still doing here, woman? You should go – get out!' She shook her head and settled herself in a chair near the door, ignoring his angry stare.

Alec placed his cup and saucer on the small table next to him and said in a calmer tone, 'You haven't answered my question, Mr Blunt. You obviously remember the fire. I understand it was your last case before you retired. I'd like to hear your description of finding the body in the church and what happened subsequently.'

'What exactly do you want to know?'

'Can you describe the state the body was in? Was there an inquest?'

'I don't see why I need to tell you any of that. I think you should leave right now!' He spoke loudly, bridling, but Ellen saw a streak of fear on his face. Now the tables were turned.

'Well, it appears there was no further investigation once you retired. Why would that be?'

'You seem to know all about it. Why don't you tell me?' Blunt appeared diminished, as if his outburst had drained his energy. He rubbed his face and stared around the room, oddly deflated.

Alec observed him thoughtfully and then nodded. 'All right, I'll tell you what I know. The newspapers reported a man had died in the fire and his name was given as Cecil Fawdon. But I've seen the autopsy report for Fawdon and he died of natural causes. Of a heart attack, as it happened. No inquest was held and there was no further investigation after you left the police. I have information indicating it's very unlikely Fawdon would have been in the church. I'd like to hear your explanation, Mr Blunt, because something is clearly wrong here.'

All eyes were on Blunt. Even the dog watched him expectantly. Blunt screwed up his face, looking like a bewildered bulldog, then said, 'Leave my house now. I've got nothing to say to you. Get out!' No one moved. He shouted again, 'Get out of my house! I won't tell you nothing more.' His voice sounded thick. Watching him, Ellen wondered if he were unwell. The light was leaching out of the room. She reached behind her to switch on a lamp and caught a glimpse of the back garden, a barren square of sickly grass. Blunt closed his eyes as if to wish them gone.

'Why don't you tell them what really happened, Percy?' Mrs Blunt's voice was quiet but there was an edge to it.

'Shut up! Shut up, you stupid cow! Say nothing!' he roared, shaking his stick at his wife, but now he was like a toothless lion.

Alec raised his eyebrows. 'What should he tell us, Mrs Blunt?'

All their attention was on her. She looked back at them with a small smile on her lips, straightening up and throwing her head back, a coquettish caricature basking in the rare glory of being the centre of attention.

'Why, he told me all about it at the time. He thought he was so clever! It was all a lie. No one died in that fire,' she said with satisfaction.

26

The words oscillated in the air, as if a bomb had exploded in the teapot. Kate's body sagged, all the breath knocked out of her. Ellen had speculated about this, hoped for this, but now that she had heard the words she was stunned into silence. Instinctively, she put a hand out to Kate. They looked at each other, their eyes wide with shock, any other reaction delayed. Alec flashed a look of triumph over at them.

Mrs Blunt ignored a strangled roar from her husband and continued in a conversational tone. She might have been describing a recipe or a knitting pattern.

'He was the first one on the scene. While he was waiting for the fire brigade, he found the body of some old drunk in the next street. He dragged it into the church and rubbed soot all over his clothes, didn't you, Percy? What a fool!' She spat these last words in a fury. Blunt watched her with glazed eyes, mumbling to himself. 'As soon as the doctor did the autopsy they knew it was a lie, but it was too late. He'd told reporters the suffragettes had murdered a man and it was all over the newspapers. His boss told him he had to retire immediately or else he faced the sack. He was lucky it wasn't worse. The war started then – everyone forgot about it. But we lost three years of his pension over his actions. Stupid, stupid man!' She looked at Blunt with loathing on her face.

Silence followed as the three of them absorbed her words. Ellen struggled to take it all in. Kate's eyes were fixed on Blunt, two red spots in her cheeks.

Alec cleared his throat and asked, 'But why ... why would he do that?'

Mrs Blunt dragged her eyes away from her husband to look at Alec. 'He saw it as his chance to lead an important investigation and get the promotion he thought he deserved. And because he hated the suffragettes.'

'They had to pay for their actions!' Blunt spoke in a dragging voice. He seemed to have difficulty keeping his eyes open. 'Bloody hooligans ... didn't care if they killed people ... a danger to society. I had to show what they're really like ...'

Kate said to him in a low voice, 'The suffragettes didn't harm people. We never killed anyone. We made sure our actions only damaged property. We were the ones being attacked, dying. All we wanted was a basic human right. For God's sake, did you not think how people would suffer through your lie?'

Blunt tried to focus on her, incomprehension on his face. 'Who suffered? He was a useless drunk ... left his family. No victims here. Don't regret it. Proud ...' Kate stared at him then shook her head in disgust. He worked his mouth as if to say more, then fell back in the chair with his eyes closed. Unexpectedly, he started snoring.

Mrs Blunt said, 'You won't get any more out of him now. He'll sleep for hours, until lunchtime tomorrow if I'm lucky. You'd better go.'

She stood up and went over to her husband. For a wild moment, Ellen thought she might be showing concern, but all she did was take Alec's card, which was still gripped in Blunt's hand. She held it out to Alec. 'Here, you should take this. His memory will be foggy tomorrow, but it's best he doesn't have your details.'

They stood up, watching her, stupid with incomprehension. Alec asked, 'Is he ill, Mrs Blunt?' She shook her head and put her hand to her lips, ushering them out of the room. The dog pricked up its ears and trotted after them.

As they followed her down the hall, she said over her shoulder, 'I put sleeping pills in his tea, that's all.' She opened the front door and stood looking at them with a satisfied expression. 'Well, that was a bit of fun, wasn't it?' she commented.

They continued to stare at her, gathered in a group in the hallway. Ellen found her voice and asked, 'Fun?'

Just then, the dog slithered past them and started to run out the door. 'Don't let it get out the front gate!' Mrs Blunt exclaimed, and Ellen quickly moved to hold the dog on the front path, squatting down to pat him. He looked at her, his body quivering, and tentatively wagged his tail. The brown patch over his right eye should have given him a raffish air, but instead he looked woebegone. Poor little thing, she thought, trapped like a slave in this house with these nightmare people. If only she could rescue him.

She looked back at Mrs Blunt. 'What's his name?' she asked.

'Jack, because it's a Jack Russell.' She made a short ha! noise which Ellen presumed was a laugh. 'He's got no imagination. Getting the idea to put that man's body in the church was the only original thing he's done in his entire life. I hate the blasted dog. It smells and leaves hairs over everything. It barks all the time. And Percy loves the thing. He lavishes all his care on it. More than I've ever got. Always feeding it titbits – no wonder the thing's so fat. But he takes it out every day for a long walk and it's the only way I get a break from him. So, the dog serves its purpose.' She looked coldly down at Jack, who flinched and pressed against Ellen's legs. Alec and Kate moved out onto the front step and turned to face Mrs Blunt.

'Why, Mrs Blunt?' Alec's voice was quiet.

'Why what, young man?'

'Why did you give your husband sleeping pills?'

She shrugged. 'I do it all the time. It's the only way I can keep him manageable and have a break for a few hours. Now I can sit and listen in peace to my favourite programme on the wireless. It starts in a few minutes,' she added, glancing at her watch. 'He's got medication for his heart, too. The doctor says he has to take the pills every day, but I usually don't give them to him, or I'll give him several in one go. He doesn't notice, he never does. For a policeman he's not very observant, but then …'

She sighed, a look of abject unhappiness flitting across her face. Blink, and you could miss it. Watching her in fascinated horror, Ellen guessed she must have had a lifetime of hiding her true feelings.

'He almost died a few months ago. He was coming back with the dog from one of their walks when he collapsed right here, where you are now,' nodding to Ellen. 'I was watching from the parlour. I saw it all. He went down, whoomph, and lay on his back staring at the sky. He was making these choking noises and his body was jerking. And I thought – that's right, go on, die, you bastard! I was waiting for him to go. I started thinking of the life I could have ... but then our neighbour heard the stupid dog barking, ran out and thumped his chest. He came back to life. I thought I would die myself that day from disappointment.' She twisted her mouth and looked at them with defeated eyes, then asked abruptly, 'Did he tell you our son was a war hero? Just another of his lies. He'd only been conscripted the week before. He got drunk in the training camp, fell into a river and drowned. Useless, just like his father!'

Kate stated, 'You hate him, don't you.' Their feeling of triumph was on hold. Mrs Blunt returned their gaze, grimly amused.

'Hate him? Sometimes, when he goes out of the room, I punch his chair. I spit in his food ... Hate him? That's not the half of it. You're not married, are you?' They all shook their heads. 'No, it shows. You look too carefree. I'll tell you what marriage is. It's a prison. Only I don't get time off for good behaviour. That's a joke told by men, isn't it? But the real joke is that marriage suits them fine. They get exactly what they want from us. Put the supper on the table, look after the children, clean the house and open our legs on demand. Oh, he was all charming and lovey-dovey when he was courting me. He used to take me dancing. I loved dancing,' her tone wistful. 'I was only eighteen. I thought he was this big, strong man who'd look after me. But once we were married ... he hit me for the first time on our honeymoon.'

She spread her arms in a gesture of appeal. By now, her words were flooding out, unstoppable. 'What could I do? It was almost impossible to get a divorce. I'd have had to prove adultery. Divorce is for the rich, for men. I could have walked away, but I'd never have lived down the shame and my parents wouldn't have taken me back. Then I found I was expecting. Like my mother told me, you make your bed, you lie in it. I put everything into my children, and I got by. Now, I'm just waiting for him to die. It shouldn't be much longer. My daughter's living in Essex and she's got a decent husband. I'll go and live with her. I can spoil my grandchildren and do what I want. Maybe I'll be happy, who knows?' She stretched her mouth in a smile and turned to close the door, saying, 'Goodbye. My programme is about to start. Come on, you.'

Jack flattened his ears at her sharp tone and walked back into the house.

Ellen said urgently, 'Wait, Mrs Blunt!' The woman stopped, halfway inside the hallway, and looked at her with dull eyes. The fire had gone out of her. 'Why have you told us all this?'

She shrugged. 'I hardly talk to anyone. You're as good as any. You don't know me, I don't know you. We'll never see each other again. It's easier with strangers. You keep my secret, and I'll keep yours. You burned down the church, didn't you?' She pointed at Kate. 'Good for you! Don't worry, I won't say anything.' She hesitated. 'Do you know what I really miss? No one calls me by my name. It's a nice name. But ever since I got married, I'm Mrs Blunt, Mum, woman, wife, hey you, stupid cow, bitch … It's like I got lost.'

Kate asked gently, 'What is your name?' but Mrs Blunt had already closed the door on them.

They stood on the front path, looking at each other with shocked faces. Alec gave a shaky laugh. 'Oh, my God!' They passed through the front gate. Ellen glanced back once and saw the lace curtain give a slight twitch.

27

Freddie was leaning against the car, one foot on the running board, gazing at the park opposite which was lit by a mellow light in the last hour before dusk. He turned his head as they came around the corner, trepidation scrawled on his face. 'About time! I was going to give it five more minutes before I came in to rescue you,' he announced with relief. He scanned their faces for an indication of how things had gone. His next words were flatter, quieter. 'Not good?' He brushed his hand against Alec's and glanced at him.

Kate was frowning and didn't appear to have heard him. Alec waited to see if she would reply, then smiled at Freddie. 'No, it's very good. No one died in the fire. It was set up by Blunt. He admitted it all.'

'But that's wonderful!' Freddie exclaimed.

Ellen's thoughts darted here and there like a damselfly, random and disorganised. She found herself wondering if Mrs Blunt had ever experienced real happiness or, more importantly, contentment. Perhaps for brief moments when her children were young? Or did she subsist on a dim recall of childhood pleasures, pitiful scraps to keep her going?

Already a hint of doubt was creeping onto Freddie's face as he continued to observe them. 'Isn't it?'

Ellen put her arm around Kate's waist and hugged her close. How absurd! Their shocked manner was more appropriate for a wake than for a triumphant outcome to the investigation. 'Yes, it's exactly as we hoped. Now we have the truth and Kate can be free of her guilt.'

'You don't look exactly overjoyed,' Freddie noted.

Kate was rubbing her neck, still frowning. She said, 'Look – can we go, and explain in the car?'

'Yes, let's get the hell out of here. I don't mind if we never see this place again,' Alec agreed, getting into the driver's seat and loosening his tie. He waited until they were settled inside before turning the car around to head for the river.

There was less traffic now and the return journey seemed shorter. Alec and Ellen filled Freddie in on what had happened, recounting the details with gusto. They had recovered from the oppressiveness of the encounter and were euphoric. Freddie listened in his usual careful way, exclaiming in all the right places.

'So, you were right all along, Ellie. Aren't you the genius! You always felt there was something fishy about the whole business,' he declared after he'd heard the full story.

Ellen smiled, but her satisfaction was increasingly tempered with disquiet about Kate's subdued manner. Her colour was sallow and she kept on closing her eyes.

'Kate, are you unwell?'

'I'm getting a migraine. It's come on suddenly. Don't worry about me. I'll just need to lie down when I get home.' Kate kept her eyes closed. Her voice was faint.

'Poor you. Does the light bother you? Here,' and she took off her scarf and placed it gently over Kate's eyes. Kate nodded her thanks and gripped her hand. Ellen continued looking at her, concerned and puzzled. She never had headaches herself, and didn't remember Kate suffering from migraines before the war. Freddie twisted around in his seat to give Kate a sympathetic look.

'I'll get you home as soon as I can,' Alec said, glancing over his shoulder. 'We're not too far from the river.'

'Ignore me, keep on talking,' Kate muttered.

Freddie broke the silence after a few minutes to say, 'No wonder you looked so shocked when you came back to the car. My God, what a man, what a marriage! It makes you shudder, really, to think of his wife being so unhappy. I don't know why she doesn't just walk out now and go to her daughter's. It's not as if she'll be destitute. Surely, anything's better than living with someone you hate.'

Ellen said, thinking about Kate's mother, 'There are lots of reasons why women don't leave an abusive husband. It's not just a lack of options, or the fear it will make things even worse. Of course, once they have children, that's it. By the time the children have left home, they can be trapped emotionally. It just wears them down over the years. I suppose they can't see a way out.' She looked again at Kate, who had her head back against the seat, the scarf obscuring her face.

Alec said, 'Do you know what's just occurred to me? If Blunt had died from that collapse a few months back, we'd never have uncovered the truth. I suppose we have the neighbour to thank for that.'

'Yes, well, you were lucky to still get him alive,' Freddie commented ghoulishly. 'From the sound of it, he won't be around much longer. Mrs Blunt will probably graduate to putting glass in his supper. Or rat poison.' Alec made a startled huh! sound. 'And you were lucky in other ways. What if she'd decided to put sleeping pills in your tea as well?'

'Bloody hell, that's a thought,' Alec replied, but he seemed more amused than shocked. 'We would have all been lying there, snoring our heads off. Trapped in Croydon!'

'No, because I'd have burst into the house to rescue you like that cartoon chappie, Popeye. I think I'd manage to defeat Mrs Blunt in a duel, although I'm not sure about the dog.' Freddie had a vivid imagination and he often let it run away into streams of fantasy. Alec laughed, looking over at him. Ellen smiled, preoccupied. Her eyes never left Kate, who hadn't moved.

Freddie turned around again. 'How's your wrist, Ellie?'

'Oh, it's—'

'Stop the car. I'm going to be sick,' Kate said urgently.

Alec sharply pulled over to the side of the road, earning a blast of the horn and angry shout from the driver behind them. They had just passed a row of shops and were alongside a small patch of scrubby grass. Freddie jumped out and pulled forward the seat for Kate, who ran a few yards to the grass, Ellen close behind her, and bent over. She started vomiting with deep groans, her body heaving and shuddering.

Ellen rubbed her back, making comforting sounds. She could see people goggling at them from the passing cars. A woman walked past with a child, averting her eyes with a disapproving expression. The boy, dressed like a little lord in velvet breeches, stared owlishly. 'Don't look,' she heard the woman command the child as she pulled him away with a tight grip on his hand. No doubt she thought they were drunken floozies, up to no good.

Kate was retching now. The spasms were dying down. Eventually she stood upright and swayed, but Ellen had her arms around her to steady her. 'Come and sit here for a moment while you recover,' she suggested, guiding her to a low wall.

Kate sat with a sigh, her face drained of colour, and shakily blew her nose. Freddie started to come over, but Ellen shook her head at him. The setting sun at their backs stretched their bodies out in crazy elongated shadows, like humanoid visitors from Mars, she thought. Her nurse training had kicked in and she relegated her distress at Kate's suffering to the back of her mind, although her body shivered in vicarious sympathy.

Kate's gasping slowed. She murmured, 'Sorry.'

'Don't be silly, my dear. You have nothing to be sorry about. Would you like a drink of water?' Ellen asked, her voice practical.

Kate made a small movement of her head to the side. 'Better not. In a while.'

'Do you think you ate something, or is this part of the migraine?'

'Migraine. Always get it.' Kate had her eyes closed again.

Ellen suggested, 'Let's just wait till you catch your breath. There's no hurry. Do you think you'll need to be sick again?' Kate gave a minute headshake. Ellen sat with her hand on Kate's shoulder as her rasping breaths returned to normal.

'Ready now to go back to the car?' she asked. Kate gave a minimal nod and stood up. Ellen supported her as they slowly walked over to Freddie, who stood waiting by the open door, dismay on his face.

The remaining drive was mercifully quick. Within minutes they were crossing the river, the sky to the west stained crimson and orange by the setting sun. Ellen glanced at it with momentary pleasure, but all her attention was on Kate who lay on the back seat, her head on Ellen's lap, eyes shielded by the scarf. Occasionally she hissed out a long breath or winced at a bump in the road. Not long afterwards, Alec drew up in front of Kate's block of flats, Ellen having quietly directed him. Her brother got out to hold the door while Alec turned around to them.

'Here we are, Kate. Is there anything we can do? Shall we come up with you?'

Kate slowly sat up and made an attempt at a smile, her eyes half closed. 'No. Soon as this is gone, want to thank you.'

'You just concentrate on getting better, my dear. We can celebrate then. Let me know if there's anything I can do. Promise?'

She nodded and eased out of the car, Ellen gripping her elbow. The door to the building was closed and Kate produced a key from her pocket, handing it to her wordlessly. Ellen glanced back to wave at Freddie and Alec before turning to unlock the street door.

28

The building was hushed, with no sign of life apart from distant sounds of a piano being played in one of the flats. They silently went up in the lift. Ellen opened the door to Kate's flat.

'Right, straight to bed for you,' she said. They walked down the hall to the bedroom where Kate subsided onto the bed with a groan, holding the right side of her face. Ellen peered around the room in the low light and found red silk pyjamas hanging on a hook behind the door. 'Let's get you into these,' she instructed.

Kate stood up and waited passively as Ellen started removing her clothing. The irony of the situation was not lost on either of them – Kate even opened her eyes briefly to look at her with a sad, wry smile. This was not how they had imagined the first disrobing, the first closeness in the dimness of the bedroom. Ellen forced herself back into a nursing mentality, clinically noting the lithe, small-breasted body, gently rounded belly, slim-hipped, strong legs. So similar to hers. She placed

Kate's clothes on the bed, helped her into her pyjamas and eased her under the covers.

'Painkillers in bathroom cabinet. French,' Kate muttered.

Ellen half-closed the bedroom door behind her before crossing the hall to the bathroom and turning on the light, screwing up her eyes at the sudden glare. The room was functional with few adornments: cream tiles, a bath, toilet and washbasin, a rail with a brightly striped towel and flannel, a small, mirrored cabinet. Behind the door, a dressing gown which she touched tenderly. There was a faint smell of chemicals and she remembered Kate used the room to develop her photographs. The cabinet was equally austere: toothbrush and toothpaste, face cream, a small bottle of pills. The French writing meant nothing to her, but she recognised the generic name and frowned. At least the bottle was almost full.

She took it with her to the kitchen, switching on the lamp in the sitting room as she passed through. After opening a couple of cupboard doors at random and noting the minimum in kitchen necessities – four plates, large and small, four cups and saucers, basic utensils – she found the glasses (four) and put one under the tap. Further searching revealed a bowl under the sink and she took that out. From curiosity, she opened the door of the refrigerator and was relieved to see a good amount of food, as well as a bottle of champagne sitting incongruously next to the milk.

When she returned to the bedroom, Kate was lying on her back in the same position.

'Here, take these,' she said, lifting her to a half-sitting position and holding out two pills in her hand.

Kate gulped them down with the water and lay back in the bed. Ellen went to the bathroom to get the towel and wrung out the flannel under the cold tap, returning to place it on Kate's forehead. She hovered, looking down at her.

Kate murmured, her eyes still closed, 'I'll be all right now. You go.'

'Nonsense. I'm staying,' she said. 'I've put a bowl and towel by your side in case you're sick again. Call me if you need anything.'

Kate did not reply. She appeared to be overwhelmed by the pain. Ellen hung Kate's clothes on a hanger she found in the wardrobe, then tiptoed out, leaving the door slightly ajar.

Back in the sitting room, Ellen looked out the window to the sky, now dressed in midnight-blue satin. Lights were coming on in the streets and she could see the beams of car headlights going around Hyde Park Corner. She stared out blankly, tapping her fingers on the glass, her thoughts tumbling over each other. What a day! It seemed she had experienced every type of emotion, from fear to triumph, from rage to compassion. This was not how she had envisaged the outcome.

She finally turned away from the view and looked around the room, dreams and hopes waltzing through her mind, before walking over to the bookshelves. After a few minutes she found the book she wanted, settled in the armchair next to the lamp and started to read.

Ellen was on the sixth chapter when she heard her name being called. Outside, the sky had turned to black. She went swiftly to the bedroom to find Kate smiling faintly in the low light from the sitting room. 'I haven't managed to drive you away yet,' she said, her voice stronger.

'Of course not!' Ellen replied. She sat down on the bed next to Kate and took her hand. 'You look a bit better.'

'Just a dull throbbing now. Before, it felt like someone was striking a hammer against my face and stabbing me in the eye with a needle at the same time. I need to be careful not to move too much or it sets off again.' There was a certain detached acceptance in her tone. She kept her eyes closed and lay immobile in the bed.

'Poor Kate!' Ellen hesitated, then asked, 'When did you start having migraines? I don't remember you having them before.'

'It happened out of the blue when I was twenty, out in France during the war. The first time, I thought I'd somehow been shot in the head and I was dying. I'd never known pain like it. Luckily, one of the other drivers also got migraines and she explained what was happening. They were bad for quite a while, but the last few years it's been much better. In fact, I haven't had one since, oh, last autumn.'

'Do they always follow the same pattern?'

'Usually. I know for some hours if one is coming. It's nearly always on the left side of my head. They last up to a day, sometimes longer. The only thing I can do is lie in the dark, sleep as much as possible and wait till I can take the next lot of painkillers. But this one feels different. I had practically no warning and it's on the right side.' She gave a small shrug, then winced. 'I had hoped they were going, but …' Her voice dwindled.

'Well, you need to be careful, because those pills are strong and quite addictive. You must wait until one thirty before taking any more. What else can I do for you?'

'You've done more than enough, Ellie. I'd like you to go home now and stop worrying about me. You're too good to me. Really, I'm not worth all your kindness.'

Ellen studied her silently, wanting to question her further but knowing this was the wrong time. After a minute, Kate partially opened her eyes and murmured, 'Still here?'

'Kate …' she hesitated.

'Yes?' Her voice was faint but clear.

'Why did you say that before, about not managing to drive me away?'

'Oh, Ellie … You've seen me in the worst of all possible ways – controlled by my guilt, pathetic, weak, vomiting, now as a sick invalid. Not exactly alluring … I can't seem to put up any front for you. You must think I'm an absolute disaster. None of this has turned out the way I expected.'

Tears seeped from under her closed eyelids. Ellen dabbed Kate's face with her handkerchief, sensing she should not interrupt. Kate sighed, then continued. 'You've been superb. So strong. You took on this investigation and found me the absolution I needed. I should be ecstatic. But all I can think is – what a stupid fool I've been! Spending all this time consumed with guilt over something that never happened. All the years I wasted – when I could have been with you. All those years away from you. For nothing. What a fucking idiot …'

Her voice faded. Ellen could listen in silence no longer.

'You have it all wrong. You talk as if you've wasted the last sixteen years of your life. That's just not true. You've done so much! Driving ambulances in the war, moving to a new country, having adventures and love affairs, learning new languages, new skills. All those experiences, yes, even the bad ones, are part of you now. They've all given you something valuable. Because – well, I believe we have a choice in life. We can hang onto our past pain and regrets, or we can face the future and make it what we want.'

She made herself stop. There was so much more she wanted to say, but this was not the time. She added gently, 'And there's absolutely nothing pathetic about you. I could not admire and respect you more. Believe me, Kate.'

Kate lay unmoving for some minutes. Ellen wondered if she had fallen asleep. But then she said, 'You should go. I need to sleep. It's the only way I can cope with this.'

'Don't make me go. I want to be here. I want to look after you.'

'Oh Ellie. I – please, it's important to me that you go.' Suddenly, she opened her eyes fully and looked at her. 'I always want you in my life, Ellen Fernsby. Go now. I'm good for nothing when I get these headaches. I need to be alone. As soon as it leaves me, I'll come for you. That's a promise.'

She closed her eyes again. Within seconds, her breathing became regular and Ellen could see she was sleeping. She went to the kitchen to fill the glass with fresh water, took it back to Kate's bedside and hung there, irresolute. It went against her every instinct to leave her alone. Finally, she bent and placed a kiss on her forehead, as soft as a breath of air. Kate didn't stir. She walked to the flat door, went into the corridor and gently closed it behind her. There was no sound on the other side of the door. She dropped her head and started down the stairs.

It was a shock to come out onto the brightly lit streets, full of people dressed in their best clothes on their way home after an evening out, or going on to a club. They laughed and chattered, flocking like birds together in their raucous groups, intent on having fun. Ellen felt as if she were a ghost walking among them.

When she turned off Piccadilly she stopped, looking down her street. She couldn't go home. She felt too restless, on edge. She needed to walk. Ellen loved London, but she had grown up in a quiet and green corner of England where the sky seemed to stretch forever. Sometimes she needed a break from the buildings, the cars, the concrete. She would often lose herself in the parks. Starting in St James's Park, she would head north-west through Green Park to the far corner of Hyde Park, miles of walking among trees and quiet space in the lungs of London. As she strode along – always with something to see, admiring the trees or the play of light at different times or seasons – she would remember pacing her cell at Holloway and her longing to be in the open air.

This was what she needed to do now. She turned south, walking past St James's Palace, a lone sentry out the front, and crossed the Mall. The great gates were closed, but it was easy enough to climb over the fence into the park.

A thin cloud had covered the sky in the last hour. No stars were visible, but the waning moon, now a thin sliver hanging low in the sky, shone through the clouds with a bright halo. As she walked towards the lake, the traffic noise faded. The silence was broken only by the chirruping of the coots, still busily feeding, and occasional honks of the geese. Ellen stood by the edge of the lake to watch them, smiling at the funny quacks of the ducks, breathing in the mild air. Her mind slowed to a full stop, a welcome stillness after so much breathless, contradictory emotion.

Just then, she heard a muffled cough and stiffened in alarm, aware she was not alone. Her eyes had adjusted to the tenebrous light and she could see two men sitting close together, rigidly still, on a nearby bench. Their fear of discovery vibrated in the air along with her relief. Ellen wanted to put her hands on their shoulders and kindly say: don't worry, I'm a fellow traveller. Everyone deserved love, even if just for a few hours, to help keep the loneliness and cruelty of the world at bay. How could it ever be wrong to freely love another adult? But she knew they wanted only to be left undisturbed in their hidden world. She walked quietly on, wishing them well, hoping the police weren't trawling the park that night.

As Ellen crossed the bridge, she paused to watch a swan silently glide beneath her. Perhaps it was the partner of the swan who died in her lap. With that thought, memories of the evening returned. Chastened, she continued over the bridge, turning left on the path hugging the southern side of the lake. She usually turned away from the Bird Keeper's cottage to wind around on the path tracking Birdcage Walk; but, this time, she continued straight ahead. She felt strongly pulled by the river, needing to absorb the life and power it contained.

Climbing the steps guarded by Clive of India, she glanced about her at the great buildings of state. A few windows on the upper floors had lights burning. Who was inside those rooms? she wondered. Overworked clerks, scratching over their papers and wishing to be home with slippers and a glass of cocoa? Or ambitious mandarins, drafting policy and plotting their next promotion?

After crossing Whitehall and skirting the buildings of Parliament, she arrived at the Thames. Westminster Bridge was busy with cars and trolleybuses, but where she had stopped she could watch the river in peaceful solitude. It was high tide and the currents moved swiftly, the dark water swirling and tumbling when it hit the bridge foundations. A long barge, loaded with crates, drifted silently by, heading east. There was a cool breeze here, and she shivered slightly, but the feeling of space and living water brought balm to her spirit.

'Good evening, miss,' she heard.

She looked up to see a policeman watching her from a few feet away. He had a friendly, lived-in face. 'Evening, constable,' she responded.

'Bit of a lonely place to be at this time of the evening. Some people say the river makes them feel sad,' he observed.

Ellen realised he was probing delicately to see if she planned to throw herself in the river. What a thought! But she appreciated his solicitude. In fact, she felt strangely moved.

'I grew up by the sea, and I always love to be by the water,' she told him. 'It gives me peace and strength, never sadness. But thank you for checking on me.'

He nodded. 'Have a nice evening, miss.'

'You too.' He walked on by, swinging his baton.

Big Ben started to mark the half hour with resonant chimes. Glancing up at the lighted face, she thought: a few hours previously they had crossed this bridge to find the truth. Now, they had their answers. It was up to the two of them what happened next. She took one last, long look at the river before turning her back on it and heading for home.

29

It was close to midnight when Ellen crept up the dark stairs. She switched on a lamp in the sitting room. There was no sign of the others. Hanging her jacket and hat on the coat stand, she went to the kitchen. They had a bottle of Irish whiskey for special occasions, and this was as good as any. She poured a measure and took it back to the sitting room, curling up on the sofa and sniffing it before taking a sip. Beth had taught her to appreciate a good whiskey, one of the happier benefits lasting from their relationship. Thinking about her now, she realised any regret she'd felt about Beth's departure from her life was long gone. They weren't well enough suited, and, truth be told, Ellen had become bored and restless in the last years. Now, of course, she knew it was a blessing she was not tied to anyone.

Hearing a floorboard creak, she looked up to see Alec in the doorway. His brown hair was tousled and he had on his vest and Freddie's pyjama trousers. Shorn of his working clothes, he was no longer the efficient solicitor or former army captain. He looked boyish, with a touch of vulnerability. 'Hello,' she said, smiling at him. 'Come and join me in a drink.'

He sat next to her on the sofa. 'How is Kate? We didn't expect you back tonight. I mean …'

'No, that's all right. She took some pills, which helped a bit, and went to sleep. That's what she does when she gets these headaches. She didn't want me to stay. She insisted I leave—' She broke off and, to her embarrassment, started weeping. Where had that come from? She never cried. Alec put an arm around her shoulders and hugged her as she sobbed down his vest. He made soothing noises, not seeming at all alarmed or annoyed. After a few minutes, she regained her composure.

'Right, I'm going to join you in a drink,' he decided. He crossed to the kitchen, returning with the bottle and a glass, settling next to her. 'Here, have a top-up. It's the least you deserve, my dear.'

'Sorry,' she said, as she dried her face with her handkerchief. 'How stupid. I don't know what came over me.'

'Don't apologise. You should never feel bad about crying. It's a good way to express your feelings or relieve tension,' Alec replied. Of course, he had two younger sisters, he was probably used to this. But his next words surprised her. 'I find a good weep can be very therapeutic. I must have cried every night for weeks over Freddie.' He smiled at her. 'You're a strong woman, Ellen, but you need to accept that sometimes you feel scared or sad. That's only human. It doesn't make you weak.'

'Hmm …' If one more person told her this, she thought she would scream. What a strange week – people crying all over the place, telling truths, talking about their darkest secrets. Not at all British. But then, what a magnificent week as well.

He added, 'I'm just saying this because I think we're similar in that way. I used to believe I had to show a strong facade to everyone, even if I was terrified or heartbroken. I've had a damned good lesson this week about myself, which I'll never forget. That's all,' and he held his glass up to hers. 'Here's to having a good weep.'

Ellen couldn't help laughing. They clinked glasses. 'To crying!' She took a sip in comfortable silence. 'I'm sorry I woke you up,' she said after a while.

'Oh, you didn't. Freddie's fast asleep, but I was still awake and heard you come in.' He hesitated. 'I just lie and feast my eyes on him as he sleeps. I can't believe my luck. I suppose in a few years I'll get used to it and we'll fall asleep like an old married couple. But, right now …' A look of amazement stole over his face before he laughed at himself. 'Enough of my besotted ravings. What made you cry?' His sympathetic look melted her last reserve.

'It's mostly because I hated having to leave her when she's so unwell, even though she insisted. But I suppose I'm also scared …'

She paused and he waited before prompting, 'Why?'

'Well, when I met her again – God, that's only a week ago – I realised how badly her guilt over the death had affected her. It's made me think a lot about how we've all been controlled by things – apart from you, I mean.' Alec made a sudden move, as if to speak, but remained silent. 'You see, Freddie felt guilty about loving anyone after Sam, and he was terrified of suffering like that again. So he pushed you away – but you know all this.'

Alec nodded. 'Go on.' He was a good listener, just like Freddie, she thought. His face was contemplative as he gently swilled the whiskey in the glass, the lamplight softening the jagged scars on his hand.

'Kate made me realise I was doing the same. I was in a long relationship with someone who left me. I've had a few affairs since then, but always with women who didn't want a commitment. I told myself it was my choice, but, really, I was scared of being hurt again. Anyway ... tonight, Kate told me she feels like an idiot because she spent all those years feeling guilty about something that didn't happen, when she—' Ellen stopped and took a sip of her drink, self-conscious.

'When she could have been with you?' he finished for her. 'Don't look surprised. Freddie and I could see what's been happening between you two.' He took her hand. 'Are you worried she's going to start feeling remorse about this, instead? She's just going to replace one guilt with another?'

She nodded gratefully. 'Yes, that's it.'

Alec pondered for a moment. 'I don't think you need worry about that. Kate's had a shock, even if it's a nice shock, and she's having trouble adjusting to it because of her rotten migraine. Once she's well again, she'll realise what's important now. How long do her headaches last?'

'One or two days, I think.' She sighed.

'You just need to be patient and wait for her. I know it's difficult for you to sit back and wait, my dear. But sometimes, doing nothing can be the best action. In love, as in war.' His smile was sad. 'But you were wrong when you said I wasn't controlled by things. In fact, I'm the worst.'

She looked at him, surprised. 'You?'

'God, yes. For you three, it was your unhappy past experiences that bound you. With me, it's been my own flawed character. When I walked in on Freddie that day ...' He bit his lip and went on, 'Well, afterwards I wouldn't answer his calls. I tore up his letters. I felt so humiliated. How dare he do that to me? I loved him so much – he was all I wanted. I thought he felt the same. But instead of talking to him, I chose to wallow in self-pity. I played at being the injured victim. And then he stopped trying to contact me. I nearly let the most precious thing in life slip through my fingers, thanks to my bloody pride. What an idiot!' he exclaimed in disgust, striking his knee with his fist. 'That day you turned up in my office – I had such a shock, thinking something had happened to him. I knew then I must go to him. You gave me the opportunity to make a decision – cling onto my stupid arrogance, or try to sort things out with Freddie. You'll never know how grateful I am, Ellie.' His words were heartfelt, his eyes shining.

'You would have done something, sooner or later,' she said wisely. 'Maybe I just accelerated it a bit.'

'Well, I had taken to hanging around Jermyn Street,' Alec confessed. 'My pride had stopped me from picking up the telephone, but I had hopes of a chance meeting. Oh, fancy seeing you here, would you like to go for a drink, that sort of thing. Perhaps we would have worked it out anyway. But, still! Thank God for you.' He held up his glass to her in homage, then added, 'Freddie is saying you and I are brilliant detectives, did you know?' A look passed between them, instant understanding.

'Well, in the end it wasn't too difficult, was it?' Ellen offered, keeping her tone neutral. 'Once we started getting some details, the story started collapsing. I think that's partly why Kate feels so bad now.'

'You'd obviously had your suspicions all along.'

'Well, yes, but I hoped more than anything. And I never thought it would be down to one stupid policeman. When did you first think there might be no body?'

'When I got the autopsy report and we'd spoken to William Fawdon. But I wasn't sure we'd be able to prove it. If Blunt – or, more properly, his wife – had refused to tell us the truth, we'd have had our suspicions, but no more. That's where we had luck, and I'm so glad for Kate's sake. That was the whole point – finding the truth for her. As well, of course, to have a reason to keep on seeing Freddie. I suspect something similar was in your mind.' He gave her a mischievous look.

'Hmm! Anyway, it was no murder mystery after all. That funny Belgian detective needn't fear any competition from us.'

He laughed. 'No, in fact it's turned out to be a love story. Less Agatha Christie, more—'

'Is this a private party, or can I join?' Freddie said from the doorway. Ellen and Alec looked over and started giggling. His pyjama top was buttoned up askew, with one side hanging down longer, and he'd fastened a towel around his waist in a sort of skirt. He looked down at himself and laughed as well. 'I think you'll need to keep some of your clothes here, darling,' he told Alec.

'Hang on! It's past midnight, isn't it?' Ellen asked. 'It's officially your birthday. Wait here.' She jumped off the sofa and ran up to her bedroom to retrieve two packages from her chest of drawers. The thought of Kate came to her in a visceral rush and she had to put a hand out to the wall to steady herself, shuddering at the thought of her lying alone in a darkened flat, in pain. When she got back, Freddie and Alec were talking, their heads close together. 'Happy birthday, Freddie,' she said, holding out the presents.

'Ooh, chocolates, lovely! We can have a midnight feast. Thank you, Ellie. And what's this?' he asked, looking at the second item tied up in paper.

'Open it and see.' She made herself smile.

He tore open the paper and shook out the garments with a shout of laughter. 'You've made me pyjamas! How clever is that?' He softly rubbed the silk material against his face before looking them over with an expert eye.

'I made them a few weeks ago because I noticed the sleeves of your old ones were getting rather frayed. But now it will be handy to have a second pair,' and she nodded at Alec.

'I'm going to put them on right now.' Freddie started removing his towel.

'But, Freddie – here?' Alec asked, glancing at Ellen with a faint blush.

'Oh, heavens, we aren't shy about that sort of thing, are we, Ellie?' Freddie said as he pulled the pyjama bottoms up over his legs. He took off his top and passed it to Alec while he buttoned up the new one. 'It fits perfectly. What do you think?' he asked, standing in front of them with a grin, hands on his hips. Ellen's professional mind was thinking how well the turquoise blue colour suited him, emphasising his eyes and warming his pale skin. But she also saw him in her mind's eye as a child, skinny and freckled with his shock of red hair: listening absorbed, lower lip caught between his teeth, as she read him a story, wandering along the beach looking for special stones and sea-shells, lying under a tree and staring dreamily up at the light shining through the leaves. He used to annoy her sometimes as a small boy, when he followed her around like a puppy; he was disorganised and untidy and often in his own world; but she wouldn't have had any other brother, then or now.

As for Alec – he was watching Freddie with a delighted smile. 'You look good enough to eat,' he murmured, then stood up, putting on the discarded pyjama top and going to the kitchen for another glass. 'Right, shove up, midnight feast it is,' he said on his return, squeezing in next to Freddie and Ellen on the sofa.

'What were you two talking about when I came in? Something seemed to have amused you.' Freddie accepted the glass from Alec and removed the lid from the chocolate box.

'Oh, we were getting philosophical about how we can be controlled by things,' Alec replied.

'Mm, yes. Well, don't forget, we all have ties that bind us. They can be for good or bad. What counts is what we do with them,' Freddie said as he sampled the whiskey. And with this pithy analysis, not unusual for him, the subject was dropped. But he continued to sit, the chocolates on his lap, with an abstracted expression.

Alec said, 'You're quiet, Freddie. What's on your mind?'

'Sorry?' He came with a start out of his world. 'Oh, I was just thinking … We could start doing a line in women's pyjamas. We already do beach pyjamas, why not go to nightwear as well? What do you think, Ellie? Would they sell?'

Alec made an amused sound in his throat. 'What?' Freddie asked.

'Nothing, Freddie.' Alec kissed his cheek. They gazed at each other as if they'd seen the gates of paradise. Ellen looked down, feeling she was intruding on their privacy. Kate, oh Kate, she thought, disconsolate.

But Freddie, always so sensitive to others, must have read her mind. He turned to her and put a comforting arm around her shoulders. 'Now, Ellie, what do you want to do about Kate?

I can manage the shop in the morning if you want to go back to her place. She's the most important thing right now. Don't worry about anything else.'

'I don't know what to do. It's been going around in my head. Kate said the best thing for her is to remain still and sleep. If I go ringing her doorbell and getting her out of bed, I might make things worse for her. And she said it can go on for hours, if not days. I don't want to phone her for the same reason.' She shook her head in confusion.

Freddie suggested, 'Well, if it can take some hours – why don't you wait until we close the shop and then go over to see how she is? That way, she'll have had all night and morning to rest.'

She nodded. 'All right, I'll do that.'

Then he turned practical. 'Now, who else wants the violet cream?'

'You have it, Freddie. I don't like soft centres. I prefer chocolates with nuts,' said Alec.

'Really?' Freddie turned to stare at him, wide-eyed, as if he'd had an epiphany. 'And I don't like chocolates with nuts …'

Ellen giggled. 'Clearly, you two were made for each other!'

By the time they made their way up to bed an hour later, she could think more calmly about it all. After all, Kate had been getting migraines for years and knew how best to deal with them. Someone hovering over her was probably the last thing she needed. God knows, Ellen hated anyone fussing on the rare occasions she was ill.

It helped that she was mellow from the whiskey. The three of them, with the same unspoken agreement, had moved onto lighter things, gossiping and swapping work stories. Ellen told some of the amusing nursing stories she'd shared with Kate. Freddie told them about the strange revelations he'd been privy to when doing fittings, while Alec revealed a hidden gift for mimicry and story-telling which had them laughing helplessly. As she brushed her teeth, she smiled to herself, remembering his description of the admiral setting out the terms of his will in tedious detail, unaware his flies were undone.

But when she turned out the light in bed, Ellen's mind and heart were again full of Kate, replete with desolate hope; with hopeful desolation.

30

Once again, the alarm woke Ellen from restless sleep, filled by dreams tinged with anxiety and foreboding. She came awake to a sickening thud of worry, thinking: Kate. But the morning rituals of bathing and dressing helped to soothe her, and she sat down to breakfast bleary-eyed, but with relative equanimity. There was no sign of the others, although Freddie's plate and cup were in the sink. As she was finishing her tea, he came up from the workroom, dressed for work and appearing remarkably fresh. 'Happy birthday, again!' she greeted him. He bent and wrapped his arms around her, giving her a kiss on the cheek. 'You're looking chipper, Freddie.'

'It's funny, you know,' he said breezily. 'When I was a boy, thirty seemed ancient to me. Do you remember when our new teacher started at school and I went home and told Dad he was an old man? And now, I feel as if I'm just starting my life. I know who I am and what I want. Life is good.'

'What's that I see?' she asked, noticing a flash of colour in his cuffs.

'Alec's present. Aren't they exquisite? They're opals.' Freddie held up his arms so she could see the cufflinks more clearly. The blue of the stone matched his eyes, and the silver finish suggested they must have cost a fair bit. 'I'll keep them all my life … Oh, I finished the cowl top for you. Do you think you can wear it in the shop today, so our customers can see how divine you look in it?'

She laughed. 'Of course.' He was holding it up so she took her blouse off and slipped it over her head.

'It goes beautifully with your white trousers. A very summery look,' he observed, satisfied.

'Well, it's the first of June tomorrow. So, what are your plans for today?'

He shrugged. 'I really don't mind, just so long as I can be with Alec and you, and hopefully Kate. Let's just see how it goes.'

The morning started quietly enough. Hester arrived with a wide smile and birthday wishes for Freddie. He recruited her to help out with the new window display, and the shared project proved useful in several ways. Watching them discuss the arrangement, as she sifted through the letters delivered by the postman, Ellen noticed a subtle change in Hester's manner. She still looked at Freddie admiringly, she was still inordinately pleased when he complimented her work; but there was a new realism in her eyes, a resigned acceptance in her manner. Thank heavens, it looked as if they would continue to work together in harmony.

Ellen turned her attention back to the envelopes in her hand, most of which were addressed to Mr Frederick Fernsby, and handed them over to him, taking the business letters upstairs. Another welcome cheque and publicity from a cloth merchant in Yorkshire. When the telephone rang, she picked up the receiver to hear her mother's voice, calling from the neighbour's phone, and shouted down to Freddie. They chatted with their parents, receiving birthday felicitations and exchanging news. Soon after, a steady flow of customers started arriving. Ellen made herself ignore the clock. Work didn't feel important after the triumphs and concerns of the previous day, but it was better to keep occupied. It stopped her from fretting about Kate.

After she'd walked out their last fitting, Freddie said, 'Look, it's only half an hour till we close. Why don't you scoot off to see Kate now?'

'If you're sure you'll be fine here ...'

'Of course, Ellie. You just make sure our Kate is all right, do you hear? I'll expect you when I see you. Don't worry about my birthday. We can do a proper celebration another day.'

'As soon as I know what's happening, I'll give you a bell. Thank you, sweetie,' and they hugged.

She ran upstairs to grab her things and was out on the street within minutes. Now, her mind could be fully occupied with Kate. As she walked along, Ellen wondered if she should take anything to her place, or simply go to the pharmacy for advice.

Thus absorbed as she came up to the crossing at Piccadilly, she realised the object of her thoughts was standing on the other side of the street, waiting to walk towards her. She gasped. They stood watching each other, separated by the river of Saturday lunchtime traffic streaming past. Kate was wearing sunglasses, which made her look exotic in the warm spring light. Her face was pale, but she looked directly at Ellen with a small smile. It seemed to take a lifetime for the policeman to stop the traffic. Finally, he blew his whistle and the crowds waiting on both sides of the street surged forward. The two women kept their eyes fixed on each other as they walked forward, meeting in the traffic island in the middle, where they stood face to face. Ellen reached out to take her hand. People were pushing past but they barely noticed.

The policeman blew his whistle again, fiddling with his white cuffs. 'Come on, ladies!' he called. 'Make up your mind, north or south?'

Kate's eyes were impenetrable behind the dark glasses. 'South,' she said and they crossed back over to Ellen's side. They walked to the back of the pavement and leant against the railings outside Green Park. Ellen needed a moment to recover. She'd pictured having to spend the weekend tiptoeing around Kate's flat as she lay in bed in the dark, in pain and distress. And now, everything had changed. She gave her head a little shake, jettisoning her gloomy imaginings and welcoming the bright reality in front of her.

'I can't believe you're here. I've been worried sick about you. I thought you'd still be in bed,' she said.

'I can't believe it either. I took more pills and managed to sleep the rest of the night. When I woke up this morning, it took me a few minutes to realise the migraine had gone. I was careful for a few hours, thinking it would kick back in, but no. It really has cleared up. It was different to my usual migraines, although I don't know if that's a good or a bad sign. Anyway, I've had a long bath and now I'm cleansed and renewed, in body and spirit. So, here I am, Ellie, just like I promised. Were you on your way to see me?' Ellen nodded and Kate leaned forward to brush her hand against her cheek. Up close, her face had a slightly bruised look, her usual lively energy was subdued, but otherwise she appeared remarkably recovered.

'Are you sure you're well enough to be out?'

'Yes, I'm fine, although I'm still sensitive to light, hence the glasses. I can pretend I'm a famous actress going incognito.' She smiled gently at Ellen. 'What's the plan for Freddie's birthday?'

'Well, he's been rather vague because none of us knew if you'd be well enough to join in, but I know Alec's coming over soon.'

'Let's go back and surprise them,' Kate suggested. She tucked her arm in Ellen's and they walked sedately back to Jermyn Street, a slow and triumphant procession. The shop was closed on their return, and they paused on the landing outside the workroom, where Freddie was bent in concentration over the pattern for Mrs Granville. He looked up, scissors in his hand, and exclaimed in surprise when he saw them.

'Kate, you're better!' He came over to give her a hug. 'This is the best news we could have hoped for. Are you up to celebrations?'

'Absolutely, Freddie,' she assured him. 'Headache's all gone.'

'I just want to finish this. I'll be up in a few minutes,' he said with a squeeze of their hands.

When they arrived in the sitting room, they walked straight into each other's arms. 'You don't need to worry about anything – I'm fine,' Kate murmured into Ellen's ear. 'I hope you didn't spend the night worrying.'

Ellen pulled her head back to study Kate's face. 'I hated having to leave you in that state. I was dreadfully concerned about you. But I have to admit, I stayed up drinking whiskey and eating chocolates with the others until late. In the end, I slept soundly,' and she gave a somewhat abashed laugh.

'Good for you!' said Kate calmly. 'Right, I have a cold bottle of champagne here for Freddie.' She went to her bag to pull out the champagne, declaring, 'Ta-da!' much like a magician pulling a rabbit out of a hat.

'I'll put it in the kitchen,' Ellen said. When she came back, Kate was sitting on the sofa gazing out the window, her sunglasses on her lap. 'Do you want me to draw the curtains?' she asked, but Kate shook her head. She was clothed in grey trousers and a white blouse, the muted colours in harmony with her energy. There was a stillness, a peacefulness, about her which Ellen couldn't remember seeing before.

Kate studied her. 'What a sight for sore eyes. You look beautiful, Ellie. Is that Freddie's new top?'

She was about to answer when she heard footsteps on the stairs, but it was Alec who came into the room a moment later, dressed in casual trousers and a shirt, and carrying a small bag. His face lit up when he saw Kate and he crossed to give her a kiss. 'How lovely to see you, Kate. Does this mean the headache has gone?'

Freddie must have heard him because he also appeared, tape measure still slung around his neck. 'Here we are now, all my favourite people,' he said, beaming. The champagne was produced and opened by Freddie with a satisfying pop. 'I'm afraid we don't have proper champagne glasses,' he apologised.

Kate replied, 'Oh, it tastes the same. We can drink it out of bowls for all I care.'

They settled down to enjoy the champagne. Freddie sat cross-legged on the floor by Alec in the chair, his arm flung over his legs. Alec raised his glass. 'Well, here's to the truth. We had the best possible outcome for the investigation.'

Freddie responded, 'That's because we were fabulous sleuths!' Alec and Ellen gave each other a brief, private smile. 'But we got the answers Kate needed, thank God.'

Kate nodded, but asked, 'Do you think there might be any consequences from all this? Could Blunt contact his old police colleagues, or make a complaint?'

'I think it's very unlikely,' Alec said. 'If he does contact the police, his lies about the death will come out, and I doubt he'd want that. He seemed nervous when I threatened him with a charge of assault on Ellen. I don't think you have anything to worry about. After all these years, and with the police file missing, there's no evidence to connect you to the fire.'

Freddie protested, 'But it's so wrong that bastard can get away with telling such lies. He caused a lot of damage. Why should he get off?'

Kate was tranquil. 'I don't want revenge. I don't want to take it further. All I wanted from this was the truth, and I've got that. It set me free.' She turned to smile at Ellen, before adding, 'In fact, it's Alec I'm more concerned about.' Freddie raised his eyebrows, looking alarmed. 'You were there in your professional role, pretending you had a client. What would happen if he complained to your firm, or to some legal body?'

'Don't forget, he doesn't have Alec's card,' Ellen said, although she knew that didn't necessarily mean anything. Alec remained unperturbed.

'I'm not worried. If he does remember my name and looks me up in the phonebook, I'll just explain the story to my partner. I don't regret for a second any small deceptions I may have practised – any porkies,' he added with an impish smile. 'If he tries to make a formal complaint, then his own behaviour will be exposed. I think, when he wakes up today, he'll probably want to forget the whole thing happened. I just hope he doesn't take it out on his wife.'

They sobered, contemplating the Blunt household. 'God, we're so lucky,' Freddie said quietly, and rubbed his cheek on Alec's leg.

Kate had only taken a small sip, but now she raised her glass, declaring, 'I'd like to propose some toasts.'

'Only two! You're allowed two wishes each,' Freddie said instantly. He'd insisted on this from a small boy, having had nightmares after Ellen read him a story about a third wish bringing disaster.

'All right,' Kate agreed. 'Well, I'd like of course to wish Freddie a very happy birthday. And my other toast is to Ellen. She made all of this possible through her search for the truth, her determination—'

'Stubbornness, I think you mean!' Ellen interjected, laughing.

'She started a process to free me from my guilt. But so much more has come out of it and … well, it's all wonderful,' she finished rather abruptly.

'I'll second that,' Alec said, raising his glass. 'Freddie and I owe everything to Ellen, but you know that, don't you?' All eyes were on Ellen, who ducked her head and took a big gulp of champagne. She tried not to cough as it fizzed in her throat. Alec went on, 'I loved doing this investigation, finding Kate as a new friend, the whole lot. Do I have another wish left?'

'Uh-uh.' Freddie gave him a cheeky grin.

'Anyway, you know what it is, my dear.' He clinked glasses with Freddie and asked, 'What are your wishes?'

'I don't need any. I have everything I want,' Freddie replied, his eyes bright.

'Oh, I forgot! I have something for you, Freddie,' Kate said, picking up her bag and producing a book on French fashion. They became absorbed in the glossy photographs. Kate talked about her years in Paris and explained the techniques involved in taking the pictures, while Freddie described the intricacies of French couture. Alec topped up their glasses and asked questions.

Ellen joined in, but mostly watched as the sitting room snuggled in with a cosy wink. The zigzag pattern on the curtains began to shimmer and dance, the roses to nod and smile. She'd always been an optimistic, hopeful person. But, right now, she was aware of an extra dimension to her sense of contentment. What had changed to make her feel like this? Obviously, a lot of it was down to Kate, but there was an added factor. Watching the others, she tried to puzzle it out.

'I'd like to make a toast as well,' she announced, but her glass was strangely empty. Kate had barely touched her drink and reached over to pour in the champagne from her glass. She had more colour and animation in her face. Ellen gazed at her admiringly.

'Come on, Ellie. We're waiting!' Freddie prompted her after a moment.

'Oh! Well, obviously I wish Freddie a happy birthday and may all his dreams come true. But my toast is to all of you. You're very dear people. I always want to have you in my life.' She stopped and gulped. Surely, she could not be about to cry again? She prided herself on being hard-headed, but lately she'd somehow turned into the sort of sentimental fool who blubbed over pictures of kittens. Luckily, the others didn't seem to notice. They regarded her with kind faces, although they appeared rather hazy. Kate took her hand murmuring, 'Always,' while Alec said, 'That's a promise, Ellie.' Freddie held up his glass. 'To the four of us.'

The champagne had been finished for some time when Alec asked, 'Is anyone else hungry? I didn't book anywhere, but we can go and have afternoon tea somewhere nice, perhaps the Criterion?' Kate and Ellen laughed. 'What?'

'We often went there in the suffragette days,' Kate explained. 'The WSPU used to hold meetings in the upstairs rooms.'

Ellen added, 'They often booked it for welcome lunches when women were released from prison. That's where they took me when I got out of Holloway. Do you remember, Freddie?'

'Then it's the perfect place to go,' Freddie declared. 'Let's face it, we all owe a lot to the suffragettes and it's where our stories began, really.' He jumped up, remembering to remove his tape measure, and they started clearing away and getting their coats and hats.

31

Out on the street, Alec and Kate walked ahead while Freddie waited for Ellen, who was having trouble closing the front door. As they set off, he tucked her arm in his and grinned at her. 'You're squiffy, aren't you, Ellie?' She maintained a dignified silence. 'Don't worry, a bit of food will sort you out. Look, what a beautiful day!'

It was true, the weather had done its best to celebrate Freddie's birthday. There was real warmth in the sun, a reminder that summer was nearly upon them. She put her face up to feel its benediction. 'We have the nicest view from here,' Freddie observed complacently, his eyes on Alec walking in front of them. Ellen laughed, but couldn't help agreeing.

The others were waiting for them at the entrance to the restaurant. The carved cupids seemed to Ellen's eyes to float over them benignly. They followed a waiter through the ground-floor restaurant, admiring the inlaid mosaic patterns on the wall and cupola ceiling, its myriad tiles reflecting back a golden haze. Freddie stopped to stare up at it and Ellen guessed he was getting inspiration for a design. They went up the stairs to the East Room and were ushered to a table in the corner.

Ellen said, 'How funny. I sat here at a meeting, just a few weeks after I arrived in London in 1913.' For so many years, those memories had been edged with sadness, with the mystery of Kate's disappearance, but no longer, she thought.

The waiter returned with hot buttered toast, sandwiches and cakes, along with a large pot of tea. There was silence while they shared the food around. 'Before I forget, my mother wants me to bring you all to tea,' Alec said, his eyes on a potted salmon sandwich.

'How nice. Maybe next weekend?' Kate suggested.

'That's when we're going away,' Freddie said, giving a brilliant smile to the others. 'Alec and I are going up to Yorkshire to visit Sam's grave, and have a little holiday. We can make it the following weekend. Oh, and Kate, we mustn't forget to arrange a time for you to take the photograph for our advertising.'

Kate nodded, but her mind appeared to be elsewhere. 'Speaking of holidays, do you close the shop at all in the summer?'

'Yes, we close for the last two weeks in August,' Ellen replied.

'What do you think about us all going over to France for those two weeks?' Kate suggested. They all stopped eating and looked at her. 'We can see the sights in Paris and visit my friends there.'

'We could take the boat train from Dover and hire a car to drive around France,' Alec responded, looking like an excited boy. 'I'd love to see the country properly, not just from a nightmare trench filled with mud. It's my birthday in August

– I'll be thirty-one. What a wonderful way to celebrate it!'

'I could visit the fashion houses,' Freddie said dreamily. 'Chanel, Schiaparelli … I hope they won't be closed for the summer.'

'I've never been outside Britain,' Ellen confessed. 'I've always wanted to see other countries.' She became lost in visions of picturesque landscapes, hilltop villages and cypress trees; lazing and meandering in the warm sun, swimming in the Mediterranean; the freedom of being on the road, going where they wanted. Two weeks with no work, just relishing life with the people dearest to her in the world.

'Well, then, this will be just the start,' said Kate.

They started discussing details of the trip, but then Freddie exclaimed, 'God, I nearly forgot, where's my head? I've got some news. I got a letter today from the Old Vic. They want to see me about my ballet designs.' After the congratulations, he said to Ellen, 'I don't know where this will lead, but I'll do my best not to let it affect the shop.'

Ellen waved a hand, unconcerned. 'Oh, Freddie, don't you worry about the business. This might be a brilliant new career for you, that's the important thing. As it happens, I've been thinking we should have more ready-made outfits and hats. That's what the department stores do. I've watched women shopping there. They like the convenience of browsing clothes in a range of sizes. They're cheaper, so we'd have to sell more of them, but we need to move with the times. We could offer your design service for select customers only.'

'Once Freddie makes his name as a designer, you'll find society women will clamour to have something done by him and be willing to pay more,' Alec suggested. 'Anyway, it looks as if the economy will be depressed for a few years yet, so having different options to make money will help. I think times will be tough for a while. A lot of people are going to be out of work.'

'At least your job should be safe,' Freddie commented. 'People will go on committing crimes, dying, getting divorced ...'

'Alec, I'd like you to be my solicitor,' Kate said suddenly. 'I've been thinking about it for days. You know I hate my father's firm. Will you do it?'

Alec hesitated. 'I wouldn't normally act in a professional capacity for my friends. It's considered a conflict of interest.'

But Kate was firm. 'Don't be silly. I trust you completely. There won't be any conflict.'

He grinned. 'Then, I'd be honoured, Kate.'

Piccadilly Circus was filled with crowds when they left the restaurant and a queue was gathering outside the next-door theatre. It was early evening. The whole day had felt dreamlike to Ellen. She wandered along with Kate, chatting about the planned trip to France and savouring the promise of the evening to come.

Freddie and Alec strolled ahead of them, close together but carefully not touching. And yet, their body language must have given them away. Perhaps their eyes lingered on each other a moment too long, or perhaps the happiness emanating from them was too obvious. A man walking past stopped abruptly and glared before spitting on the ground towards them. As he continued past Ellen and Kate with a sour face, they caught the tail-end of his comment: '... should all be locked up.' His companion, a woman with tightly waved hair, nodded vigorously, the feathers on her hat bouncing in unison.

Kate stared angrily at them while Ellen kept a loving lookout on Freddie and Alec, oblivious in their own world. A shadow passed over them, a momentary eclipse of the sun.

'What are your plans for this evening?' she asked, when they reconvened in the flat.

Alec said, 'There's a Ralph Vaughan Williams concert at the Wigmore Hall. We might see if we can catch it.'

'And Ellen and I are going for a swim in the Serpentine,' Kate stated.

'Oh … right! I'll go and get my swimming costume,' Ellen said, surprised but pleased. She ran up to her bedroom and rolled her costume and cap into a towel, hesitating then adding a top and fresh underwear into a small bag.

When she came back to the sitting room, Freddie announced, 'We've decided we're going on a picnic to the seaside tomorrow, while Alec still has the car. We'll head off from here at eleven. Sound good?'

'Sounds fabulous,' Ellen agreed. On impulse, she went over and put her arms around them, hugging them close. Alec kissed her cheek, while Freddie put his forehead against hers and smiled into her eyes. They stood this way for several seconds, arms entwined in a silent communion, before she separated and moved over to Kate, waiting by the door. She put her hand on Kate's shoulder and paused. The two men returned her look with peaceful smiles, their arms around each other's waists.

Ellen felt a sudden rush of joy, so strong it seemed only a fragile cord kept her tethered to the earth. 'Have a lovely evening, my dears,' she said. Kate blew them a kiss, then they went down the stairs.

32

'I have a confession to make,' Kate said, as they walked up to Piccadilly. Ellen stopped and looked at her serenely. This last week had been so thought-provoking and tumultuous that her capacity for surprise had been exhausted. But her eyes widened when Kate went on to say, 'The thing is … I don't actually know how to swim.'

'Oh!' That wasn't what she had expected.

Kate pulled her by the hand to keep on walking. 'You don't need to look quite so flabbergasted, Ellie,' she said with a shamefaced laugh. 'After all, compared to thinking I'd killed someone, this is pretty small beer! My father refused to let me learn. He said there was no need for it and, anyway, it wasn't "ladylike". When I first met you and you said how much you loved to swim, I made a vow I'd learn. But things got in the way … So I wonder, will you teach me?'

Ellen turned her face to Kate as they paced along. 'I'd love to, Kate.' She felt deeply moved by the trust Kate had shown in her. 'But you'll need a swimming costume. I have a spare. I can go back and get that—'

'Oh, don't worry, I bought one years ago. It's accompanied me on all my moves, because I always intended to have lessons. Hopefully, it's not too moth-eaten,' she added with a rueful look.

They passed through a loud group of society types milling around outside the Ritz, owning the pavement. Pedestrians were forced to creep around them at the edges. Ellen stopped suddenly. 'Look, Kate, it's one of Freddie's designs.' She remembered the client from last summer, a bashful debutante with a coldly ambitious mother. Freddie must have seen something behind her timidity, because he'd made her a dress with a plunging back in silver lamé. And here she was, sparkling boldly and screeching with her companions. She'd certainly lived up to the dress.

They moved on and soon arrived at the crossing where they'd met earlier in the day. 'Now we go north,' Kate said. Once on the other side, she asked, 'What exactly is it about swimming that's so important for you?'

'Well, it gives me a sensation of freedom,' Ellen replied, thinking it through as they turned down White Horse Street. 'Although I admit, there's not much of that in a swimming pool full of screaming children! The best is when I can swim outdoors, somewhere quiet and wild. The water feels like silk on my skin. I'm in my element, a part of nature. It just feels … so right. But it seems to have a healing power as well. I'm always peaceful and full of energy afterwards.' She laughed self-consciously. 'I don't know if that makes sense.'

'Yes, it does. How did you learn to swim?'

'My father taught us when we were children, in a small river near our home. He was so patient, he'd spend hours with us. We always looked forward to our lessons. Do you know, he was the only man in our village who taught his daughter to swim? The other men used to rib him about it. He told us that, not long before we were born, the girl next door had fallen in the Broads and drowned. She couldn't swim, of course, unlike her brothers. Her parents thought modesty was more important than a girl's life. My father vowed it would never happen to his children. But then, it became so much more for me than just a tool of survival.'

'What can I do for you in exchange for my swimming lessons?'

'You don't need to do anything, Kate. Oh, I know, you can show me Paris.'

'I'll do that anyway! No, it needs to be something equivalent. Some skill I can teach you. I want us to be equal in everything.' She seemed oddly insistent.

Ellen puzzled over this for a moment, then turned to her with a cleared face. 'Teach me to drive. I've always wanted to learn.'

'Gladly! It's a deal,' and they stopped outside Kate's building to solemnly shake hands. 'Come on,' Kate said, her eyes hidden behind the sunglasses, 'I'll get my things and we can head straight off.'

But when they came into the lobby, Kate was hailed by the porter sitting at his desk, who broke off from a harassed discussion on the telephone. 'Miss Shergold, I'm glad I caught you. What a day I've been having! Just one thing after another— No, not you. Please hold one moment,' he said into the receiver.

'George, this is my friend Ellen Fernsby. You'll be seeing a lot of her,' Kate said.

'Pleased to meet you, Miss Fernsby.' George nodded at her distractedly. He stood up, shifting crutches under his arms, and Ellen saw that one trouser leg was pinned up. He was a spry man with pockmarked skin and an anxious expression. 'I'm terribly sorry to say the lifts are out of order. It happened at lunchtime, and poor Miss Taylor was trapped for nearly an hour before we freed her. It was most unfortunate – well, you know her heart is rather weak. We had to sit her down with a nice cup of tea. Mrs Robinson is kindly looking after her. I'm trying to get the engineers out, and of course they're coming up with every excuse why they can't come until tomorrow. I hope it won't inconvenience you too much.'

Kate reassured him, 'You don't need to worry, George. We'll be fine. I'm sorry you're having problems. I'll let you get back to your phone call.'

After they passed through the lobby Kate said, 'Up the apples and pears we go.' Their smiles acknowledged a mutual awareness of beginnings and shared memories. The stairwell was lighted by large windows, and the elegant iron work on the bannisters made Ellen conscious of the contrast to her flat above the shop. Once they were starting on the second floor, Kate commented, 'George is a good man, but he can tend to go on a bit.'

'He'd be a perfect match for Hester. The two of them could chatter to each other all day long. Did he lose his leg in the war?'

'Yes. Apparently, they were worried he might not manage when he started in the job, but he soon proved them wrong. He's pretty nimble. He gets around as quickly as anyone. When he's not fussing, he's quite interesting. He spends his spare time exploring London and can tell you the history of any given place— Oh, Mrs Blavatsky, let me help you,' she broke off to say. They had come around the turning to see a white-haired woman ahead of them, holding onto the bannister and carrying a large bag of groceries.

'Kate, you too kind! You very good girl,' the woman exclaimed, a weary smile lighting up her face as Kate took the bag and offered her arm. Ellen tactfully hung back as Kate helped the woman to her flat on the third floor and carried her bag inside. She emerged after a few minutes, politely regretting she could not stay for tea and promising she would pop down soon.

As they resumed their climb up the stairs, Ellen asked, 'Where's she from?'

'She's a refugee from the Russian Revolution. Poor woman, she's had a bloody awful time. Her husband was killed by a mob, she lost contact with her son, doesn't even know if he's alive, and she lives on a pittance. But she's always cheerful, a real lesson in coping with adversity.'

'You took a photograph of her, didn't you? One of your portraits. I thought you caught her spirit very well.' Ellen had pictured Kate leading an isolated life and was comforted by the vignettes she'd witnessed of domestic harmony and kindness. The thought of Kate being sad or lonely was unbearable.

'That's right. Clever of you to remember. She has an interesting face and I think she welcomed the attention. I took George's portrait the other day, too, although I haven't developed it yet.' Kate hesitated, as if to say something more, but they were arriving a little puffed at her front door.

As soon as Kate closed the door, however, she interrupted Ellen's reflections by firmly kissing her. 'There! I've been wanting to do that for some time,' she murmured. They melted into the embrace. After a while Kate pulled back with a regretful look. 'I'd better shake a leg if I'm going to have my swimming lesson.' She disappeared towards the bedroom.

Ellen hung her coat and hat in the hall and wandered over to the window. The book she'd been reading the previous evening was still lying on the chair, but she couldn't think about that now. In fact, she wasn't really thinking about anything. Her mind was a curious blank, apart from a low hum of anticipation, skipping over any rational analysis or expectation. She sat on the edge of the armchair to gaze out at the view, enjoying the warmth on her face. The sun was dipping towards the horizon, although they had a good hour or more of light left. She shut her eyes, vaguely conscious of Kate coming into the room and going out again.

'Do you remember agreeing I could take your portrait?' Ellen opened her eyes to see Kate setting up a camera on a tripod. 'This won't take long, I promise, but when I saw you sitting in this light, I thought it would be a perfect opportunity. You don't need to move or do anything. Just pretend I'm not here.' Kate did things with the camera and squinted at a small instrument in her hand. 'This photograph will complete my portfolio. I can take it to the studio next week. Now, I need to take a few shots to check the light. Just ignore me.' Her low talk was soothing.

Ellen forgot her usual stiffness in front of the camera as she gazed out at the view. This was her favourite time of the year: an explosion of warmth and light and life after the winter, and with the covenant of the summer to follow. She never wanted it to end. Kate called her name and she turned her head to smile at her, barely conscious of the camera clicks.

'There, all done. That wasn't so bad, was it? You're a natural in front of the camera.'

'On the contrary! You made it seem so easy.'

Kate carried the camera and tripod out of the room and emerged a moment later holding a bag. 'Right, time for my first lesson,' she said. Ellen took out her rolled-up towel and they left the flat without bothering to put on coats or hats. They quickly passed downstairs and through the lobby, where George was ploughing through an explanation about the lift to an elderly man.

As they walked along, Ellen looked with interest at the grand houses, fronted by large carriage lights and covered entrances. One particularly impressive building had pineapples carved into the iron fence. Butlers or maids could sometimes be glimpsed at the doorways. It was like another world to her. A regular customer lived around here, a haughty woman who insisted on nothing but black satin, she recalled. They arrived at Park Lane, busy with Saturday evening traffic. 'I hear that's going to be a posh hotel,' Kate remarked, nodding her head at a large building site on their right.

After they'd crossed and entered Hyde Park, Ellen asked, 'How are you feeling after the migraine? You look amazingly well, considering.' It was true. Kate had colour in her cheeks and her usual lively energy had returned.

Kate's smile was radiant. 'I usually feel quite peaky afterwards, but not today. I suspect it was more a reaction to all the events of this last week. As if it marked the end of a crisis for me. Does that sound silly?' Ellen shook her head. 'Anyway, I feel marvellous, in mind and body. This is a new chapter in my life. I know it.'

The crowds were dissipating in Hyde Park. Just a few people were left promenading along Rotten Row. The sun provided a golden haze as it filtered through the great trees.

Riders passed them galloping their horses on the way back to the stables, the sand flying up under their hooves.

Ellen said, 'We're close to my favourite statue. I'd like to show it to you.' After a few minutes they came to a rose garden and stopped at the fountain. 'She's Diana, the goddess of hunting. Have you seen her before?'

'No, I can't believe I missed this section of the park. She's a beauty, isn't she?' Kate replied.

The naked body of the huntress was strong and functional, yet harmonious. She stared with careful concentration along her arrow. Water trickled out of sculpted shells into the fountain. No one was around to disturb the quiet.

'I always loved this statue, but it meant even more to me when I found out it was sculpted by a woman. Does that sound ridiculous?' Now it was Kate's turn to shake her head.

'Not at all, Ellie. We need examples of female triumphs. God knows, we're starved of hearing how other women break free. It's a hard, isolated life going against the restrictions forced on us. We're told to stay in our place, be quiet and obedient. The punishment, if we don't, can be savage. I always love to hear when a woman achieves something, other than being a "good wife and mother", of course.' She spoke these last words with a passing frown.

'Like Nancy Astor being an MP, or Amy Johnson achieving her solo flight?' Ellen suggested. 'I always think the suffragettes were my heroes. Not just the Pankhursts – all of the women. I mean, look at Hilda. No one knows about her, outside her circle, but she showed such courage. What an inspiration to us all.'

'Exactly. It gives you hope you're not alone, doesn't it? Being queer is part of it, but it's more than that. It's about women demanding an equal space in the world.'

'God, yes,' Ellen agreed. 'Not being confined or repressed. Not creeping through life like poor Mrs Blunt. Not just surviving, but actually thriving. Meeting life on our terms.'

Kate grabbed Ellen's hand and laughed. 'Right, now we've sorted out the role of women in the world, shall we go and have that swimming lesson?'

33

They walked on towards the Serpentine, passing a large willow tree, its branches spreading and drooping down to the ground, creating a cave-like canopy. Ellen noticed a flock of sheep cropping grass in the distance, probably the ones she'd seen in the street the day before. Then she got down to business. 'They're going to open a lido in a few weeks, with proper facilities for women swimmers, but until then, we have to get changed in the lavatories. Here, take my bathing cap, it'll keep your hair dry.' They emerged a few minutes later in swimming costumes, their clothes bundled in their hands.

'Hmm, your costume is more flattering than mine.' Kate looked her up and down.

Ellen supressed a giggle at the shapeless woollen garment hanging loosely on Kate's graceful body. 'Well, at least I can't see any moth holes!' she remarked brightly. 'Let's leave our things on this bench.'

A few passing people gave them startled looks, but Ellen was used to it and ignored them. Kate didn't seem to notice, her eyes fixed on the water gleaming palely in front of them. 'I'm calling on my suffragette spirit. I can do this,' she muttered, a mixture of mischief and determination. They stepped down to the water's edge, observed by a heron standing in a frozen pose nearby.

'I'll show you how to float first. That's the essential part,' Ellen suggested. The shallow water was a comfortable temperature, although it became cooler as they walked in up to their waists. 'Now, you're going to lie on your back in the water. Don't worry, I've got my hand under you, I won't let you sink. No, put your head back, if you raise it sharply you'll start to go under. Move your arms out from your side. That's it.' After a few false starts, when Kate flailed around and started to go under, she managed to float. 'How does it feel?'

'Not bad. I think I'm getting the hang of it.'

'All right, I'm going to slowly take my hand away so you can float on your own, but don't worry, I'll be right here. You trust me, don't you?'

'With my life,' Kate replied, a picture of concentration.

Ellen moved her hand away, watching her closely. 'Good. You need to gently move your arms and legs, not a lot, just to maintain the float. You've done it, Kate! You're floating on your own! Gosh, you're a quick learner,' she commented, impressed.

'This feels nice,' Kate started to say, but at that moment they were hailed by a loud voice.

'I say, ladies, should you be in the water? Are you in trouble?'

Ellen said impatiently under her breath, 'Oh, fuck off, stupid man.' Kate stood up, the water dripping off her in rivulets, laughing silently. They turned to see an officious-looking man peering at them from the path.

'You should come out now! I'm sure you're not allowed to be here. You might drown,' he called over to them, flapping his hands in an alarmed way.

'I swim here regularly. There's no risk of drowning,' Ellen said, forcing politeness into her voice.

'No, really, you must leave the water. This isn't right!' he insisted with an astonished expression. No doubt he was used to women always obeying his instructions. Ellen turned her back on him and rolled her eyes at Kate. He said, in a changed tone, 'You're those disgusting sapphists, aren't you? It's unnatural ...' They heard him stomping off.

'Good riddance! Have you had enough, or do you want to go for a bit longer?' Ellen asked. They looked at each other, a long look of understanding.

'More, please,' Kate replied.

It was trickier teaching her how to tread water, but eventually Kate was managing to do this for several seconds, proud surprise on her face, before she lost the rhythm and started to sink. But her arms had goosebumps and Ellen noticed she was starting to shiver.

'I think that's enough for today. How about you dry off and get warm?' she suggested. 'I'll just have a quick swim before I come out.'

On her own, she confidently stroked out from the edge. The calm waters of the Serpentine embraced her, blue-green and slate, impenetrable and wise. She watched as the heron flew over her, head tucked into the long, snake-like neck, its vast wings momentarily blotting out the sun which grazed the horizon. How primordial it looked, like the picture book of dinosaurs she'd pored over as a child. A cormorant suddenly popped up a few feet away. She let out an explosive laugh of surprise and continued to move through the water.

On any other day, these scenes would have brought Ellen a wordless pleasure, an almost mystical sense of being at one with nature. At any other time, she would have settled into a rhythm of movement and breathing, her mind slowing to a peaceful crawl. But not today. Not now. Her mind was focused on one thing only. She stopped and looked back at the shore, her arms moving in circles as she watched Kate emerge from the lavatories and sit on the bench in the sun, rubbing her head with a towel. She could no longer hold back her feelings. The dam had burst, the steady stream was an unstoppable torrent. She was drawn to Kate as instinctively as an animal seeking food or shelter. Never had anything in her life felt so right, so fundamental. She could wait no longer.

'How are you feeling?' she asked when she joined Kate on the bench ten minutes later, dried and clothed.

'Very pleased with myself!' Kate replied. 'I'm starting to get an idea now why you love swimming. It's something about the weightlessness, being free from gravity. I'm looking forward to the next lesson. And what about if you have your first driving lesson tomorrow? I'm sure Alec will lend us the car. We can find a quiet street when we go for the picnic.' Ellen made a sound indicating agreement.

Kate kept her attention fixed on her costume as she rolled it up in her towel. 'Do you have plans to see Myra?'

'No. I finished that some days ago.'

Kate turned to look into Ellen's eyes. 'Is that so?'

'Yes. I want only you. No one else matters,' Ellen said boldly. There! Now it was out in the open. It could not be clearer.

Kate made a move towards her, but was brought up short by shocked tutting from an elderly couple walking past. Instead, she threw her head back and gave a shout of joyous laughter. 'Oh, Ellie, Ellie! I went to Hilda's funeral looking for my old friend, and instead I found a glorious woman. The woman of my dreams. If only ...' and she gave a slight shake of her head, gazing at Ellen. 'But no more "ifs", no more regrets about the past. Let's go home.'

'Yes.'

They were silent on the journey back to Curzon Street. They would have plenty more to discuss, a lifetime of conversation; but right now, the time for talking was past. Occasionally their bodies came together, drawn by a power stronger than magnetism, as they retraced their steps, striding in unison. The lobby was empty and silent.

'Come on,' Kate said, holding out her hand. Ellen remembered how that hand had pulled her along as they raced from the police in their suffragette days. They climbed the stairs steadily, side by side, increasing their pace until they ran up the last flight to arrive, laughing and breathless, at the front door. 'Welcome home, Ellie,' Kate said.

The light woke her. They'd forgotten to close the curtains last night, and the dawn light was sliding into the room. Ellen turned her head to look at Kate, who lay on her back, dark hair tumbled on the pillow, one arm flung above her head in trusting sleep. She gazed, enchanted, before reluctantly easing out of the bed and padding to the bathroom. Their swimming costumes were hanging over the bath and Kate's towel had fallen on the floor. She hung it neatly on the rail, then sat on the lavatory to pee. As she washed her hands afterwards, she watched herself in the mirror, her normally pale cheeks flushed, her eyes glowing. The cat who got the cream, she thought. Her reflection in the mirror looked back with a knowing smile.

Slipping into Kate's dressing gown, she went out to the kitchen to put a glass under the tap, waiting for the water to run cold then thirstily drinking it down. A few crumbs on the counter bore witness to their late-night snack. She wandered back to the sitting room and stared out at the pink, wispy clouds. Even as Ellen looked, the light was changing from pearly grey to a more substantial blue.

Her vision seemed acute, as if the air were crackling: the sharp edges of the buildings, the tiled rooves, the verdancy of the park. Down below, the life of London was stretching and stirring in miniature, a doll's house of activity. Over in the distance was the silver ribbon of the Thames, and there, a bus creeping along Piccadilly, glowing like a red jewel.

A group of swifts wheeled around chasing insects. Breathtakingly fast, they swooped down to the surrounding buildings before abruptly changing direction. As she stood watching, a few flew directly past the window, inches away from her nose, their wings stretched out like arrows. For a fanciful moment, Ellen imagined they had been shot from Diana's bow.

She felt exultant. Her future stretched ahead like a promise. She threw her arms out and twirled around. She wanted to embrace the world. Her goodwill extended outwards, like a gossamer web, to all humanity. She wanted to open her arms and soar over the city, swimming in the currents, the wind on her face, free like a bird.

But first, she would fly over the rooftops to Jermyn Street, hovering protectively as she looked down on Freddie and Alec. Ahead of them lay countless acts of insult, rejection and cruelty; perhaps violence, loss of liberty – or even death. For now, they lay in each other's arms in their circle of love, in the sleep of the innocent and the brave. If only she could surround them with a magical shield. They would need all their courage and love to get through. But they'll do it, she thought with conviction. We will make it.

When she returned to the bedroom, Kate had not moved. But as she went over to close the curtains, she heard her name spoken, and turned to find Kate watching her sleepily through half-open eyes.

'It's early yet. Come back to bed, you gorgeous thing,' she said with a lazy, reminiscent curve of her lips. She opened her arms invitingly.

Ellen turned to finish drawing the curtains, smiling to herself. Outside, the sun began its slow arc through the sky.